A. N. BOYDEN AND EM JAY

Anyone But You

First published by Tangled Sheets Publishing 2025

This novel is entirely a work of fiction. The names, characters and incidents portrayed in it are the work of the author's imagination. Any resemblance to actual persons, living or dead, events or localities is entirely coincidental.

A. N. Boyden and Em Jay asserts the moral right to be identified as the author of this work.

A. N. Boyden and Em Jay has no responsibility for the persistence or accuracy of URLs for external or third-party Internet Websites referred to in this publication and does not guarantee that any content on such Websites is, or will remain, accurate or appropriate.

Designations used by companies to distinguish their products are often claimed as trademarks. All brand names and product names used in this book and on its cover are trade names, service marks, trademarks and registered trademarks of their respective owners. The publishers and the book are not associated with any product or vendor mentioned in this book. None of the companies referenced within the book have endorsed the book.

First edition

ISBN: 979-8-99-888512-9

This book was professionally typeset on Reedsy.
Find out more at reedsy.com

We all have a "That Man Over There."
We're just lucky enough not to be
stranded on an island with him.

A. N. BOYDEN

Contents

Preface

Warning: Coconuts aren't the only thing falling!

This spicy age-gap rom-com includes a morally gray billionaire, an emotionally exhausted assistant, forced proximity, tropical mayhem, and enough tension to make your e-reader sweat. Anyone But You brings a new meaning to Love Island! This book is ideal for mature readers 18 and up! Please be mindful of any tropes or triggers!

Tropes:

Age Gap Romance
Billionaire Romance
CEO x Executive Assistant
Forced Proximity
Enemies to Lovers
Curvy/Plus-Size FMC
OTT MMC

Content Warning:

This story contains themes of memory loss and scenes involving a parent in a nursing home setting, intense sibling rivalry, fraud, identity theft, exploitation, bribery, assault, death, food scarcity, traumatic injury, discussion of assisted suicide, depression, anxiety, discussion of murder of a parent, significant age gap relationship, ageism, graphic language, and graphic open-door sex scenes. Please read with caution.

1

That Man Over There

Victoria

I pinched the bridge of my nose as tears streamed down my cheeks.

"I can't stand that man. God, please let him get hit by a fucking garbage truck or a food truck or something," I whispered. I had my third argument of the day with Mr. Ramsey and had to sequester myself in the supply closet at the end of the hall to avoid bludgeoning him to death with my stapler.

"I'd beat his motherfucking brains in with that stapler. Then I'd open it and staple his fucking lips together, so I don't have to hear another damn thing come out of his mouth!" I seethed.

"Join me in my office once you're done fantasizing about murdering me with a stapler. We have work to do. Stop using company time for your little bitch fits," Mr. Ramsey complained through the door.

I bit down on my knuckles to prevent myself from screaming in frustration and repeatedly drove one of my heels into the floor like a petulant child. I had no one to blame for my current situation but myself. I could've resigned a year ago when I realized Knox Ramsey and I had clashing personalities. I could've walked into his office and dropped my letter of resignation on his desk with a polite smile and a fuck you before filing an EEOC complaint, but the money was good— good enough to endure his toxicity. I'd be out of here like a deadbeat parent if I didn't have to supplement my mother's nursing home bill with my income.

At the tender age of 50, my mother began exhibiting signs of dementia after undergoing a hysterectomy. The signs were subtle at first. She would misplace her keys, purse, and the television remote. As time progressed, my mother often lost her train of thought and struggled with communication. The moment she began hallucinating, I knew something was terribly wrong and rushed her to the hospital. I explained all of my mother's symptoms to the overworked resident, who looked as if she wanted to tell my mother to scooch over so she could get in the bed with her. She bobbed her head as I rattled off my mother's symptoms, and she remarked that my mother was exhibiting signs of dementia. I laughed in her face. How could a healthy fifty-year-old woman have dementia?

We were referred to a neurologist and blindsided when the results returned. My mother was diagnosed with early-onset dementia due to complications from the anesthesia from her surgery. Two years later, she was completely reliant on assistance with her activities of daily living and could no longer safely live at home. It broke my heart to admit her to a nursing facility, but my siblings proved to be unreliable, and

24-hour in-home care was more costly and less reliable.

"Suck it up, Tori, and do it for Mom," I chastised myself as I swiped angrily at my tears.

Thank God I don't wear makeup to work anymore. What would be the point when I had to run to the supply closet or the restroom for my daily mid-afternoon cry?

* * *

Just to inconvenience Mr. Ramsey, I took fifteen minutes for myself in my office to recuperate. I slumped into my office chair and spun around until I was staring at the downtown skyline that was splashed with red, orange, and pink from the setting sun.

A buzz from my desk distracted me. I opened it and fished out my personal cell phone. It vibrated in my hands several times, and I wasn't surprised to see my best friends going back and forth about our upcoming trip to Miami.

Brittney: I don't know about y'all, but I'm already tipsy!

Alyssa: Trust and believe I'm right there with you!

Me: Sadly, I am not.

Brittney: You're still at work, aren't you?

Me: You know it.

Alyssa: You're better than me. I would've burnt off on your boss at 5 o'clock on the dot!

Brittney: Alyssa, you know Tori isn't gonna leave until Mr. Ramsey says she can leave the Big House.

I snickered and shook my head as I responded to their texts.

Me: Shut up, Britt. I'm leaving in thirty minutes.

Alyssa: Standard thirty minutes, or CP Time thirty minutes.

Me: CP Time.

Brittney: Okay, fuck around and miss your flight. You'll be crying while Alyssa and I are in Miami looking for our hoochie daddies.

Me: You don't have to worry about that. There's nothing that'll make me miss this flight.

Alyssa: How much do you want to bet Tori hasn't packed yet?

Me: Don't waste your money because my bags are packed and by the door.

I lied. I was nowhere near packed. My bedroom floor was littered with bikinis, sarongs, tiny shorts, tank tops, maxi dresses, and sandals. It wouldn't take me long to pack because there was a method to the madness—pick everything up, toss it all into the suitcase, and figure it out later.

I rolled my eyes when my instant messenger pinged in the background.

It's That Man Over There. He can wait.

Brittney: You're a bags-are-packed-at-the-door lie.

Alyssa: Her clothes are all over her bedroom floor.

She's not lying.

I had met Brittney and Alyssa during my freshman year of college when I joined a journalism club on campus, and we'd been inseparable ever since. They knew me inside and out and felt more like sisters to me than my own.

Which reminds me...

I shot a text to my trifling sisters, reminding them I'd be out of town for a few days.

Me: I'll be out of town for five days starting tomorrow. Can

4

you two please check on Mom while I'm away?

Faith: Where are you going?

Me: Miami...I told you this...twice.

Hope: I will if I have time.

Me: You only visit her on her birthday and Mother's Day. Make the time.

Hope: Like I said, I will if I have time.

I almost texted her that she'd make the time to be at the reading of the will so she could get her cut, but I decided to keep my mouth shut to avoid an argument.

Me: Sure. On another note, can you two throw in on Mom's bill next month?

Faith: Why? Do you need money? How are you going to Miami if you don't have money?

Hope: Why would you ask that, Victoria? You know we don't have money like you do.

What money? I could only afford to take a vacation because of the quarterly bonus I received from That Man Over There. I lived in New York, and if my apartment wasn't included in my lucrative employee package, then I'd be fucked, and Mom would be on the streets.

Me: Don't worry about it.

I tossed my phone into my desk, grabbed the leather portfolio binder my boss had gifted me for Administrative Professionals' Day and a stapler, so he knew I wasn't playing with him, and trekked to his office.

He grinned like an idiot when I entered.

"I see you've brought the stapler."

"You've been warned," I threatened, snapping the stapler in his direction before sitting in a leather accent chair in front of his desk. "You have ten minutes, and then I'm leaving. The next time you see or speak to me will be a week from now."

Knox

"The next time you see or speak to me will be a week from now."

Miami.

I'd like to believe those words didn't just slip from her lips. My sexy yet delusional executive assistant thought I'd allow her to jet set to Miami with her drunk friends so she could flounce around in barely there bikinis, fuck other men, and twerk on tabletops.

I'm not an idiot. I've heard what goes on during those girls' trips to Miami. She can't go.

I'd been monitoring Victoria's online activity on her employee laptop for the past month. I'd watch her mouse drag across the screen and grind my teeth when she'd add a risqué bathing suit to her shopping cart. My favorite was a red triangle string bikini that would look striking against her deep, rich skin. It'd show a lot of ass, too—another reason she couldn't go. I didn't want any men looking at what was mine.

Thinking about going a week with no contact with Victoria was maddening.

No calls? Texts? Emails? Nothing?

My unhealthy codependency wouldn't allow it. It was why I resorted to nefarious tactics just to get a hit of Victoria Caldwell, no matter how detrimental it was to my health and safety. I'd call her early in the morning just to hear her groggy, freshly woken voice. I demanded excessive overtime for the chance to linger in her vanilla perfume a little longer and to share late-night dinners with her, even if they were work-related.

I was a masochist in many ways, always needing to be on the receiving end of her vitriol. The more she raged, the more excited I became. A therapist had volleyed the term 'energy vampire' once before and coupled it with "narcissism" when I brought up Victoria. That was the first and last time I lay on a shrink's leather couch.

I'll do anything to prevent her from going on her trip, even if that means devising a bogus mandatory business trip. The trip will be unforgettable. It'll be her and me basking in the lap of luxury.

"I have a feeling we'll be seeing each other sooner than that."

"I highly doubt that. What do you need, Mr. Ramsey?"

You coming on my dick, but I guess I can't say that, can I?

Wordlessly, I slid a leather folder in her direction. Her eyes narrowed once it met its resting place in front of her. Silently, she placed her hands on the folder and slid it back to me. I grinned and skated it back. "We can do this all day, Victoria. As always, I know you have last-minute packing to do; it'd be a shame if you had to stay late."

"*You* are the reason I pack last-minute."

"Don't blame me for your poor time management skills."

"Poor time management? Really? Because my last evaluation said that I have excellent time management skills," she quipped, sliding the Folder of Doom back to me.

The Folder of Doom could be anything—a new acquisition, a business meeting with a cantankerous client, a gala invitation, and, in this case, a business trip.

"Take the folder," I insisted, shoving it back.

"Whatever is in this folder can wait until I return."

"Victoria!" I snapped, using an authoritative tone that meant I didn't have the time or patience to engage in a squabble. She huffed, snapped up the folder, and flipped it open. I gazed at her beautiful face, taking in her striking features while I waited for Mount Victoria to erupt. A perfectly arched eyebrow slowly ascended her forehead. Her eyes widened as she read the pages, and her button nose twitched like a bunny now and again. Those red pouty lips that I dreamed of sucking on at least five times a day folded inward. Agonizing silence continued for another minute before she snapped the folder closed and placed it on the desk.

"I think it's time for me to speak to the Board," she said softly.

"And why is that?"

"Because you are clearly unfit to run this company as Chief Executive Officer. You should exchange the Italian designer suits and the penthouse office for a straitjacket and a white padded room because there's no way in Hell you thought I'd agree to go on this trip!" she barked.

"It's mandatory, Victoria."

"Mandatory for you, not me," she argued.

"I'm considering another hotel acquisition, and I need my right-hand woman with me."

"You *need* a lobotomy," she hissed, spewing her venom at me.

She's getting worked up. I should schedule a couples massage for us promptly. A Swedish massage on the beach sounds heavenly.

I slipped into another one of my fantasies as she ripped me apart. Her pouty lips rapidly moved, and her arms waved around frantically, but her words of disdain never reached me. All I could think of was a lovely house, two kids, and a hamster named Hamlet.

Maybe not Hamlet; that might be too on the nose. We'll have to name it a stupid small critter name like Bubbles or Cheeks. Are my fantasies tipping into delusion? That bitchy therapist would say yes, but as the old adage goes, "Winners never quit, and quitters never win." We can have this if Victoria's willing to give me the time of day.

I sighed and relaxed into my chair as her tirade continued. My eyes darted to the stapler she unhinged before bouncing back to her luscious lips. I couldn't fear for my life because everything she did seemed to endear me. Her anger was red hot and volatile, making my dick stand at full attention. I bit back a groan when an insult slipped through.

I think this solidifies that I have a nasty degradation kink. Who fucking knew? Well...to be fair...the therapist did say that. Perhaps I was too harsh with her.

"I know you're stupid, but let me help you out one more time: I'm not going on this trip. I have *approved* time off, and I'm going to Miami. Go...to...Hell."

"The car will arrive promptly at 7:00 AM to pick you up from your apartment."

"I won't be there," she insisted, standing to her feet.

"I'll bring the donuts you love!" I shouted after her retreating form. She slammed the door hard with such force that the meek employee at the printer nearly jumped out of his skin. My eyes narrowed when Victoria paused to speak to him. He touched her arm and rubbed it soothingly.

Note to self—fire him. Oh, wait. The little twerp is Blankenship's executive assistant. I can't just get rid of him. No bother. He isn't a threat. He can never get a rise out of her like me. I have a plan to ensure Victoria doesn't make it to Miami. I just have to duck the next time she sees me.

9

2

Miami Bound

Victoria

I was relieved when I exited my apartment building and was greeted by my Uber driver and not my living nightmare, Knox Ramsey. What frustrated me the most about Knox was that if he weren't such a dick, I would've thrown him a little something.

I'm not a fucking idiot. I know that man has been cuckoo for my Cocoa Puffs since he interviewed me, and I'm not ashamed to admit I landed the job because the man wanted to bend me over his desk.

I was seriously one "Thank you for applying, but we found another candidate" email away from selling feet pictures and my used underwear to the freak nasties on the Internet.

Truthfully, I wouldn't mind the bending. Knox Ramsey was a fine piece of work. He towered over me, even when I wore stilettos, making me feel small and vulnerable around him. There had been times when we rode the elevator together, and I became damp between the thighs thinking about him slamming me against the elevator walls and taking me down.

In my defense, this little fantasy almost always happens when I'm ovulating. Some things can't be helped.

He was 49-years-young, stayed active, and was a sharp dresser with a panty-melting smile. He reminded me of Clark Kent when he donned his glasses when he was too helpless to order more contacts. He had the same jet black, wavy hair and strong jawline. We worked overtime a few weeks ago, and the man nearly made me drool when he slowly rolled the sleeves of his dress shirt up, exposing solid forearms.

In my defense, I was ovulating...I think.

The Lord in Heaven knew I was tempted a few times during our business trips. All I had to do was knock on his suite door, and he'd drop his drawers, but all the late-night clandestine fantasies went out the window as soon as the man opened his stupid ass mouth.

That's fine. I'll get that itch scratched while I'm in Miami.

Instead of thinking about Overlord Ramsey, I texted my girls on the ride to the airport.

Me: I'm on my way to the airport!

Alyssa: You're cutting it a little close.

Me: No, I'm not. Two hours is plenty of time to get checked in and through security—perks of flying First Class.

Brittney: Did your work daddy buy your ticket?

I frowned.

Me: First of all, don't call him that. You may refer to him as: "Bastard," "Dirty Old Bastard," "That Man Over There," or "Tall, Dumb, and Ugly."

Alyssa: Girl, stop. We've seen your boss. I don't know about his intelligence, but I'm guessing he has to be pretty

11

damn smart to successfully run his business as CEO. The man is far from ugly. It might be the shot I took to the head before leaving my house this morning talking, but he's a 10 out of 10.

Brittney: Fo sho.

Me: Girl…it's 6:30…in the morning…

Alyssa: And it's 6:30 in the evening somewhere else. Miss me with the bullshit. I'm officially on vacation!

Me: All right. You're gonna fuck around and be too inebriated to board the plane.

Brittney: She's gonna be drunk and sad watching the plane taxi away.

Alyssa: Hell nah. Y'all are not leaving without me. I'll call in a threat. All the planes will be grounded.

I snorted and exited our group chat when I received an incoming text message from Dirty Old Bastard. I rolled my eyes at the attachment of an open box of donuts from my favorite bakery located two blocks from our office.

Sometimes, when Knox wasn't being a complete monster, I'd find a treat on my desk from him—usually in the form of a heavenly soft and sweet powdered sugar donut. The last time he left me donuts was to apologize for making me do a ton of preparation for a meeting that he ultimately bailed on. It took me *weeks* to assemble the massive expense report and presentation, only to be the only attendee at the meeting. Without informing his executive assistant, Knox decided to take the clients to a working brunch followed by golf, leaving me at the office hotter than a hot comb on Easter Sunday morning. I was still pissed when he returned to the office that afternoon with a box full of fluffy, delectable donuts. I snatched them from him without hesitation and devoured three, which resulted in him nicknaming me Tori Montana due to the epic mess I made with the powdered sugar.

Tori Montana...Knox can be funny when he wants to be, but those moments are few and far between.

Knox: Look what I got you, Tori Montana.

Me: You're messaging me outside of work hours *and* on my personal phone. I meant what I said when I said I didn't want to hear from you. Just for that, I'm taking FMLA when I return.

Knox: Let me save you the trouble. Your FMLA has been denied.

I frowned in disgust.

Knox: Stop frowning. You're too pretty to frown.

I groaned and threw my phone into my purse.

This man knows me too well, like on some lover-type shit, minus the sex. I guess it's bound to happen when you spend over sixty hours a week with someone. You unintentionally learn everything about that person—their likes and dislikes, quirks, mannerisms, and favorite deli order. A week away from Knox will do me good. It's just what the doctor ordered.

* * *

"Good morning. My name is Tiffany, and thank you for choosing Premiere Flight Airlines. Put your suitcase on the scale, and we'll get you checked in," the preppy agent said.

"Good morning," I grunted as I lifted the suitcase onto the platform. I said a silent prayer that I wasn't over my limit.

"Forty-eight pounds even. You won't have a lot of room for

13

souvenirs," Tiffany mentioned.

As long as I can fit a magnet for Knox in the suitcase, then I'll be fine. Ugh. Why am I thinking about bringing him anything back?!

Knox had a quirk about collecting novelty magnets from every place he visited. He once overshared that his parents used to do it when they went on road trips when he was a child. He wanted to keep his father's memory alive by continuing the tradition.

It's not a big deal if I buy him a magnet. It's a nice gesture that won't break the bank.

"May I have a name and ID?"

"Victoria Caldwell," I confirmed, slipping her my driver's license.

"And where are we traveling today, Ms. Caldwell?"

"Miami." I beamed.

"How fun!" she exclaimed. "I went to Miami a couple of years ago for Spring Break and had the best time of my life. I mean…I returned with a little souvenir I couldn't unwrap until nine months later, but it was a memorable experience."

Not this woman getting knocked up on Spring Break. No judgment. I just wouldn't mention it in a professional setting, which makes me question if I'm really down to clown in Miami. Yes, contraceptives exist, but they can also fail. At least if Knox knocked me up, then I wouldn't have to worry about child support.

I sighed.

Why am I thinking about this man? Knox and child support shouldn't be in the same sentence.

"Um…Ms. Caldwell?"

"Yes?"

"I don't have a booking here for you."

"I beg your pardon?" I asked, now on high alert.

"I see here that your ticket was canceled last night."

"Who canceled my ticket? I didn't do it."

"Let me...look at the notes here."

I watched Tiffany's face morph from curiosity to downright confusion.

"There's a note here that says that your husband called and said you died. The ticket was canceled, and you were refunded."

"I'm not dead! And more importantly, I don't have a husband!" I shrieked.

"No surprise there," someone mumbled behind me. I whirled around and found an unfortunate-looking man with a beard that looked like it was playing Connect Four. I shot him my best "fuck around and find out" glare before returning to Tiffany.

"There has to be some sort of mistake. Is there another flight to Miami today?" I asked, logging into my email to find the cancellation confirmation.

"I'm sorry, but all the flights today are booked. In fact, some are overbooked."

I went cold when I received an incoming call from Knox.

This...motherfucker...

"Hello?" I whispered, swallowing back all my rage.

"Good morning, Victoria. Come outside. We have a plane to catch."

"Did you call the airline and tell them that I died?!"

"I did. Come outside."

"Why would you do something like that?"

"I told you our business trip was mandatory, and you thought I was joking. Get it in gear, Victoria. We can't idle forever in the pickup area. It's rude."

"Pickup area?"

"Yes, outside the terminal. We're flying privately from another airport. Let's go. Your donuts are getting cold."

I hung up the phone with a trembling hand.

"Are you okay, Ms. Caldwell?" Tiffany asked.

"I'm not okay, and neither will Knox Ramsey be once I'm done with him."

3

Bribery

Knox

I'd like to say Victoria was a little pissed as she exited the airport, but it would be a lie. She was *incensed*. Her eyes cut into a sharp, rabid glare, and her knuckles were stretched tight around her luggage that she dragged along like a dead body.

My dead body, I'm guessing.

Her right eye twitched in rage, and her steps were fast and violent.

I wonder what type of flowers they'll have at my funeral. I should be more scared, especially since I know Victoria wants to strangle me, but she's...fucking adorable.

Tired of being dragged like a corpse, the bag tipped over onto its side. The burgeoning suitcase I knew was filled with skimpy bikinis and cut-off shorts threatened to burst open at the seams. I watched her stop dead in her tracks and glare at it. I knew she was calling the suitcase every foul name in the book in her mind.

She prefers "bastard." She loves calling me a bastard. And when she's absolutely not in the mood for my bullshit, she calls me a "dirty, old bastard." I'm not dirty; neither am I old. I'm only 49. A slight correction is warranted. My thoughts regarding everything I want to do to my executive assistant are dirty — downright filthy is a more fitting description.

After a moment of fighting, Victoria snapped the suitcase upright and continued her wrathful march towards my SUV. She hoisted herself on the running boards and rapped her knuckles against the window.

"Come outside, Knox. I just wanna talk," she said softly. Too softly if you asked me. A chuckle spilled from my lips.

I rolled the window down a fraction, but kept it high enough that she couldn't fit her fist through.

"I'm not falling for that one."

Victoria smiled tightly and leaned into the window. "Do you know what I want right now?"

"A donut?" I offered.

"To crush your old ass balls into dust," she answered.

I shuddered but kept my composure. "If you wanted to touch my balls, we could arrange—"

"Go to Hell!" she spat.

Such venom...I love it.

"Victoria, there's no point in stalling. We have a flight to catch. Get in the truck," I demanded, nodding at the available seat beside me. I cleared my throat, trying to ignore how her intoxicating and deliriously sweet perfume seeped into the car.

"What part of 'go to Hell' don't you understand?"

"All of it," I replied.

She grinned, and her fingers clung tightly to the window. "Go to Hell with gasoline drawers on. If you think, for one minute, that I'm gonna get in this truck, then you've lost your ever-loving—"

"One hundred thousand," I interjected, cutting off her well-wishes for my soul.

Victoria blinked rapidly. "Excuse me?"

"I'll give you a $100,000.00 bonus once we return to New York. Get in," I remarked, unlocking the door.

She hopped down and created some distance between my idling truck and herself. She paced in a circle and spoke to herself erratically. The words tumbled from her luscious lips like rapid fire. I could barely keep up. I did catch her saying, "Do it for Mom."

Do it for Mom? Is her mother in financial straits?

Eventually, Victoria's shoulders slumped in resignation. She opened the passenger door, slipped inside, and filled the SUV with the scent that was uniquely hers. I nodded at my driver through the rear-view mirror, and he fetched Victoria's massive suitcase and hauled it into the trunk.

"I want you to know that I despise you with every fiber of my being."

I rolled my eyes. "Tell me something new, Tori Montana."

"Stop calling me that. It's Ms. Caldwell."

I sighed. "Ms. Caldwell is so boring," I taunted. I was waiting for a snarky comeback, but Victoria's buzzing phone had stolen her attention. Her nose did that twitchy thing it did when she was pissed off. "Are you messaging your friends?"

"Yep. Just telling them how my sadistic *husband* canceled my flight and bribed me with an obscene amount of money to accompany him on the business trip I had no plans of attending."

I smiled softly, finding an opening to tease her more.

"I just had a thought. Mrs. Victoria Ramsey has a lovely ring to it. Don't you think?"

"Only if you drop dead as soon as we say 'I do.'"

I chuckled. "Now, where's the fun in that? I'd at least like to make it through our wedding night."

"What's the point?" she mumbled as her fingers flew furiously across the screen. I peeked over, and she was typing in all caps and exclamation marks. I could barely contain my smile when she inserted several knife emojis. "You'd never live long enough to get the kitty."

"Oh? Tell me more."

"I'd imagine we'd be in some penthouse of a swanky hotel. The guests would still be in full swing, enjoying the open bar reception downstairs. I'd propose a toast to our new beginnings, hand you a flute of poisoned champagne, step over your twitching body, and slip into bed. I'd sleep easily that night knowing I was a billionaire."

This trip will be...gratifying. Seven days on a tropical island with the most beautiful woman on Earth? My dick is getting hard just thinking about it.

"You know. That was extensively thought out for a woman who claims to hate me."

The SUV lurched forward, and the driver pulled into the roundabout. Victoria tossed her cell phone into her purse and turned to address me.

"Mr. Ramsey."

"Knox," I corrected. There was no need to be so formal. She'd be mine after the trip, after all.

"Mr. Ramsey," she asserted. "This is a business trip."

"I'm glad you caught on."

"That means you are to leave me alone unless it's business-related. That means no emails or calls before 8:00 or after 5:00. I don't want to hear or see you if it's not about business. I don't even want you to breathe in my direction if it's not about business," she informed as she spoke with her graceful hands. "I better be able to convince myself you're dead until something business-related comes up."

So cruel. I can't get enough.

I leaned a little closer.

"I want to hear you say it," Victoria demanded. My mouth dried.

She's sexy when she gets dominant.

"I will not breathe in your direction unless it's about business," I recited diligently. "I promise."

"Good."

We both shared a look. It was wordless, but we knew what it meant. There wasn't a chance in hell I'd keep my word.

All of this is simply posturing from her, but I'll let her think she's won...for now.

"Do you have a copy of the itinerary?"

"It's in your email."

"Of fucking course it is," she mumbled under her breath. "You planned on abducting me this whole time, didn't you?"

I shot her a pointed look. "Do you really want to piss yourself off with a rhetorical question like that?"

"I'm not pissing myself off. *You're* pissing me off. I'm praying for your downfall, Knox."

"I'm sure you are. I'm just not sure it's a good idea since we're always together," I mentioned, raking my eyes over her. She glared out the window. In the reflection of the tinted

21

glass, I could see her lips turned down into something like a pout. "Where you go, I go. And if I go down, then we'll go down together."

It's because I can't let her go. I don't mind monopolizing her time and enjoy pushing her to the edge. I can't help myself. The further she tries to distance herself from me, the tighter my grip. But the question remains...how can I let her know it's not just banter? How can I close the gap between us?

"We'll see about that," Victoria grumbled.

Maybe a little praise will do the trick.

"You're a good assistant, Victoria. More than good, actually. You're very capable. I'm lucky to have you. I don't even mind the cursing and death threats."

Things will be different on the island. I'll show her a different side of me. She'll relax, and I'll finally let her see Knox, the man, not Knox, her overbearing, boundary-crossing boss.

She glanced at me with cautious, brown eyes and nearly stole my breath. "I'm the best assistant you'll ever have."

"You are," I co-signed with a nod.

"You'll never find someone better than me."

"I wouldn't dream of it."

She's too cute. Look at her resolve bleeding away because of a bit of praise and a pat on the back. I can praise her more. I can talk her through it. I can pound her anger out while praising her for taking me so well. And just like that, I'm hard.

I glanced away, cursing myself for underestimating my self-control around her.

This will be an exciting adventure, indeed.

4

Diabolical AF

Victoria

Alyssa: Yooooo! That man is diabolical!

Brittney: That man is a psycho! Get away from him, sis!

Me: Yeah, that's kind of hard to do when we're 40,000 feet in the air.

Alyssa: You need to give that man your two-week notice IMMEDIATELY.

Brittney: Alyssa, that man literally called her airline and told them she died so he could force her on this trip. Do you think he's gonna let her go just like that? That's like trying to divorce a desperate ain't shit man.

Alyssa: Shit. You're right, Britt. He's desperate af. That man will knock her head off.

While my friends are right to be concerned, Knox isn't THAT crazy.

Brittney: What if he's trying to traffick her??

Alyssa: I'm calling the laws.

Me: All right. Let's calm down. What would you even tell

23

them? My best friend's boss strong-armed her into going on a business trip and paid her $100k to go?

Yeah, I'm no fucking idiot. I made that man transfer me $100k before arriving at the airport.

Brittney: Damn. You shouldn't have taken the money, Tori.

Maybe not. But your mother also isn't in a private pay memory care nursing home.

Me: I'll turn it down next time. Anyway, I know y'all are probably itching to hit the beach, so I'll talk to you two later. Have a drink for me and send me pictures.

Alyssa: We'll check in with you often. Keep your head up, sis!

Brittney: Make his pockets hurt while you're there!

Me: That was a given.

I tossed my phone aside and returned my attention to the sorry-ass excuse of an itinerary.

"Victoria."

"Don't talk to me, Knox," I said, scrolling through the document on my work tablet, which I purposely left locked in my office because I *knew* I wouldn't be doing any work while on vacation.

That's another strike against him. He knows I don't allow him in my office. My office is my private sanctuary—a safe space from him, if you will.

My brows furrowed deeper and deeper the more I reviewed the cockamamie itinerary that Knox pieced together.

"Knox?"

"Oh, I can speak now?"

"For now…what's with these large gaps in the schedule? And why is it so vague?"

"I don't find it particularly vague."

"Knox…this shit literally says there's a morning meeting tomorrow from 9 AM to 10 AM, and then it says we have "free time" for the remainder of the day."

"It also says TBD, and the schedule is subject to change."

"How long have I been working for you, Knox?"

"A little over a blissful year," he replied with a sarcastic smirk that made me want to wind up my pimp hand.

"That's right. So, you know, or you should know, that this itinerary is unacceptable. As much as it kills me to admit this, despite all the bullshit you put me through, you and I work as a well-oiled machine, but that's because we have *structure*. This fly-by-the-seat business is not going to work for me."

He stroked his clean-shaven chin as he considered my words. "What do you do to wind down, Victoria?"

So, he's just going to pass over everything I just said?!

"I go to Miami to wind down," I spat, getting worked up again. He smiled once more.

Knox doesn't know it yet, but he's two seconds away from being strangled with his tie.

"I'm aware that the itinerary is a little…flexible, but you know what they say about all work and no play. I assure you that Bali far exceeds Miami."

"Not if I'm with you," I countered.

"Relax, Victoria. It's not the end of the world. Plus, you were paid handsomely for your attendance. You have $100,000.00 more than you did before you woke up this morning."

Shit. I can't argue with him there. That money will cover Mom's rent for a year.

Remembering that my mother would be cared for without me stressing tamped down my anger.

"You're right," I mumbled as I continued to scroll.

25

"Of course, I am."

I raised my palm to pause him when I made it to the accommodation portion of the itinerary.

"Knox Jamarcus Ramsey."

"That's not my middle name," he sighed, massaging his temples.

"Tell me your middle name, and I'll stop giving you random names," I insisted.

"I refuse."

"All right then, Knox Kayden Ramsey. Why is there only one room booked?"

"That was all that was available on such short notice."

"I'm not sharing a room with you."

"We're not sharing a room; we're sharing a common space. The suite has two bedrooms."

Nope. This isn't going to work for me because a few cocktails might convince me that a good rage fucking is in order. At least if I'm located on a different floor or at the opposite end of the hotel, we wouldn't be as easily accessible when we're drunk, horny, and lonely.

Knox

The next afternoon after our overnight layover, I nursed my bourbon as I read the latest crime novel, ranked #1 on the *New York Times* Best Sellers list that week. It wasn't the best I'd read—predictable by page 50, but the dialogue was engaging enough.

My eyes flicked up from the pages when I heard Victoria moan softly in her sleep.

How high on the delusional scale would I have to be if I

imagined she was dreaming of me?

Rather high.

I'd gotten off easy after the stunt I pulled. I was still breathing, had all my limbs, and could see out of both eyes. I'd expected to at least receive a decent-sized lump to the back of my head.

Thank God for donuts and wealth, or I'd be a dead man.

It might be my narcissism talking, but a part of me believed that Victoria didn't mind accompanying me on this trip. Of course, she protested and threw a tantrum like the petulant woman child she was. Still, I couldn't help but notice when she left her tablet behind to use the restroom that she'd been researching excursions. I had no desire to go horseback riding on the beach, but I'd do it if it meant I could spend time with her.

The plane jolted, and some of the amber liquor splashed on my white dress shirt.

"Shit," I mumbled, reaching for a napkin.

"Shut up, Knox," Victoria mumbled in her sleep. I rolled my eyes and continued dabbing at my shirt. The jet lurched again in a way that made me feel uneasy. I glanced at Victoria, and despite the worsening turbulence, she was still sound asleep. The jet shuddered again, and my fingers sank into the armrests like a spooked cat with its fur raised and claws out.

This is not normal. Something's seriously wrong.

I threw up the shade and was relieved to see the engine wasn't on fire, but my relief was short-lived when the jet took another jerky dive, and my stomach dropped to my toes.

"Fuck this shit."

I freed myself from the seat belt and was about to approach the cockpit when the flight attendant rushed towards me.

"Sir! Please remain seated and secure your seat belt."

"I need to speak to the pilot."

"Please return to your seat," she said. She was trying to appear calm, but the sweat on her brow and the downward twitch of her lips betrayed her.

She's afraid.

"I'm speaking to the pilot one way or another. Maybe you should take your own advice and fasten your seat belt."

"Unfortunately, sir, I need you to return to your sea—"

I brushed past her, determined to speak to the pilot. My intuition told me that there was a probability that the plane wouldn't make it to its intended destination.

That can't happen; Victoria's with me.

She could've been in Miami with her best friends, but my selfishness could endanger her life.

A garbled commotion echoed from the cockpit.

"Sir? Sir? Oh, fuck! Oh, shit!"

The yelling didn't abate but became increasingly panicked and nonsensical with each passing second.

No one wants to hear "oh, shit" from their pilot.

I rushed to the cockpit and ignored the attendant's frantic calls. Nothing could've prepared me for the scene I stumbled upon. I didn't know what to expect, but I hadn't expected to find the seasoned pilot convulsing in his seat with his eyes rolled into the back of his head. The co-pilot, who couldn't be more than 25, hovered over him while red lights buzzed and flickered on the dashboard.

"What the fuck is going on in here?" I demanded, pushing closer.

The young pilot looked at me with tears in his eyes.

"H-he just started shaking," he explained, his hands trembling like a Southern church lady with a tambourine.

"Yeah, no shit. He's having a seizure, dumbass. I want to know why you haven't taken over? I don't know if you've noticed, but it's getting rocky out here, kid," I said, wrestling the deceased pilot out of the chair onto the floor.

"Is…is he dead?"

"We'll all be dead if you don't get this plane under control." The young pilot looked at the controls like he'd never flown a plane. "Please tell me you know what you're doing," I spoke softly.

He licked his lips and swallowed roughly. "It's my first…it's my first week. I've never flown internationally before."

I ran a hand through my hair and tried to remain calm so I could take control of the situation. It was no different than handling a work crisis.

Except that we're 40,000 feet in the air, and there's a possibility that we'll plunge to our deaths.

"Th-that's not all, sir," the co-pilot stammered.

I narrowed my eyes at him and clutched the back of the pilot's chair when we took another unfortunate dip.

"Lay it on me, kid."

"We have bigger issues on her hands."

"Such as?" I questioned.

"One of the engines failed, and I'm fairly certain the other won't hold us until we reach somewhere safe to land."

I never thought I'd use my age as an excuse for not comprehending the basic English language, but there was a slim chance I misheard the young pilot.

Did he just say one of the engines failed, and the other is about to go out? He didn't say that. I'm 49, and my hearing isn't what it used to be.

"I'm sorry. I think I misheard you, kid. Can you repeat that?"

"One of the engines failed, and I'm fairly certain that the other won't hold us until we reach somewhere safe to land," the co-pilot whimpered.

"I need you to calm down and regain control of this plane. I don't know much about planes, but I know that in the event of engine failure, the plane can glide. Can you radio for help?"

The jet pitched, setting off more alarms.

Fuck.

"Knox!" Victoria shrieked, helplessly calling my name.

I closed my eyes and took several deep breaths to calm my nerves, but that was challenging to do, thanks to the pilot's pathetic sobs that he didn't want to die.

"Knox! Where are you?"

My eyes snapped open, and I knew I had to take control of the situation as best I could.

"Hey! Put your hands on that goddamn joystick, or whatever the fuck you call it, and try not to kill us all! Deal?" I ordered before rushing back to our seats. The look of sheer terror on Victoria's face was gut-wrenching. She was terrified—rightfully so—and all I could think about were those escaping zoo penguins in that children's movie directing you to put your head between your knees and kiss your butt goodbye. It was time to prepare for the worst-case scenario.

This plane is going down.

I sat beside Victoria and offered her a practiced smile—the same smile I'd use when a board member asked too many damn questions.

"Knox, something's wrong, isn't it?" she whispered, tears cresting her lid.

"Of course not."

"Don't fucking lie to me, Knox. You're wearing that same smile you wore when Buchanan was digging in your ass about profit margins."

She knows me too damn well.

Her breath shuddered, and she whispered, "Oh, my God," when I reached under the seat and retrieved the life preserver. "None of that matters. What matters now is that you keep calm. You will be okay," I assured her as I tugged the vest on her. I secured it—ensuring all the snaps were fastened across her chest and midsection.

"We're going to die," Victoria whimpered as reality set in for both of us. "Fuck! We're going to die!"

"We're not dying, sweetheart," I said, not even believing my own lie. I didn't know the precise odds of surviving a plane crash, but the ones I'd seen sensationalized for shock and awe on network news made me believe the odds weren't in our favor.

Tears fell freely from Victoria's eyes, and the painful regret I felt bloomed in my chest, spreading through me like wildfire. I placed my hands on her face, and she looked into my eyes. Her pupils dilated as adrenaline coursed through her system.

"Hey. Guess what?"

She sniffled and shook her head. "I-I don't have time for your bullshit, Knox. Can't you fucking let me die in peace?" she cried.

I shook my head and grinned. "I have to pay you hazard pay for this. You're welcome."

She scoffed and muttered under her breath that I was a bastard as I rechecked her attachments and carefully scanned for holes in the life preserver between the violent shaking of the plane.

Hey. At least she didn't call me a dirty old bastard this time.

As reality settled in that we were going down, Victoria's sobs overtook, and she began hyperventilating, tugging at her life vest in a desperate attempt to breathe. I wrenched her fingers away from the clips and held them tightly.

"Tori Montana, you're the strongest, smartest, and most unfuckwithable person I know. There's nothing you can't handle. I promise. I'll make sure you're okay, but you have to take deep breaths because *when* we survive this, we'll need that big brain of yours to help us get out of this mess. Okay?"

She nodded gently, and I patterned deep breaths for her until her breathing leveled out.

"You'll...you'll be here, right?"

"I'll be here every step of the way. I won't leave you—not for a single second," I promised.

"W-why aren't you in your life vest yet? Put it on! Do you want to die?"

I smiled.

Well, if I'm going to die, I might as well make it count, right?

Without further thought, I leaned over, pulled her in, and pressed our lips together.

They're soft. I always knew they were, but fuck, the physical confirmation was needed. So fucking worth it.

Victoria was stunned—frozen in time like a statue while the jet continued to fall out of the air. I deepened the kiss for a moment when she didn't move away. I finally released her when I realized I only had precious moments left.

"I think I deserve a little taste of Heaven before I go to Hell."

She was silent, staring at me while our fate hung in the balance. I took the opportunity to pull on my life preserver and secure myself in my seat. She didn't react until I offered her a flirty wink.

Victoria's face scrunched up, relieved of shock as anger replaced it.

She's making my favorite face; if it's the last face I see before I take my last breath, I'm satisfied.

"You son of a—"

5

Jack and Rose

Victoria

I opened my eyes and blinked rapidly, hoping my double vision would clear sooner rather than later. The smell of smoke, gasoline, and salt invaded my nostrils as my eyes focused on the wreckage that grew farther and farther as I was dragged away. We crash-landed into the ocean, and I was shocked we survived, but even more stupefied by the kiss. The last thing I remembered was Knox's lips on mine.

Initially, I was stunned when he cupped my face and kissed me. It was unexpected but not necessarily unwanted. My eyes rolled in the back of my head when his tongue caressed mine. The bourbon on his tongue made my head swim, or maybe it was 100% Knox that had me swaying. I fantasized about kissing my boss more than I cared to admit. I was willing to do anything to shut his stupid mouth, even if it meant mouth fucking him so good his toes curled in his Italian loafers.

Okay...let me be so fucking for real that's not the reason, and I know it, but your girl just fell 40,000 feet out of the sky—let me be delusional.

I had snapped out of my shock when he moaned softly and deepened the kiss. I had no choice but to return his gesture. Our tongues tangled in a last-ditch effort for comfort and reassurance as we realized our time was coming closer and closer to an end. He broke away, and my tongue slid across my bottom lip, lapping up whatever was left of him. He slipped on his life preserver, buckled himself in, and winked at me. My blood boiled when I realized that man gave me the best kiss of my life and I was seconds away from dying. All I could imagine was how good his head game must have been before it was lights out.

"Victoria, keep your eyes open for me," Knox rumbled.

There he goes ruining shit for me again. Can't a woman fantasize in peace?

"J-just so we're clear—"

"I know. You hate me," he panted as he swam us to shore.

"That, and we're not having a Jack and Rose moment."

He chuckled through his labored breaths. "C'mon, Victoria. I can smell the romance in the air."

"I'm sorry to tell you that the 'romance' you're smelling is jet fumes. There was nothing romantic about *Titanic* or our current situation," I proclaimed.

"Expound."

"The movie highlighted how most people regard poor folks."

"And how is that?"

"Their lives are expendable. I'm mad that Jack saved Rose—he never had a chance."

"Thank God. I can stop swimming," he replied in that teasing tone that made me want to dot his eye more than once. "I'd hate to be Jack—saving a woman I'd never have a chance with."

"Knox Nigel Ramsey—"

"That's not my middle name," he huffed.

"Knox Ezekiel Ramsey, you ruined any chance you had with me when you canceled my flight."

"I don't know about that, Victoria. That kiss said otherwise."

I could've responded with something snarky, but the blood dripping into my eyes took precedence. I lifted a hand, touched my forehead, and yanked it back with a hiss.

"You hit your head upon impact."

"Wow! However would I have figured that out without you?" I drawled.

He snorted.

"I should save myself the trouble and drown you now. I need a break."

He paused to catch his breath as we bobbed in the water.

This man needs to get a move on. I've seen enough Shark Week to know exactly how this will go!

"I can swim," I said, maneuvering behind him.

"What the hell are you doing, Victoria?"

"We can't stay in the open water like this. We'll be sitting ducks for sharks. Hell, there might be barracudas or something in here," I explained as I surveyed our surroundings. My heart fluttered with hope when I noticed an island in the distance. If we were lucky, we'd make it in one piece, and if God chose to show us a little mercy, we wouldn't be met by a lost cannibalistic tribe.

I grabbed the back of his vest and swam with one arm towards shore.

Thank you, Mom, for the swimming classes at the Y.

My tears blended into the ocean, adding to the saltiness as I thought about my mother. Knox's bribe money was there, and my salary was directly deposited twice a month. Her rent would be taken care of, but there was a possibility I'd never see her again.

What if no one finds us?

"Victoria...I'm sorry," Knox whispered, voice thick with emotion.

I hadn't realized I was sobbing as we approached shore. I abandoned Knox and crawled on shaky hands and knees on hot, white sand to safety. The beach appeared deserted, and the shock and reality of our situation began to sink in. I was stranded on an island with my boss from Hell.

Knox

"I hate you."

My heart dropped in my chest. Victoria had said those three little words so many times over the past year, but never with such insult—never from the heart. And it stung like a motherfucker.

"Victoria, I'm—"

She held a hand up, halting my apology, forcing the words to die in my throat.

"I-I don't want to hear sorry, Knox. Your sorry isn't going to save us."

She was right. I could say sorry until I was blue in the face, but it wouldn't change our situation or how she despised me.

I nodded at the wound on her head.

"Let me bandage that up," I murmured.

"How do you plan on doing that?" she questioned skeptically.

I held up the first aid kit I salvaged from the wreckage. I had clipped it to my vest before I swam us toward shore.

I had expected her to deny my assistance and tell me to fuck off and die, but to my surprise, she motioned for me to proceed.

"All right. Let's see what we got," I said, crouching and opening the kit. I was relieved to find that everything was encased in waterproof packaging. I moved efficiently, tearing open a package of antiseptic wipes and bandages. "This is alcohol base, so it might burn. Well, maybe not as much as the salt water."

Victoria's "I don't give a fuck" face, mixed with the blood that was steadily pumping from her forehead, prompted me to shut the hell up and tend to her wound. She winced periodically as I cleaned her injury.

"What is that?" she asked when I cracked the lid off a small tube.

"Liquid stitches."

She shook her head. "Don't use that. Just bandage me up."

"It'll leave a nasty scar if I don't."

"We may never see civilization again. I don't give a damn about a scar. We should save it for more serious injuries."

I nodded and proceeded to work my magic. I tried to ignore how Victoria trembled like a leaf before me, but the shaking was so violent that I'd have to close my eyes not to notice.

This is all my fault. She could've been in Miami with her friends, having the time of her life, but instead, she's wet, injured, and afraid for her life. I don't even know where we are—somewhere in the Pacific if I had to guess. But how helpful is that? How many microscopic islands dotted the Pacific Ocean? We need a plan—water, food, shelter.

Locating a drinkable water source would be my number one priority. We wouldn't survive long without it. If we were lucky, it would rain, but then we'd need a receptacle to collect rainwater.

"W-we need to find water," Victoria stammered. I held back a smile. Did I hire her because I thought she was smoking hot and I wanted an assistant who was easy on the eyes? Yes, but I knew from how she domineered our interview that she was a competent woman with a take-no-shit personality.

"We do," I agreed as I finished bandaging. "Someone will find us," I said confidently.

"How can you be so sure?" she snapped.

"Billionaire CEO Knox Ramsey goes missing after never arriving at his destination? Someone is bound to be looking for me."

She glanced up at me and scoffed. "Trust me. They wouldn't look for you if they knew you like I did."

"Fair enough. I'm going to look around and see what I can find. Maybe something washed ashore. Stay put."

I left her and returned to shore, giving us both some much-needed space and time to think. Just as I arrived, I noticed something approaching—a lone figure in a life raft.

Another survivor? No fucking way.

I didn't think it was possible for my mood to sour any further, but my anger bubbled up when the young co-pilot, who was responsible for our crash landing, pulled the raft ashore.

"God! That was a fucking nightmare. I thought I was going to die. I think I shit my pants. I can't tell with all the water—"

Wisely, he stopped speaking once he noticed the thunderous

look on my face.

"Of course, after dooming us all, you somehow survived."

"Hey! It's not my fault the engines failed!"

"Well then, whose fault is it? Aren't you required to perform pre-flight checks?"

"The captain performed our pre-flight check."

"Did you sign off? I know there must be a checks and balances system." I closed my eyes and sighed when the kid looked away sheepishly. "You didn't…did you?"

"I didn't, but it's not from my lack of trying! He told me he knew what he was doing and wouldn't let some green-behind-the-ears kid fresh out of flight school check after him—his words, not mine."

I was about to give him a piece of my mind when my eyes strayed to the contents of the life raft. I was shocked to see a flashlight, rope, scissors, coffee, and a coffee pot.

"You managed to salvage a few things from the wreckage. I guess you're not a useless piece of shit after all, huh?"

He scoffed. "Guess not."

I narrowed my eyes. "You and the deceased captain are responsible for us crashing—don't get too fucking cocky."

"You don't have to keep reminding me," he drawled with a childish roll of his eyes.

"Did the flight attendant survive?"

"No—she perished."

"Okay…so it's just the three of us."

"The three of us?" he asked curiously.

"Yes, the woman I'm traveling with."

"But I only see you."

"She's right fucking—"

I turned to point at Victoria, and that's when I noticed she

40

was no longer where I had left her.

Oh, fuck.

6

Honey Pack

Knox

Where did she go? Maybe she had to pee? I told her to stay put!

I heard a scream echo from beyond the trees just as my mind raced toward the worst-case scenario. My heart kicked into overdrive, and my feet moved before my brain could process what was happening. All I knew was that Victoria's hardheaded ass was in trouble.

"Victoria!" I shouted, breaking the plane that separated the beach from the jungle. I called her name several times, but she didn't respond.

What if she's hurt? What if a wild animal has gotten to her? What if she fell into quicksand? Fuck! Why does she have to be so goddamn stubborn? Can't she take instructions for once in her life?

I slowed my sprint when I noticed her flailing around aimlessly, swiping at her face and hair with tears streaming down her face.

"There you are! Jesus Christ, what part of stay put don't you—" I stopped speaking when she offered me a silencing, tear-filled glare. "Not the time. Okay, message received. What's the matter?" I examined her quickly, relieved that she wasn't bleeding or injured. She seemed fine, at least physically.

"Get…it…off!" she shrieked, starting back up with the windmilling, looking like she was participating in a mosh pit. I narrowed my eyes and took a closer look.

"You've got to calm down so I can help you. Stop freaking out," I said, trying to soothe her and stop her rash movements. I held her arms by her sides. Her chest heaved with little effort, and her brown eyes were red from tears. I couldn't help but smile.

She's so cute. Even when she's covered in…

"Oh, is it the spider webs?"

She nodded weakly from exhaustion, thanks to a combination of her adrenaline dump, fear, and impromptu cardio workout.

"All right, all right. I've got you," I whispered, pulling the webs from her body. I checked every inch of her to ensure no creepy crawlies remained. When I was satisfied, I resumed my ass-chewing. "What were you thinking? What part of stay put sounded like run off into a jungle and get yourself killed? You could've gotten seriously injured!"

I huffed and waited for her to spit her deadly venom at me— to scream and curse at me and tell me everything was my fault, but she didn't. Instead, her eyes welled up with fresh tears. They streamed down her face, marking a path through dirt, grime, and traces of blood. I felt like even more of a shithead when sobs wracked her frame.

Maybe I'm being too harsh. We did crash land into the ocean

43

thousands of miles from home with no provisions, communication, and little to no survival skills. We're both trying to do the best we can with the shitty hand we were dealt.

"Hey, look…I'm sorry, Victoria," I apologized, rubbing the back of my neck anxiously. Guilt swaddled me once more when her crying intensified. I did the only thing I could in our situation and pulled her into a hug. I rested my cheek on top of her head as her tears soaked my shirt. "I'm sorry," I whispered again. "I know you're doing your best."

"I really am," she offered breathlessly between sobs. "I-I was looking for food and water because God only knows if we'll ever be rescued. W-we might be stuck on this fucking island forever." She pulled out of my embrace and fixed those enchanting eyes on me. "What if we're never found?"

I rubbed her arms soothingly. "Then…I guess you have no choice but to become my island wife. I'm sure we can find a talking crab to officiate our wedding."

"Listen to me when I tell you, you should've died in that plane crash," she remarked.

"Then you would've been left with the co-pilot, who is partly responsible for us crashing."

"That's fine. I'd turn him into my little bitch boy."

We cracked inappropriate smiles at each other because, despite our dire situation, we knew it was true.

"I can see it. That boy doesn't have a spine. As you would say, 'It's giving invertebrate.'"

I doubled over when she punched me in the stomach.

"Fuck you, Knox." She giggled.

"Fuck me," I groaned, trying to swallow down the bourbon from earlier. "And here I thought I was afraid of your stapler."

"You better thank whatever god you believe in that I don't

have it, or I would've unloaded the clip in you. I would've pieced your ass together like Frankenstein."

I closed my eyes, pulled myself up, and sucked in a deep breath before opening my eyes again. "Is this a bad time to tell you that I'm wildly turned on right now?"

Victoria

My eyes ticked down, and I regretted it immediately.

And here I was, afraid I'd run into a snake in the jungle. Oh, I ran into a snake all right—more like a fucking anaconda. Damn...no wonder this man cuts up the way he does. I have to stay away from this man. I've never been one of those women who were dumb over dick, but I can see my IQ tanking a little after getting hold of him.

"What are you doing?" he asked curiously.

"Patting myself on the back for never showing up at your hotel room in the middle of the night. Good job, me."

Knox chuckled and put his hands on his hips like some caped superhero no one asked for. "I would've obliged."

Tell me something I don't know.

"All right, King Dong, you need to put that thing back in its cage. Think depressing thoughts like how I'm turning in my resignation if we're ever found."

"You're not resigning, Victoria," he said confidently.

"Bitch, yes, the fuck I am. I'm getting a book deal, a movie deal, all that. I don't have to work for you anymore once I get done snotting and crying on TV."

"Bullshit," Knox challenged.

"Knox Peterson Ramsey—"

"That's not my middle name," he complained.

"Knox Emilio Ramsey—"

45

"Again, not my middle name."

"Knox Whatever-the-fuck-it-is Ramsey, I will get on TV and tell them people that I ate the fucking flight attendant—don't try me."

Knox turned a deep shade of red before laughing uncontrollably. "That's...you...you can't be serious," he stammered through his laughter.

"I'll tell those people she tasted like chicken and that I had to do what I had to do to survive—don't play with me, Knox."

"It sounds like you'd do anything for money," he remarked.

"Including working for you," I hissed.

"Okay...hear me out," he said, folding his arms over his chest. "I'll accept your resignation, but I'm offering you another proposal."

"No, I won't marry your funky ass either."

"I smell?" he asked, sniffing his armpit. "Oh, geez. That's rank."

"Yeah, that stress sweat is no joke."

"Tragic body odor aside, become my sugar baby."

That's an attractive offer, but no.

"I'm not bussing down for your old ass for money."

"But you'd do it for free?" he challenged with a raised brow.

Can't this man just suffer a heat stroke and leave me alone?

I waved my hands, trying to regain control of the situation. We were on a runaway train to Fantasy Land.

"I know the last five minutes have been playful, unserious banter to distract us from a very real situation, but we need to get serious, Knox Wolfe Ramsey."

"You were close that time."

"Really?" I asked in disbelief.

"No, not really. You couldn't be further."

"You're lying," I accused.

"I'd give you my wallet to confirm, but it's lost at sea along with the rest of our shit."

Thanks for the reminder, dipshit.

"I know you're scared," Knox said. "This is…an unreal situation, and I'd be lying if I said I know how to get us out of it. But I'm here and willing to do whatever I can to keep us alive and thriving until we're rescued."

"What if we're not rescued?" I asked softly. His face pinched with uncertainty. He raised his arms out to his sides.

"Then welcome to our new life."

The tears returned, and Knox had me in his arms in seconds. My shoulders shook. "I-I can feel your dick against my stomach," I said through my tears.

"I apologize," he said, scooting back just a smidge.

God, if you plan on me being stranded on this island with this man for the rest of my days, then let a falling coconut take me out now!

I waited a few moments, but the head-smashing coconut never came.

"I need you, Victoria."

I need this man to stop asking me for a pity-stranded-island fuck.

"I know I'm the big boss at the office, but we need to work together here." My crying had reduced to sporadic sniffles. "Believe it or not, I can't be efficient without you, whether in the office or on a remote island."

"My pay should reflect that," I responded.

"Your benefit package is out of this world. You're compensated better than most executive assistants. Not too many CEOs pay for their assistants' apartments. Especially assistants they aren't fucking."

My brows knitted together. I was curious.

"Why do you pay for my apartment?"

"I'll tell you when we get home—whatever version of home that might be. It might be a high-rise or a hut."

I pulled out of his arms and instantly missed the warmth despite how hot and humid it was. He provided a different kind of warmth—a comforting coziness that made you feel that everything would be okay. I wanted to pretend that everything would be fine, but the reality was that someone might become sick, get hurt, or be injured.

What happens if it's Knox? According to my Naked and Afraid meter, the co-pilot has a low survival rating. What will happen if I'm left all alone? That's what I fear the most. I can't think like this—catastrophizing and expecting the worst. The negativity won't do us any good. I have no choice but to put on my big girl panties and make the most of an awful situation.

"Knox, we need to come up with a game plan."

"Agreed."

"What kind of survival skills do you have?"

"I did a few years in the Boy Scouts."

"I didn't know that. How come you never told me?"

"Mmmm, maybe because you never asked, and you spent more time threatening to kill me with your stapler than getting to know me," he answered.

Valid.

"Okay, fair. That's good. My confidence in you and your survival abilities has skyrocketed."

"What about you?" Knox queried.

"My TV stays on the *Discovery Channel*."

"Really?" he asked, sounding impressed.

"Yes, Knox, really."

"Hmph. I took you more for—"

"Let me stop you right there, Knox Hamilton Ramsey. I swear to God, if you say *BET, OWN, The Impact Network, Zeus,* or any other heavily melanated television station, then I'm killing you. When I'm rescued, I'll tell them you died on impact, and that impact was my fist."

Knox cleared his throat and shifted on his feet. "I was going to say *Lifetime* since you're so dramatic."

"Mhm. *Lifetime* my ass. Keep playing with your lifeline, Knox."

"Is this a bad time to tell you that I'm still turned on?"

I looked down once again and sighed.

I mean...good for him, I guess. He's old as fuck and can get it up and maintain without a honey pack.

7

Scooby Doo Bullshit

Victoria

I closed my eyes and imagined what a double shot of tequila would taste like at the moment. My tongue moved across my bottom lip, searching for the coarse sea salt I'd chase away with the liquor and lime. A growl bubbled in my throat when Tweedle Dee and Tweedle Dum interrupted my fantasy with their bickering.

Seriously, these two fight more than Knox and I fight!

I rolled my eyes when a shoving match ensued.

We...are...doomed.

I put my fingers in my mouth and whistled, catching their attention. "What's good?"

"Nothing's good!" the co-pilot, Josh, exclaimed.

Knox and I glanced at each other before rolling our eyes.

At least King Dong gets me.

"Let me rephrase. What seems to be the problem?" I asked.

"The kid here thinks it's a great idea to split up," Knox

informed me as he ripped off what was left of his dingy white dress shirt, leaving behind his white undershirt and bulging biceps and forearms.

"Split up?" I asked in disbelief when I finished objectifying my boss. "What kind of Scooby Doo bullshit are you on? We will not be splitting up," I insisted.

"We need to find a water source," Knox mentioned.

"But we also need to find food and look to see if there are other inhabitants. We can divide and conquer and split the tasks," Josh expressed.

I see I need to speak to this man like those silly little interns we get that can't tell their ass from a hole in the wall.

I clapped my hands together and fixed the co-pilot with a sweet-as-pie smile until Knox snorted in the background and made an under-the-breath comment about how Josh shouldn't fall for my smile.

He's talking a little too much shit for a man who starts stuttering when I bend over to pick something up.

"Josh, I want to start by recognizing that we're only alive because of your aviation skills and quick thinking under pressure."

"Are you serious?" Knox interrupted, sounding like a squealing pig. "This idiot—"

"Keep talking, Knox, and you'll get a handful of sand in the face," I threatened. I was satisfied when he clamped his mouth shut.

He knows I'm good for it.

"As I was saying, we're alive because of you, and I appreciate your valiant effort. I may not know everything about wilderness survival; however, we must stick together as we familiarize ourselves with the island. There's no telling what dangers we may encounter. It could be anything from wild animals, poisonous insects, indigenous inhabitants, or quicksand—you name it. We'd be foolish to believe we can go trekking in the jungle alone—"

"Wait...didn't you go into the jungle alone?" Josh pressed, an amused smirk resting on his lips.

See...that's why I should've let Knox knock your head off your shoulders.

"He got you there," Knox muttered.

My smile widened as I attempted to keep my cool. "Yes... Josh...I did go into the jungle unaccompanied, and look what happened. I'm speaking from a place of experience. We need to stick together, at least for now. Acquiring water is our number one priority, followed by food and then shelter. We can kill two birds with one stone by searching for water and food simultaneously. You did amazing by recovering useful items from the wreckage that we'll be able to utilize."

"I did," he boasted triumphantly.

Don't get too full of yourself.

"You did. Now, do me a favor and gather the coffee pot, flashlight, scissors, first aid kit, and rope."

"What do we need the coffee pot for?"

"The coffee pot is currently the only receptacle we have. We can use it to carry water or food. Also, don't go into that jungle eating things willy-nilly, especially if you don't recognize them. That may be your last meal."

Josh nodded and returned to the raft he dragged to shore.

"A compliment sandwich? Really?" Knox asked.

"It worked, didn't it?"

"Someone has been taking the HR-mandated leadership modules seriously."

52

"And I know someone who doesn't and usually waits until the last minute to complete them."

"The active shooter training is bullshit; it's the same song and dance. The people in the video stick around too fucking long after hearing the initial gunfire, and they don't do the best job of running for their lives. It's unrealistic," he complained.

"Tell me about it! I'd be knees to chest!" I exclaimed.

He snorted. "Thank goodness for the panic room behind the bookcase in my office."

I blinked rapidly as I tried to compute what the hell he just told me. "I'm sorry…what's behind the bookcase?"

"A panic room."

"And how come you've never told me about this panic room?"

"Because I didn't want you to get to it first and lock me out."

I crossed my arms over my chest and kicked at a brown and white hermit crab shell, sending it flying a few feet away from me.

"Real talk?" I stated, tilting my head to the side.

"Always."

"I would've slammed that door shut like John Kramer did to Dr. Lawrence Gordon in *Saw*."

"I expected nothing less," Knox said, chuckling. "It was an amazing movie for its time—very original."

"Eh, I was four when it was released."

"That's depressing to hear," he muttered.

"Why?"

"I was 28 when it was released," he admitted, cringing as he went down memory lane.

My overwhelming urge to call him a dirty old bastard for lusting after me was put on the back burner when a sudden thought came to me. "Hey, Knox?"

"Please don't make fun of my age."

"No, I'm being serious. Are you on any medication?"

"Besides a daily vitamin supplement? No. My last physical was three months ago, and I received a clean bill of health."

"Thank God," I murmured.

I don't need this man dropping dead on me because he didn't have his pressure medication.

"What about your vision? I'm assuming you don't have spare contacts with you."

"I'll survive without them."

"Are you guys ready?" Josh asked, ambling towards us.

"As ready as I'll ever be," I mumbled.

My eyes widened when Knox grabbed my hand and laced his fingers in mine.

"Wh—"

"I can't have you running off."

He's just looking for an excuse to touch me. I should snatch my hand away, but who am I to deny him such a simple pleasure when he may never leave this island?

Knox

"I...I need to take a break," Josh announced, groaning feebly as we searched for provisions.

I slapped at two mosquitoes on my forearm and grinned in triumph at the sight of the smeared blood and smashed insects. We'd been walking for nearly three hours, and I had to be covered in over one hundred mosquito bites. I was tired, sweaty, and itchy, and not in the mood for anyone's bullshit.

"We just took a break ten minutes ago," I said, throwing him an unimpressed glance over my shoulder.

"It doesn't matter if it was ten or two minutes ago. I need a break."

"No, we need to keep pressing forward."

"Ramsey," Victoria said.

She only calls me by my surname when there's zero room for argument.

I relented.

"Five minutes, and then we need to keep moving."

"Thank fuck," Josh whimpered, plopping down on a log for respite.

"I wouldn't do that if I were you," Victoria said as she wiped her forehead with the bottom of her shirt, revealing her soft belly and belly button ring.

"And why not?" he asked childishly.

"Because bugs love living in those hollowed-out logs. There's no telling what might be in there—ants, termites, beetles, spiders—"

"Shit!" Josh yelped, jumping from the log and slapping at his legs. "Fucking fire ants! Just get it over with and kill me now!"

"Don't tempt me, kid," I mumbled as I observed our surroundings. Our food search hadn't been as successful as I'd hoped. Everything we'd come across was, at the very least, questionable. I thought we'd hit a minor jackpot when we stumbled across some fallen coconuts. However, Victoria warned us that fallen coconuts had to be carefully examined for cracks and damage due to the potential risk of contaminants. I spent the next thirty minutes cracking open brown coconuts that all proved to be spoiled.

We're off to a great fucking start, and at this rate, we'll have to rely on what we can catch out at sea.

"Are you all right, Victoria? I haven't heard much from you. Usually, I can't go more than ten minutes without hearing a complaint."

She shrugged.

"I think I should've taken advantage of the free gym membership in my employee package and cut back on the donuts."

"Way to take personal accountability," I praised playfully.

"How much further will we walk in this direction before doubling back?"

I sighed and placed my hands on my hips. "We need to go as deep as we can. Returning to the beach without fresh water isn't an option."

"We might have an alternative if we don't find water," Josh offered.

"And what is that?" I questioned, keeping my expectations low to avoid disappointment.

"We were carrying cases of water on the jet. There's a possibility that there might be some water bottles floating around the wreckage. We planned on returning to the wreckage to scavenge for supplies anyway."

"How many cases were there?" Victoria asked.

"Six. They were 32-count."

"That could last us a while if we're conservative," she spoke wistfully.

I shook my head. "I'm not trying to be an asshole, but we shouldn't get our hopes up and should remain focused. If, by some miracle, we find some bottles floating at sea, wonderful, but we must keep our expectations in check. More likely than not, that won't occur."

"I don't see how you worked for him. He seems like such a

Debbie Downer," Josh complained to Victoria, trying to get some sympathy points from her or kiss her ass. It was difficult to tell. The boy seemed to have a kiss-ass nature about him.

Victoria glared at him, and I'd expected her to hurt his feelings with one of her snarky remarks, but I was sorely disappointed when she said, "I wouldn't lean against any trees if I were you."

"Why not?" Josh asked.

She scoffed. "For the same reason I told you not to sit on the log. "Let's get moving."

I followed and fell in step beside her. "You could've defended my honor back there."

"There was nothing to defend. It was a valid inquiry," she expressed. "I'd work for the devil as long as he paid me a fair, livable wage with benefits."

"I pay you a fair, livable wage."

"My point exactly."

We continued our lighthearted "bickering" while on our hunt for water as a way to keep distracted. Josh complained that he felt left out of the conversation, and Victoria told him he should be grateful that he was breathing.

Ten minutes later, I nearly dropped to my knees and kissed the ground.

"Is this a mirage?" Victoria asked.

We had our answer when Josh released a piercing victory cry and ran toward what I believed to be a freshwater oasis fed by a 20-foot waterfall. He jumped cannonball-style and broke the surface a few seconds later.

"Whoa! This water is so cold!"

"What about the taste?" Victoria asked as I shedded my clothes.

"It's the best-tasting water I've ever had. Think Evian, but ten times better!"

That is good enough for me.

I was about to follow Josh's lead when Victoria stuck her arm out to block me.

"Vic—"

"Give it a few minutes."

"Why?" I asked curiously.

"He jumped in and has no clue if predators are in the water."

A chuckle started low in my chest and soon became a full-blown gut-busting laugh. I wagged a finger at her—still coming to terms with how devious my sexy assistant could be.

"You're fucked up, you know that?"

"It's called survival of the fittest. Give it about twenty minutes. That's enough time to see if an alligator will snatch his ass up."

Victoria

Thank God I had the good sense to get vacation braids, I thought as I floated in the crisp water. The palm fronds and overgrown vegetation provided a natural canopy that blocked some of the sun's harsh rays. The waterfall was crystal clear, catching the sun in each drop that cascaded from a cliff. I was at peace for the first time since the crash. The sight was so majestic and astounding that I had nearly forgotten we weren't in Bali and were stranded on what now appeared to be an uninhabited island.

I closed my eyes, obscuring my vision of Knox getting his *GQ Magazine* on underneath the falls. The water beat down on him like it was his personal shower. He slicked his wet hair back with his hands and blew water out of his nose and mouth. The water sluiced down his bare chest and well-defined abdomen, threatening to trigger my own little waterfall.

Now, if he just loses the designer boxer briefs, then we'd be in business. Never mind. It's probably best that I focus on finding something to eat instead of thinking of gobbling up my boss's dick.

I closed my eyes and tried to think pure thoughts instead of Knox Ramsey opening my third eye. I began sputtering when someone's childish ass splashed water in my face.

"What the—Josh, quit playing around!" I fussed after recovering from him splashing a tidal wave of water in my face. I swiped at my face angrily. "I *know* you were that badass kid running around the community pool being a menace. You had to sit in time out every five minutes, watching the rest of us have fun because you were doing too much."

I heard Knox chuckle in the background and grumble something about me projecting.

And I am. I was the badass little kid, but that's neither here nor there.

"What's a community pool?" Josh asked inquisitively, pushing his auburn hair out of his face.

Mr. Alligator, you can come take him now.

"Think of the pool at your parents' country club, but without the servers, cabanas, and luxury loungers, and everyone is invited, no matter their financial status," Knox explained.

Josh cringed, and I wanted to punch him in the face. He caught the unimpressed look on my face and changed his tune with the quickness. "That...that sounds...exciting," he said with a tight smile.

Translation: Bless your heart.

On our three-hour hike, Josh couldn't help but tell us that his father was basically Daddy Warbucks and would be looking for him, which was terrific for me because that doubled the odds we'd be found.

"We should start heading back," Knox said, filling the 50-ounce stainless steel carafe from the waterfall.

We need to find a way to carry more water back with us. Rationing 50 ounces of water between three adults a day isn't ideal, but neither is making a six-hour round-trip journey for water every day. We can hollow out the coconuts and fill them with water, but carrying them will be a pain in the ass. Knowing Josh, he'll probably trip and drop his coconuts on the ground. We won't be in bad shape if we find some young coconuts.

We gathered our belongings and dressed—the men opting to make the journey back to the beach shirtless.

I'll give it a month before I'm walking around in a grass skirt with my titties out. I don't give a fuck.

We began our hike with renewed vigor. We were hydrated, cooled down, and had scrubbed away all traces of dirt, grime, and sweat from our misadventures.

"Knox, give me your shirt."

"Why?"

"Because I said so."

"Because I said so…please," he taunted, tossing me his shirt. I rolled my eyes and tucked my lips in to hide my smirk as I tied the arms of his dress shirt around my waist. "What are you doing?"

"I'm bringing coconuts back to the beach. We might not be able to drink them; however, we can hollow them out and use them for bowls and—"

Josh shrieked. "Oh, what the hell? What the hell?"

"What is the matter with you, kid?" Knox growled.

"Th-there was a snake!"

"And you didn't kill it?" I asked.

"Kill it? I wouldn't go anywhere near it!"

I sucked my teeth in disappointment. "Well, there goes our dinner."

"I'm not eating snake," he argued. I shrugged.

"That's fine with me—more for me and Knox. If you want to starve, then be my guest."

"Josh, if you see another snake, instead of crying like a little bitch, you need to let either me or Victoria know so that we can take care of it. Eating a snake may not be ideal, but it's protein that our bodies will need to survive. It's no big deal. I heard it tastes like chicken."

"I second that," I agreed, moving through the vegetation.

Ten minutes later, Josh had located a berry bush. "These look delicious," he said, picking a few of the berries off the bush. He was about to toss a few in his mouth when I stopped him.

"Don't eat those!"

"Why not?" he snapped, becoming frustrated.

"Let me see them." He begrudgingly handed the berries over, and I sniffed them. "No. These aren't good."

"Why not?"

"Stop asking questions and listen to what she says," Knox drawled, unamused by Josh's endless inquiry.

"Don't discourage him, Knox. He has a right to ask questions," I said.

"Okay, NatGeo," he snorted.

"It's *Discovery Channel*; get it straight. Anyway…where was

61

I?"

"Denying me food once again," Josh whined. I narrowed my eyes at him.

I'm trying to be patient with this little boy, but he's about to get punched in the stomach, too.

"Smell these and tell me what you smell," I said, pushing the berries toward him. His nose crinkled. "What do you think?"

"They smell bitter."

"Correct. The rule is to stay away from any berries that are green, yellow, or white. To be fair, you should avoid some red and purple berries, too, but the trifecta for sure. Also, stay away from berries that smell bitter or whose branches have a white, milky sap when you snap them. Do you understand me?"

"Yeah, whatever," he huffed. I smiled in satisfaction when Knox grabbed Josh by the back of his neck. "Ow, ow, ow, ow, ow! Let me go!"

"Quit being a disrespectful piece of shit and listen to what she tells you. She's trying to save your fucking life, dumbass," Knox hissed in Josh's ear.

"I'm sorry. I'm sorry. I'm sorry," Josh repeated.

"Don't apologize to me—apologize to her," Knox demanded, spinning him in my direction.

"I'm sorry, Victoria. Will you accept my apology?"

I nodded and tossed the berries onto the ground.

"Show a little fucking respect for the person who's trying to keep you alive," Knox remarked before storming off.

Josh rubbed the back of his neck and rolled his head around clockwise and then counterclockwise. "What is wrong with that guy? I think he has anger management problems."

"Probably, but when Knox gets like this, his blood sugar is

low. If I were you, I'd be as quiet as a church mouse and stay out of his way," I warned.

"No shit," Josh murmured, following behind me.

We need to find food ASAP because if Knox grabs me on the back of my neck like that? It's going down.

8

Salvage

Victoria

"We have water—we're making progress," Knox announced once we returned to the beach. "We didn't secure food as planned, but it's not the end of the world."

He was about to continue his pep talk when Josh raised his hand, interrupting him. "Yes, Josh?" he answered with a sigh.

"How long can we survive without food?"

"Good question. Would you like to answer, Discovery Channel?"

"Answer yourself, Boy Scout," I huffed, folding my arms over my chest.

He's not the only one whose blood sugar is running a little low, especially after a six-hour hike.

"Fair enough. Conservatively, about three weeks," Knox answered.

"We're fucked."

I glanced down at my toes that sank in the warm sand and

caught movement out of my peripheral vision. It was a hermit crab moseying along the sand without a care in the world. We could eat them, but we'd have to find and consume a fuckload to make a dent in the calorie intake needed for three people to survive on an island.

I bent down to pick it up and examined it.

"What do you have there, Victoria?" Knox asked.

"It's a hermit crab. Where there's one, there's more."

"Thank God. I'm starving," Josh said, reaching out for the crab. I gave him my meanest stank face and pulled the crab out of his reach. "What do you think you're doing?"

"Being a selfish prick. That's what he was doing," Knox growled, frowning in disappointment.

"That's what I'm saying. Your greedy tail was about to be hunched over with the shits. You can't eat these raw. They have to be cooked, meaning we need more supplies so we can build a fire."

"Okay. You and Knox can return to the wreckage, and I'll stay behind and gather hermit crabs," Josh suggested.

"No. You're going with me—"

"Knox, it's fine."

"It's safer for you on the beach," he insisted.

I waved him off. "We work better together, and the last thing we need is you stroking out in the ocean because he got on your nerves, and Josh can get in less trouble if he's on hermit crab duty," I reasoned. Knox nodded resolutely and retrieved our life vests. "What's the matter?" I asked, accepting the orange reflective vest that could be seen from space.

"Nothing," he mumbled, glancing at Josh, who walked the expansive beach on the hunt for crabs.

Something.

"Is it Josh?"

"It is. My gut is telling me not to leave him alone. He reminds me of a toddler, and it makes me wonder if his father bought his pilot's license."

I sighed and clipped myself into the flotation device. "At this point, it wouldn't surprise me, but honestly, I think you're overthinking as usual."

"Maybe," he responded skeptically. "Let's head out. We only have a few more hours of daylight. We need to grab as many items from the wreckage as possible, but let's not overdo it. Only grab items that'll be practical."

"Aye, aye, Captain," I responded with a lazy salute, forcing a grin from him.

"Always with the smart mouth."

"You say that as if your toxic ass doesn't love it," I teased, helping Knox push the raft past the shore into the shallow end of the ocean.

"You say that as if you're not equally toxic."

"I'm not toxic," I argued, accepting his outstretched hand. "I'm reactionary. There's a difference." I climbed into the raft and waited for him to join me.

"You're toxic because of *how* you react," he remarked, pushing us away from shore.

"And you just be doing shit, Knox. Real talk? You're talking shit about Josh and how he got his pilot's license, and I wonder how you're the CEO and owner of a billion-dollar company. Seriously, Knox, you could've flown to Miami and stalked me on my vacation instead of doing the absolute most."

"Huh...I didn't think of that," he murmured as he rowed us to sea.

I rolled my eyes.

Of course, he didn't.

"How mad would you have been if I crashed your little girls' trip?"

I shrugged. "I wouldn't be stuck-on-a-remote-island-for-the-rest-of-my-life mad. However, I would've used you as a personal ATM for the duration of my trip."

"I expected nothing less from Tori Montana."

* * *

Sweat dripped in my eyes as I cut through the thick fabric of the seatbelt from the seat I'd occupied earlier. I had no idea what we'd do with seatbelts, but I figured it could come in handy. If I had to guess, we'd been at the crash site for over two hours. So far, the raft was filled with items from the galley, including an assortment of sodas, a bottle of champagne and bourbon, bottled water, a stainless steel pitcher, some silverware, including a steak knife, the ice drawer, some ready-made meals that wouldn't last more than three days, and liquid antibacterial soap. Knox found a couple of pillows, blankets, soaked toilet paper rolls that would have to be dried out, matches, and the body wash and shampoo dispenser from the shower.

"Victoria! Look what I found!" Knox announced after breaching the water's surface. He swiped his dark hair out of his face and cleared the seawater from his eyes. I snarled when he held up my work tablet in the air.

"That's great, Knox. Take it and shove it up your ass!"

"It still works! Good thing I sprung for that waterproof case, huh?"

This isn't all bad. I might have a night or two of entertainment. We won't have WIFI, but I did download a few movies from Netflix onto my tablet a few days ago.

"That's great news. Did you find anything else?" I asked, tossing a belt into the burgeoning raft.

"There's a lot of debris on the reef, but I haven't found anything that would be of immediate use to us. Have you found anything we could use for fishing?"

"Nope. If we were on a commercial flight, there would be netting on the back of the seats that we could utilize. I'll keep looking."

He shook his head. "Let's call it and head back. We can try again tomorrow morning. We've been out here long enough and have some food that'll last us a few days."

"Sounds good. I don't know about you, but I vote we wait until tomorrow to build a shelter. We've expended enough energy today."

"Agreed," Knox responded tiredly. I threw the scissors into the raft before slipping into the water.

"I'll pull first," I volunteered, grabbing the rope on the front of the raft.

I know one thing for certain: I'll be in the best shape of my life in a month.

My mind replayed the day's events, from discovering that That Man Over There canceled my flight to swimming to shore with our salvaged loot.

I have yet to accept that this is my reality—that I'm destined to live out the remainder of my life away from civilization. It's only Day One, and surviving in these conditions with minimal supplies

*and random facts I've memorized from the Discovery Channel
for a week will be a major feat. I want to hate Knox for what he
did, but I know guilt is eating away at him. I can see the pain in
his dark eyes that begs me for my forgiveness. I may not 100%
forgive him by tomorrow, but the way I see it, the pent-up anger
and animosity will weigh me down like an anchor dropped to the
ocean floor. Instead, I'm choosing acceptance and peace.*

Knox

"Ain't this 'bout a bitch!" Victoria expressed, punching a fist
into her open palm.

"You owe me fifty bucks."

"What the hell do you want me to pay you in? Seashells?
I can't fucking believe this," she complained, kicking at the
sand.

Josh was…dead.

"This is your fault, Victoria. I told you he shouldn't have
been left alone."

"I'm sorry. I didn't think we'd have to babysit a grown-ass
man. All he had to do was wait two hours, and he could've
had one of these Fancy Feast dinners."

I snorted. "The meals are better than cat food."

"Says you."

I stared down at Josh, who had turned blue in the face and
lips from eating the berries Victoria had specifically warned
him to stay away from.

Note to self…always listen to her.

I glanced up when I heard Victoria sniffling. "Are you
crying?"

"It's just—" she hiccuped, "he went out like Seneca Crane in

The Hunger Games. I liked Seneca—he had a redemption arc."

"I don't know what the fuck you're talking about."

"Of course you don't," she said, breath shuddering. "I was a child when *SAW* came out, and you were in the workforce."

I sighed and shook my head. "What are we going to do with him?"

"Eat him, duh," she said through her tears.

"What the—"

"I'm joking. It's not a joking matter, but a little dark humor never hurt anybody. Um…we should send him out to sea with a little homegoing ceremony. We'll have one of those luxury Banquet meals you love so much at the repast. I call dibs on the bourbon."

"Now, wait one damn minute," I said, climbing to my feet. "You don't even enjoy bourbon—I should have it."

"Who says I don't enjoy it?" she asked, wiping a tear away from the inside corner of her eye with her shirt.

"You make this godawful face every time you drink it."

"So now I'm ugly?" she questioned with a raised brow. In a matter of seconds, all sorrow had dripped out of her tone and was replaced with the venom I lived for.

"Yes," I said, blocking my abdomen with my arms. She smirked.

"Pussy." I lowered my arms and flinched when she made a sudden move. "Two for flinching," she said, punching me in my arm twice.

"You shouldn't beat on the elderly."

I chuckled when Victoria rolled her eyes. "I love how you're elderly when it's convenient for you. But let me call you elderly, and you're sliding down the walls."

"It's no different than when you play your Black Card."

She opened her mouth to protest and stopped herself. "You know what? Fair."

"Do you remember that one evening I was craving fried chicken? I asked if you wanted some for dinner, and you went off on me."

"I said fair. You don't have to take a stroll down memory lane."

"No, I have to get this off my chest. You need to know how devastated I was. We had to order pizza instead. That next evening, I binged on an 8-piece family meal while watching *My 600-Pound Life*."

"Yeah, that tracks. I do the same thing when I know I'm about to throw down and don't want to feel guilty. I tell myself, 'Well, at least I can wipe my own ass.' I get pretty emotional when they meet their goals, though. I be rooting for them."

"Likewise. But enough about that—we need to take care of Josh properly."

"I don't want to be *that* person, but you and Josh are about the same height, and you only have the clothes on your back. You might want to consider taking his clothes."

"I can't do that," I said uneasily.

"Bet," she replied. She crouched down and began to undress him.

"What are you doing?"

"If you don't want the clothes, then I'll take them." Seconds later, Josh was left in only his boxers.

"Why stop now? You might as well take the boxers, too," I remarked.

"Man, if you're gay, just say that."

"I can assure you, I'm not."

"I didn't ask for your reassurance. We should get some

flowers. You should be good at doing that since you're—"

"Let's remain focused, Ms. Caldwell."

Victoria snapped her head back and glared at me skeptically. "Okay, Mr. Ramsey," she replied, exaggerating the syllables.

"Let's take care of the young man and give him a proper sendoff. Grab his arms, and I'll grab his legs."

* * *

"Dearly beloved—"

"Knox McKinney Ramsey."

"That's not my middle name."

"Dearly beloved is used for weddings, not funerals," Victoria reminded me.

"Thank you. Where would I be without you?"

"In the Underworld where you belong."

"I'm the one who saved you from drowning in the wreck."

"I didn't ask for that. You could've let me go on to Glory peacefully."

"Yeah, right," I huffed.

"I do have a question. How did you manage to survive the crash unscathed?"

I snorted. "That is not the case. My back is screaming louder than you when you discovered someone drank the last of your coffee creamer."

Victoria sucked in a breath. "Listen, I was already having a shitty morning, and I was looking forward to my morning coffee. You needed to send out a memorandum about respecting co-workers' property. Not only was my name written on the bottle in permanent marker, but the asshole returned the empty bottle to the fridge. Who does that?"

"It was me. I did it," I confessed, avoiding her heated gaze that routinely made my blood simmer and my dick swell.

"Don't get killed on this island. It's just me and you. I'll send you off just like Josh."

No, you won't. You'll miss me too much.

"Noted. Let's get started. There isn't much I can say about Co-pilot Josh. He was a pilot, and he occasionally provided comedic relief. Unfortunately, his life was cut short before we could witness his full potential. I'm certain he'll be missed by his loved ones. Amen." I turned to Victoria, who was clutching a hibiscus bouquet in her hands. "It's your turn."

"Josh Jayden McClure—"

"Is that his full name?"

Victoria shrugged, her shoulders meeting her ears. "No, but it's better than Co-pilot Josh."

"I beg to differ."

"Overruled. Josh Jayden McClure, I am saddened by your unexpected yet avoidable departure from this world."

What a lovely and subtle way of saying I told you so.

"I hope you didn't suffer and that you find peace in the next life. Ashes to ashes, dust to dust. Amen."

"Amen."

A few minutes later, Josh was floating away with the tide.

"What are you doing?"

"Pouring one out for the homie," Victoria said, pouring some champagne into the water before taking a swig. I followed suit and poured a shot of bourbon into the ocean.

"Rest easy, homie," I said.

Victoria snorted and sprayed champagne from her mouth.

She laughed and wiped her mouth dry with the back of her hand. "Don't ever say that shit again."

"Don't worry. I won't. It didn't feel right when I said it."

"Good," she responded when the giggles ceased.

"I have a proposal."

"Let's hear it, Knox."

"I propose we eat, drink excessively, and fool around. I feel vulnerable and need to be comforted after sending off my best island friend."

I swallowed roughly in anticipation of rejection when Victoria stared at me for what felt like an eternity. "Okay."

"Okay?"

"Okay...I'm feeling a little vulnerable, too."

9

Usher

Victoria

Josh's unexpected passing took a bigger toll on me than I initially thought. I was oddly protective of him, maybe because I thought he was a little touched in the head. Knowing his ass went to Heaven because it wouldn't be right to send him to Hell kept me from sobbing.

The champagne has been doing its job, too.

"I have a confession to make."

Knox and I had been going back and forth like Usher for the past hour with our confessions—things we never told a soul. The confessions were nothing too heinous. They ranged from stealing candy from the convenience store as a child to receiving helpful stock market tips from a business colleague just days before a particular stock crashed.

They did Martha dirty. That's all I have to say about that.

"Go ahead, Knox," I slurred, taking another swig from the nearly empty bottle.

75

"S-sometimes…I buy you jewelry."

My head swiveled on my neck in his direction.

What did this man just tell me?

"Um…you're gonna have to run that by me one more time."

"I'm at the store buying myself a new watch, and then I'll happen to see the matching Hers watch, and I buy it thinking about how it would look on your wrist."

This man is insane in the membrane! But I'm kind of living for it. It might be the alcohol talking, but I've never had anyone obsessed with me like this, and I don't think I mind.

"W-what did you do with the watch?"

"It's in my safe, along with all the other pieces."

"All the other pieces? How much jewelry did you buy me?"

"You'd think I was crazy if I told you."

"I got the hint you were crazy when you told the airline I died, so you might as well fess up."

He sighed and threw back another shot—no grimace.

He's hammered.

"The first purchase was a pair of diamond hoop earrings. I overheard you speaking to one of your friends on the phone. You mentioned, 'the bigger the hoops, the bigger the hoe.' I saw a pair of hoops while shopping and couldn't resist. From there, I spiraled."

"How much money have you spent?"

"In jewelry?" he asked.

There's more?

"Well—" He paused to hiccup. "I saw some dresses that I thought would complement your figure… and some heels that would show off your pedicures you love to get… and—"

Please tell me this man bought me a penthouse. Please tell me this man bought me a penthouse.

"—and some... some lingerie?"

Never mind. This man is weird.

I stared at the ebbing waves, unable to meet Knox's pleading gaze. I felt like shit for judging him because we were supposed to be in our vulnerable space. "How much have you spent?"

"Well over a million," he confessed. I sucked in a breath before letting it out slowly. "Say something...please."

I could hear the fear of rejection in his voice loud and clear.

"I find all of this odd considering how we're always at each other's necks. Why do you always go out of your way to make me angry?"

"Because your anger lights a fire inside of me. My blood courses through my body, my heart thumps in my chest, and sometimes I feel like I'm on the verge of passing out."

I see Knox is going to Heaven, too, along with Josh and all the dogs.

"You're giving yourself high blood pressure arguing with me all day," I spat.

He shook his head in drunken defiance. "You're like an adrenaline rush."

"You're a masochist, Knox."

"My therapist said that," he mumbled.

"Hmph."

At least he's seeing a therapist.

"I fired her."

Correction: at least he saw a therapist.

"You should think about rehiring her."

"Do you have any feelings for me, Victoria? Any at all?"

I glanced away and stared at the four hermit crabs that were in a standoff in their makeshift prison cell.

"I don't appreciate being angry and stressed, Knox. It may

have been fun and exciting for you, but there were some nights I lay awake wondering why the hell my boss hated me. Sometimes, it was difficult for me to get out of bed in the morning, but I kept at it because I had to pay for my mother's nursing home rent."

"Your mother's... in a nursing home?" he asked slowly.

I nodded. "She's in a memory care unit—the one you have to pay the big bucks for."

"H-how old is she?"

"Fifty-three."

"My God. Is it genetic? You do tend to be a little forgetful sometimes. We should get you screened."

I rolled my eyes. "I'm sure we can find an MRI and a CT machine somewhere out here."

"You know what I meant," he whispered, pushing his dark hair away from his face. The salt had made the strands a little stiff, and his fingers didn't glide through them like usual, resulting in him jerking at the tangled strands at the end.

Again...thank God for vacation braids.

"It's not genetic. A reaction to anesthesia caused the dementia. It later developed into Alzheimer's. She's why I get up every morning and put a smile on my face for you despite everything. I hate when we fight—it's distressing to me."

The silence grew between us as I stared into the bonfire we made.

"I-I'm sorry, Victoria. I didn't mean to cause you so much pain. I thought you enjoyed going back and forth with me just as much. It felt like twisted foreplay to me."

"Twisted is right," I answered softly.

"And your mother... your poor mother. I'm so sorry. How

will you pay—"

"It's fine. The money you bribed me with will cover her expenses for nearly a year. Maybe we'll be found by then."

"We will be," he remarked with drunken optimism.

Maybe...

I gulped down the last of the warmed champagne and tossed the bottle behind me. It landed with a loud thud in the sand.

"I have a confession to make."

"Go ahead, Victoria."

"I, too, ate fried chicken the night after we had pizza."

He narrowed his eyes at me as if I were a monster. As if he didn't just confess that he'd gone on a million-dollar shopping spree for me. "I can't believe you," he hissed.

I laughed as Knox spent the next five minutes bitching about how guilty I made him feel about the fried chicken comment as we prepared for bed. We hadn't gotten around to building a shelter and would sleep in the raft for the time being. I settled on one side, and he settled on the other. It was a tight squeeze, and our forced proximity was unavoidable. Not that I minded, considering a light breeze had settled in, and the blankets we retrieved from the wreckage were still damp. It was the forced proximity that made me trail my fingers down his chest through the wispy black and silver hairs.

He cleared his throat.

"Victoria? What are you doing?"

"I believe it was you who mentioned fooling around," I answered, trailing my fingers further. "I agreed, and I always keep my promises," I whispered, squeezing his impressive bulge. My lips cut off Knox's soft moan.

Knox

It had all been a dream. The airport, crash, beach, Josh Jayden McClure—all of it. It was the only explanation for why Victoria Caldwell's lips were on mine. She moved them veraciously as if we were longtime lovers, and she knew exactly what I wanted and needed. She knew that I enjoyed being teased with soft nibbling. My bottom lip was trapped between her teeth, and I didn't want her to let go for fear the dream would be over too soon.

Her lips were enough to send every drop of blood in my body south, and when her tongue slid across mine, giving me a taste of the dry sweetness of the Brut, my balls tightened in preparation to come as if I were a trigger-happy teenager again.

Not yet.

She reached into the waistband of my boxers.

"Is this okay?" she whispered against my lips.

In my dreamlike state, I managed a consenting nod and groaned deeply seconds later when her hand wrapped around me. My dick pulsed and twitched excitedly in her hold— simultaneously appreciating her touch and wanting more— wanting to be buried inside of her.

My brain short-circuited at the first long and languid upward stroke and completely melted by the downstroke. Dream or not, it'd been nearly a year since I'd been with a woman. All thoughts of being with another woman went out of the window when Victoria entered the picture. As soon as we met, she consumed me, and I knew just any woman wouldn't do. I was convinced that no woman could satiate me like her.

I rolled my hips at the same sluggish pace as her tongue and smoothed a hand down her side to her ass. I squeezed her firmly and dug my fingers into the soft, malleable flesh. I'd spent countless working hours stealing glances at Victoria's ass every time she walked past in one of her pencil skirts. It always looked so damn appetizing.

I broke our kiss, hitched her leg over my hip, and buried my face in the crook of her neck. Her skin smelled of sea salt and the faintest hint of her vanilla perfume that I couldn't get enough of. I licked a long stripe across her neck before gently sucking at the base of her throat.

"Oh...fuck, Knox."

The waves in the background were resounding and threatened to drown out her tender moans, but my name on her lips pierced through, muffling the background noise.

I need to be closer....

I rolled her onto her back in a swift motion and wedged myself between her parted thighs. She embraced me, circling her arms around my neck and her thick thighs around my lower back. I rocked against her once, pulling another moan from her, and paused to unbutton my dress shirt that she'd commandeered for herself. A kiss trailed every loosened button until I reached her navel. I dipped my tongue in her belly button to tease her a little before sucking her piercing into my mouth—imagining it was her clit.

I traveled back up her generous body and peeled away the shirt, exposing her ample breasts. I latched onto her dark nipples as my dick hung heavy between us. I grabbed myself and nearly winced from the sensitivity and tugged her nipple between my teeth for a quick nip before laving it with my tongue.

"That feels so fucking good," she murmured, sinking her fingers into my hair. Her nails scratched against my scalp, sending a chill down my spine.

"Of course it does," I replied with a playful taunt. She responded with a roll of her eyes before kissing me. I abandoned myself and slipped a hand between us. My fingers met the warm wetness that soaked through her panties. I brushed against her clit and marveled at how her thighs clamped around me from the slight contact.

"May I?"

She nodded frantically, peering at me with the most seductive eyes ever. With a crooked finger, I tugged her panties aside, exposing her glistening folds. Like the lustful man I was, I couldn't prevent my tongue from moistening my lips in anticipation of finally getting a taste of Victoria Caldwell. I always imagined we'd be in my office when I'd indulge in my first taste of her. In my fantasy, she was bare-bottomed in my executive chair, spread wide with her legs crooked over the armrests. I'd be on my knees in front of her, servicing her while emails and phone calls went ignored.

"Actually," she said, pressing her hand against my forehead, preventing me from face-planting in her pussy. "Let's not."

"Why not?" I queried.

"I'm big on hygiene, and I feel disgusting."

"You don't look disgusting, and you certainly don't smell disgusting."

"Knox Neveah Ramsey—"

"You know god damn well that's not my middle name," I seethed.

"—I haven't had a proper shower in 24 hours."

"We bathed at the waterfall," I reminded her.

"That's a typical response from someone who thinks swimming in a chlorinated pool is the same as taking a bath."

"It's not?" Victoria kissed her teeth loudly as I chuckled. "I'm kidding. I'd have you know that I use washcloths, too," I boasted, climbing back up to be face-to-face with her.

She smiled tiredly. "I'm impressed."

"As you should be," I said, returning King Dong to my boxers. *Victoria's words, not mine.*

"Honestly, we should rest. It's been a long, eventful day," I suggested, buttoning up her shirt.

"It has," she mumbled, slapping at a mosquito on her arm. "I know what I'm doing tomorrow."

"What's that?" I asked, settling beside her.

"Looking for something in the jungle that'll be a natural mosquito repellent."

"That'll be lovely," I replied, yawning and wrapping an arm around her. Moments later, I realized that Victoria had fallen asleep when I didn't receive a response. We had our first day stranded on a remote island in the books. Unfortunately, we lost a soul, but I prayed we'd continue to thrive until rescue came for us.

10

Tiger Woods

Victoria

"How long have you been up?" I murmured when I felt a slight tug at my braids. Every morning, Knox checked to ensure I had nothing crawling in my hair. I didn't fuss about it. I was grateful to have a personal primate.

"A while," he answered roughly.

Hours.

Knox had developed insomnia shortly after our arrival. He was always on the lookout for potential predators that would come and drag us out of our lovingly crafted hut by our ankles.

That's what Knox calls our little shanty... lovingly crafted. The man has a way with words when he wants to.

It took three days and a shit ton of mud, sticks, and palm fronds to piece it together. Truthfully, it took three days because we had different opinions about where to set up shop. I didn't think it was logical to build our shelter on the beach only to make six-hour daily trips to get water. I voted to build our shelter closer to the water source, and Knox reasoned that we needed to stay on the beach in case a ship passed or a helicopter or plane flew over. In my opinion, we were both right—we needed accessible drinking water and to remain visible.

"Lie down and get some sleep," I said, pulling him down so his head rested on my chest. His arms wrapped around me tightly, and like every morning, I didn't want to get up. I didn't have to wake up to inconsiderate phone calls, fight through traffic, or ensure that briefs were printed and tucked into their padfolios for a meeting, but work still had to be done. His stomach growled loudly.

"I'm so fucking hungry," he groaned.

"I'll tell you what my mom said when I was up past my bedtime and wanted something to eat—you can't be hungry if you're asleep."

"Please don't tell our future children that. Just call me, and I'll make them a peanut butter and jelly sandwich," he said teasingly. I smacked my lips and shoved him off me.

"That peanut butter and jelly sandwich might be hard to conjure out here."

"Funny you doubt the sandwich but not the children," he whispered, voice growing heavy with sleep.

"I am not having children by you on this island for them to come out like Donnie Thornberry."

"Who is Donnie Thornberry?"

"Go to sleep."

I moved to leave when he grabbed me. "Don't go too far," he insisted.

"I won't."

He nodded sluggishly before passing out and giving me some peace and quiet. I "brushed" my teeth before leaving the hut by furiously rubbing my teeth with a piece of cloth and some coconut paste I made. I contemplated what Knox said about children and snorted. I didn't see that happening. My Depo shot would only last two more months, but I doubted my body could sustain a pregnancy given the lack of nutrition and rapid weight loss. We'd only been on the island for a month, and I had probably dropped thirty pounds.

I'm not really tripping about the weight loss because I look good as fuck, but a bitch is starving and malnourished.

We'd been surviving off nuts, hermit crabs, coconuts, and some unidentifiable-to-me fruit we found further past the waterfall. We caught two fish, but they were both on the smaller side. By the time the fish were cleaned and cooked, they were barely worth the work it took to catch them. We attempted to kill a few parrots by throwing rocks at them, but we had no such luck.

Knox had also lost noticeable weight. The bulk that took dedication and early morning hours to obtain started thinning out, leaving behind lean muscles, taut abs, and single-digit body fat.

The man also needs sunscreen because he's starting to look like a leather handbag.

I undressed, tossed Knox's dress shirt onto the sand, and submerged myself in the ocean to relieve myself and give myself a precursory scrub down. I rolled onto my back, floated underneath the pink and peach sunrise, and prepared for my morning devotion. I didn't grow up in a religious household, but I had to give thanks for the land, plants, ocean, sea life, and... That Man Over There. I prayed for my friends, who were most likely mourning my disappearance. I prayed for my mother's health, and saved my little prayer for my sisters.

I hope they're doing all right, I guess.

Finally, I prayed we were found, but if we weren't, we were blessed with knowledge and adaptability to survive the island.

* * *

I'd been foraging for nuts in the jungle for a while when I heard a sound that made my heart pump twice as fast. I looked up and grinned when I found a bird's nest above my head.

"Ohhhh, you precious... little... babies," I whispered, dumping the nuts onto the ground. I counted eight birds in total. They were young—barely past the hatchling stage, but protein was protein. I eyed the nest that was precariously perched on the branch and drooled. It was a lot lower than the previous nests we'd found. "Mommy didn't tuck you in the tree so good, huh?" I cooed, looking for a long stick. "That's okay. She'll learn next time."

I took a few steps back, mindful not to get too close to the trees because of snakes, and jabbed at the nest. My tongue stuck out as I stood on my toes and worked my magic. "Come on. Don't fight it," I grunted.

I grinned stupidly when the nest full of squawking baby birds tumbled to the ground. I pumped my fist like Tiger Woods at a PGA Tour and rushed to grab the birds before something jacked our meal. Three of the birds had died from blunt force, and three more were injured. I snapped all their little necks with the quickness.

"Knox is going to be so happy," I murmured, filling the nest with the nuts I'd dropped.

I ran back to the beach and started a fire. An hour later, the down feathers were scraped off; they were clean and roasting over an open flame on a skewer.

"Too bad we don't have barbecue sauce."

Knox

My stomach twisted in knots from the hunger I couldn't quite find relief from. I curled into the fetal position and tried to think happy thoughts, but something kept pulling me out of my sleep. My nose twitched repeatedly, catching the scent of something delicious… like meat.

It's just a dream. It has to be a dream.

"Knox! Wake up!" Victoria shouted. I jolted upright and nearly hit my head on our low ceiling.

"What's the matter?" I asked, clearing the sleep from my voice as I left the hut. My mouth dropped when I realized where the smell was coming from. Saliva seeped out of my mouth and down my chin. I wiped away the trail on the back of my hand and slowly approached, praying this wasn't a figment of my imagination. "Where did… what—"

"The birds took a fortunate tumble out of a tree," Victoria responded gleefully—the happiest I've seen her since we crashed. I licked my lips and watched her divide our meal, which consisted of nuts and hatchlings. My brows furrowed when I counted how many she intended to give me. "I'm no Gordon Ramsay, and we don't—Gordon."

"Excuse me?"

"Gordon. Is that your middle name?"

"No."

"As I was saying, I'm no Gordon Ramsay, but I stuffed the seaweed inside the bird, hoping it'll give it a little razzle-dazzle," she said, handing me an elephant ear with six chicks.

"I'm not taking that."

It was her turn to look confused. "What do you mean you're not taking it? Is it a moral dilemma or something? Their deaths were quick and painless."

"Why did you give me so much?"

She squinted at me and shielded her darkened face from the sun with her hand. "Because you expend more calories than I do," she said.

"I don't give a shit. There are eight birds. There's no reason why we can't each have four."

Victoria shook her head furiously. "You need more protein and calories than I do."

"Vic—"

She jumped to her feet. "Stop fucking arguing with me and take the fucking food! Quit trying to be so fucking chivalrous and think about the big picture! You do more manual labor and expend more energy and calories than I do. This is about survival; I can't make it any simpler than that. I'm a thick bitch, and I can afford to lose more weight, but pretty soon, you're gonna be looking like Tom Hanks in *Cast Away*!"

"It took him four years to get like that."

"I don't give a shit. I don't care if it took four days, four months, or four years—at this rate, I'll outlive you, and I don't want that!" she yelled. Her chest heaved up and down from anger and frustration, and all I could do was stand there like a big oaf, struggling to find the words to say. "Just... take the food, and consider it a blessing because technically, our lunch should've been hermit crabs, fruit, and nuts. Don't forget to give thanks," she mumbled.

"Thank you," I whispered, accepting the leaf. I sat on my log across from her and waited to dig in until she joined me. My instinct was to devour the hatchlings, but I savored them instead, unsure when I'd taste real meat again. My stomach was happy, but my soul wasn't.

What did she mean when she said she didn't want to outlive me?

"I think you're better at this surviving thing than me," I mentioned, hoping it would be enough to open the dialogue back up. I received a grunt as she chewed on an underdeveloped wing. "It's very possible that you might outlive me. What happens then?"

She discarded the bones into a coconut bowl and motioned for me to do the same. She'd undoubtedly attempt to make stock or soup from them.

"It doesn't matter what happens to me if you're not here, now does it?"

"It matters to me, especially when you're being so... so selfless. If, God forbid, something happened to me, I have no doubt that you'll be capable of taking care of yourself."

"It's not about my capability, Knox. Physically, yes, I can take care of myself. Emotionally, no. I don't want to do this alone. So, stop being such a dickhead and consider what's best for both of us."

I chuckled humorlessly. "I never thought I'd see the day when you'd desire to have me around."

She shrugged casually. "What can I say? You grew on me like barnacles."

I grinned. "May I ask you something?"

"May I say no?"

"You may not."

"Gone 'head."

"Why do you refer to me sometimes as That Man Over There?"

Victoria snorted, and soon, her sweet giggles followed behind it.

"I call you That Man Over There when I'm at my wits' end with you. I'm so flustered that I don't even want to say your name. The 'over there' part comes from not wanting to be near you. Hence: That Man Over There."

"That makes perfect sense. Thank you for clearing that mystery up for me."

We finished our sumptuous meal, and I prepared the raft for my daily scavenging adventure. I was about to shove off when Victoria approached me.

"Will you bring me back something nice?"

My heart split in two because I could hear the hopefulness in her voice and see the pleading in her eyes.

"I will."

She nodded, and I could tell she didn't believe a word that came out of my mouth.

And why should she?

"Here's your water," she said, offering me a few water bottles that were filled from the waterfall.

"Thank you. I'll be back. Stay on the beach."

And because it felt like the most natural thing to do, I kissed her. She tensed but eventually returned my affection. Besides touching and holding each other, we hadn't been intimate since our first night on the island. Truthfully, we had bigger things to worry about, and I didn't want to make her feel obligated to be affectionate with me. I figured it'd happen on its own time—when the moment was right.

This moment feels so fucking right.

I broke away first, leaving her a bit stunned, and shoved off into the water before she could call me a Dirty Old Bastard or That Man Over There. Instead, as I rowed away, I found her smiling as she grew in the distance. It was foolish of me to make her any promises, but I did, and I'd do my best to fulfill them.

11

Million-Dollar View

Victoria

"He has officially been promoted from That Man Over There to That Man Stranded Out at Sea because where the hell is he?" I growled, looking at the expanse of the ocean. I was trying not to freak out, but it was becoming late, and the orange raft was nowhere in sight.

I'll never forgive that son of a bitch if something happened to him. We have a rule not to go farther than the wreckage. I shouldn't have been so fucking self-righteous and ate the damn birds!

"He's fine. That man is literally a roach. Him and his antennas will be back, bothering me, and keeping me sane," I murmured. I had a strong urge to strap my life preserver on and swim out to the wreckage to search for him, but the voice in the back of my head was telling me to trust him and give him some time.

I left our "condo" with the "million-dollar view," as Knox loved to call it, and checked on the sun-drying coconut meat I planned on turning into flour. I squatted over the drying mat Knox weaved together for me from palm fronds and rubbed the dried flakes between my fingers. Satisfied, I scooped the flakes onto a slab of rock and used another rock to grind them into fine pieces. I whistled the tune to "Don't Worry, Be Happy" as I tried to remain upbeat about my task at hand. Later, I planned to make a crude pancake from the flour with some of the sweet fruit we found. Personally, I felt the little dry-ass cakes left much to be desired, but Knox always requested them, ate them with a smile, and sent his regards to the chef.

I paused my grinding to wipe away tears on the back of my arm. Since our arrival, there wasn't a day when Knox didn't tell me that he appreciated me and my efforts. It was all I ever wanted from him—an acknowledgment that my work mattered... that *I* mattered outside what I could do for others. That was always the role I found myself in, even as a child. My mother had deemed me the "responsible" and "independent" one when, in reality, I had more common sense than my older sisters, which translated to me taking on more burdens than my little shoulders should've borne. My problem was that I was too selfless for my own damn good.

I looked out at the ocean, and relief flooded my body when I spotted Knox in the distance. I never thought I'd live to see the day I was excited to see him — but in just a month, I'd gone from wishing he'd catch a case of crippling gout after an all-nighter to praying for his safe trip, his return, and... another kiss.

I wanted Knox...badly. It was something about how that man took care of me that made me as feral as my deceased cat, Nala, who would go into heat so severely that you'd find her with her ass tooted up in the air. She didn't give a shit what was behind her—human, couch, cat-scratching post—she wanted it. My mom kicked her ass out for trying to throw it back on the Christmas tree. She said, "That freaky bitch has to go." A few months later, I saw Nala happily trotting around the neighborhood with her full, heavy belly swaying.

I could feel Nala's pain, but the hygiene situation on the island hadn't been the greatest. We ran out of the soap we recovered from the jet a few days ago. We'd been careless with the soap initially and went from using it on our entire bodies to washing only the "important parts" with our dwindling supply. We were always sweaty, sticky, covered in bug bites and sand — and often compared our underarm body odor to see who had the most pungent "onion burger" smell, as Knox graciously coined it. I rolled my eyes when I thought about how extra he was when he would smell my armpits. He'd start choking and hacking, and once, he even rolled onto his back and imitated having a seizure. I didn't even bother punching him in the gut because we both knew it was his ass stinking up our condo with the million-dollar view. Maybe smelling each other and laughing at our musk was weird, but it was our way of coping and laughing at a situation we didn't have the power to change. It was our way of saying, "It's okay. I understand." But at some point, I had to get out of my head and acknowledge that we were two stankin' ass motherfuckers who needed to fuck. The body odor and sweat weren't going anywhere, and neither were our libidos.

* * *

95

Some time passed before Knox returned to shore. My concern grew when he nearly collapsed into the water while exiting the raft. I rushed towards him with a water bottle and abruptly stopped when I saw what was in the life raft.

"Oh, my God, Knox," I whispered as I slowly approached.

"I promised you… I'd bring you back something nice," he said between tired breaths.

"Where did you find it?"

"A reef about a mile past the wreckage. It took me a while to swim down and get it because of the sharks in the area."

"Sharks… there were sharks?"

We've never had issues with sharks before.

"They weren't huge, but I managed to get you a three-footer," he said, proudly holding the shark up. I smiled and put my fingers up, mimicking taking a photo of him with his deadliest catch. At the moment, I didn't know what made me happier, the Blacktip reef shark Knox bagged or my fully intact suitcase. All I knew was that it was on and popping.

Knox

I'd barely gained my land legs again when Victoria threw herself on me. The momentum knocked me off my feet and we collided onto the ground. I hardly registered the seashell digging into my lower back because her lips were just that fucking hypnotic. I thought the greatest thrill was hearing Victoria tell me to go to Hell with gassy drawers on, but being on the receiving end of her tender affection topped the fucking cake.

I'll gladly swim in shark-infested oceans every day if this is the result.

"Thank you. Thank you. Thank you," she whispered against my lips.

"No—fuck! What was that for?" I exclaimed, holding my cheek.

"Swimming with sharks, really, Knox Abraham Ramsey?"

"That's not my middle name," I said, sighing and rubbing the pain away from the slap.

Thank God she's weak and malnourished. I would hate to see the damage if she were operating at full strength.

"My belongings weren't that important to risk your life!"

"Bringing you the slightest comfort of home was worth the risk."

The heated glare on her face slowly melted away. "Losing you is not worth the risk," she said softly.

"I understand," I replied. "Who else will carry the water from the waterfall?"

She rolled her eyes and climbed off me.

Okay, maybe I should've just kept my mouth shut because I obviously ruined the moment.

I pulled myself to my feet and watched her wrestle her suitcase out of the raft with glee as if she had found a chest of sunken treasure. I secured the raft and beamed proudly at the shark. Catching the shark was my greatest accomplishment. Fuck the money, the mergers and acquisitions, and all the material bullshit; nothing could compare to spearing a shark with a bamboo stick and bringing it back home to the missus.

"Knoooooooox," Victoria called sweetly, catching my attention. "Look what I got!" she exclaimed, holding a bag full of snacks in the air. My mouth watered with excitement when I noticed the Three Musketeers in the plastic zip bag among the other goodies. But then a thought came to me.

"Why did you pack so many snacks in your luggage?" I questioned.

"I don't know. I just had this feeling, you know? Like this feeling that my plane would end up crashing and I'd be stranded on a remote island with my psychotic boss slash island husband, and I needed to be prepared," she said mockingly.

"Island husband, huh? I think I missed that memo."

"Along with the HR-mandated trainings. Why are you bleeding?" she asked suddenly, pointing at my leg.

"That Three Musketeers is sounding delightful right about now," I said with a smile, hoping to distract her from the shark bite to the back of my calf. I sighed when she crooked a finger and beckoned me to her. I complied, and she silently motioned for me to turn around.

"Knox Kilroy—"

"Not my fucking middle na—"

I was cut off when she slammed the bag of treats into my chest and stormed off to our hut.

Correction... condo.

I tore open the bag, rifled through it like a trash panda, and snagged the chocolate bar. I ripped it open and devoured half the bar in one bite. "Fuck me," I whispered blissfully, closing my eyes as an orgasm exploded in my mouth. I seized when an intense burn shot up my leg.

"That's unpleasant," I complained, taking another bite out of the chocolate bar, this time smaller to savor my treat.

"Quit being a baby. It's just rubbing alcohol. I don't think you need stitches."

"Then I think I'm justified in saying that you overreacted," I murmured as I inventoried the remaining treats.

Chips, popcorn, cherry licorice, the treats seem endless. I wonder...

"Island wife."

"Please don't call me that." She laughed softly as she bandaged my leg.

"On a scale of one to dead, where would I fall if I ate these peanut M&Ms?"

"Silent treatment," she answered, securing the bandage.

"That's what I thought," I said, moseying over to her suitcase to see what else she packed. "What's that?"

She peeked around me. "Tell me you don't get bitches without telling me you don't get bitches. It's a vibrator, Knox."

"That's obvious. I'm referring to the case beneath it."

Victoria crouched on the balls of her feet and retrieved the box. She hunched over it, blocking my view.

"Everybody get the fuck down right now! Move it! Down!" she yelled, pointing a gun at me. I dropped the bag of snacks and my body down to the sand. Victoria fell into a snorting fit before returning the firearm to the case. "Somebody has never seen *Set It Off*. Knox, get off the ground."

"Why the hell do you have a gun?" I asked, slowly climbing to my feet.

"We literally live in Gotham City. I always carry, even on vacation." She fell silent, and I could see the wheels turning in her head. "Can you do me a favor, Knox?"

"No."

"What if it'll end my suffering? What if I fall off a cliff and I hit the rocks, but I'm still alive, but my wounds are fatal?"

"Then I'd do what must be done, but there's no reason to have this conversation."

"You're right...let's head to the falls and wash up before

99

dinner."

* * *

"This feels amazing, Knox. The only thing we're missing is hot water," Victoria sighed as she washed her braids with a coconut-scented shampoo and conditioner. I hummed softly as I washed my own hair. I could feel life slowly returning to the dried strands and felt almost human again.

"Here."

Tears welled up in my eyes when Victoria handed me a brand-new toothbrush and toothpaste. "I don't know who is enjoying your suitcase more—me or you," I remarked, accepting the toiletries.

"Me. Hopefully, I won't be subjected to your dragon breath every morning now."

"Ditto," I responded, squeezing a dollop of toothpaste onto the brush. "Why do you pack extra toothbrushes?" I asked out of curiosity.

"Just in case one falls in the toilet," she mumbled around her toothbrush.

"How many times has that happened to you?"

"Enough."

"What's this?" I asked, accepting an unraveled loofah. Victoria spat into the water before educating me.

"This feels like history repeating itself. It's an African net sponge. Do you require a demonstration?" she asked tauntingly.

"A PowerPoint would be preferable."

I squatted to retrieve a bottle I thought was soap—until Victoria's aht-aht-aht echoed throughout the alcove.

100

"Give me that," she demanded, snatching the bottle away. "What's yoni wash?"

She fixed me with a devious smile. "Oh, you're about to find out."

12

Mr. Ramsey and Ms. Caldwell

Victoria

We fell onto our "bed," with me straddling Knox. His mouth covered mine hungrily, sending shivers of desire racing through me. It had only taken three seconds for realization to hit Knox like a Mack truck. He cleared his throat and offered to wash on the other side of the fall while I cared for my "yoni."

And take care of it, I did!

I washed thoroughly until I felt like a woman again and put in a little razor action. My pussy was face-riding ready.

Knox pulled away, and I chased his lips until he stopped me. "What's the matter?"

"Are you sure about this?" he asked cautiously, eyes sharp and assessing.

"I wanted to fuck on you when you made it your personal mission to give me daily aneurysms. You swam the depths of the ocean and were bitten by a shark to bring me food and my belongings. Not only did your survival score go up, but your fuckability score skyrocketed." He sighed, and my eyebrows shot up in surprise.

"In my fantasy, I had you spread out on my executive desk. I miss my desk."

I snorted and trailed down his body, kissing him feverishly. "What else happened in your fantasy?" I asked, finally reaching his happy trail.

"You were moaning loudly as I slammed into you, and I encouraged you to scream at the top of your lungs because no one would hear you because everyone had left for the evening." I slowly pulled down his boxer briefs, taking my time and giving myself a little show. I nestled my nose in the pubic hairs I *knew* would be drenched in my pussy juices momentarily. The hair was soft and smelled like my body wash, as if he had spent the night and didn't have time to run to his place to shower before work.

"Tell me what else, baby," I encouraged, leaning back to free his dick. I sucked my bottom lip between my teeth and held back a moan when it sprang out, already leaking, and slapped his abdomen.

Knox had what I'd classify as *ID Channel* dick. He had the kind of dick that'd make me hide in his trunk and murder a little bit.

I hope this man is ready to be soul-tied to me.

"You'd yell at me and call me a piece of shit. You'd tell me that you hated me, but I didn't give a shit. You could hate me all you wanted because your hate didn't keep you from leaking down my dick. Fuck, Victoria," he groaned when I licked the stream of precum that trickled down his veined shaft. I hummed my satisfaction and slurped the crown of his dick into my mouth.

I always knew that, at some point, I'd be swallowing down Knox's meat, but I always thought I'd be on my knees under his desk or in a penthouse suite on the company's dime. Never in a million years did I believe I'd be drooling down the eighth wonder of the world with my ass in the air on a deserted island.

But honestly, I wouldn't have it any other way.

Knox's calloused fingers slid into my braids. His grip was tight, possessive, and unrelenting—like he never wanted to let me go—like I was his plaything for him to do whatever he wanted to. I gagged around him when he thrust up, jabbing me in the back of my throat. I didn't fight it and let him fuck my mouth. It felt like a well-earned but appreciated punishment for all the back talk I gave him over the year.

"Tell me you hate me, Victoria." I shook my head and choked, sending saliva spilling out the side of my mouth. I couldn't breathe, let alone talk. "Tell me you hate me, Tori," he repeated through clenched teeth. I denied him and reached for his tightening balls that I juggled in my hand. He yanked me off his dick, and I gulped down air. I winced when he sat up and caught my already aching jaw in a powerful grip. My jaw screamed in pain as he brought my face to his. "Your boss gave you an order, Victoria." Knox's demands accelerated my need for him, nearly pushing me over the edge. My eyes fluttered closed when his fingers skimmed my protruding nipples over the turquoise satin night shirt I had chosen to wear. He shoved his hand into my top, subsequently popping a button. I wanted to curse at him for tearing up my clothes, but instead, I melted into his touch when he cupped my breast. I had expected pain, but experienced nothing but pleasure.

"I hate you... so fucking... much," I whimpered.

"I hate you, too… so fucking… much," he whispered in my ear. I grinned widely and bit my bottom lip because, despite the harsh words, I felt nothing but passion and reverence from him as he kissed softly along the plane of my jaw.

"Show me," I urged. "Fuck me like you hate me."

Knox

"Show me. Fuck me like you hate me," Victoria pressured. I ignored her and trailed my nose down her neck as I groped her breasts. I felt as if I were back at the office again, getting high off her perfume as soon as she entered my space. Fuck Folgers in your cup; I wasn't fully awake until I caught the scent of her pheromone-like perfume. "Knox," she whispered.

I'm sorry, Victoria. I can't fuck you like I hate you because the simple truth is that I love you, but I can fuck you like I can't live without you.

I brought us back down to the mat and wedged myself between her thighs after I lost my boxers completely. From my position, I could slide into her easily and have us panting and writhing on the mat in no time at all, but there was no urgency for me. There were no board members breathing down my neck, no time-sensitive calls or emails I had to respond to, and none of those fucking HR-mandated learning modules to complete.

As they descended, my fingers skimmed down her night-shirt, popping open the pearl buttons. Each button release revealed a swatch of brown, supple skin. I left traces of wet marks against her flesh as my tongue made its descent. I paused at her lower abdomen and massaged between her folds. She inhaled a deep breath through her nostrils and released it with a pleasured whimper.

"I imagined my first time tasting you would've gone a little differently. You were supposed to be in my office chair with your legs splayed open, hooked over the arms. I was supposed to be on my knees, wringing out orgasm after orgasm from you as your arousal dripped down my lips, chin, and neck."

"Y-you...you're one nasty motherfucker," Victoria panted.

"The nastiest," I agreed, dipping two fingers into her. I could've gone with one, but something told me from the way her arousal coated my fingers and trickled down the digits just from a little massage that she could take more than one. Her walls clung to me desperately as I dragged my fingers in and out of her leisurely. Soft moaning filled our "condo," and I couldn't help but think about how amazing she'd feel on my dick.

I worked her pussy some more, stretching and scissoring my fingers inside her. I needed to taste her—lick her up and down like my favorite scoop of vanilla bean ice cream, but I was holding out for the good stuff.

I pressed the heel of my palm into her lower pelvis and thrust my fingers into her with wild abandonment.

"Oh, fuck, Knox," Victoria moaned as she squirmed under my ministrations. She bucked underneath my touch and attempted to scoot away.

"It's Mr. Ramsey, Ms. Caldwell," I reminded her as my fingers sped up. Her head thrashed back and forth as I continued to coax her first orgasm of the night out. I grinned in satisfaction when I was rewarded with her strangled cries and splashes from her pussy that dampened the mat beneath us and suddenly made me thirsty. "Turn around and get on your hands and knees," I instructed. She flew up, wrapped her arms around my neck, and kissed me with newfound vigor. Her lips parted mine, and her tongue went on a soul-searching journey like she wanted to possess me.

I'm yours, is what I hoped my actions relayed.

"Turn around and get on your hands and knees," I whispered. "Get all the way down, and put that ass in the air." She moved slowly, still recovering from her orgasm. She yelped in surprise when I harshly slapped her ass. I chuckled when I earned myself a heated over-the-shoulder gaze.

She should know by now that all she's doing is stoking the flame.

I wasted no time burying my face into her parted cheeks. I ran my tongue the length of her drenched slit and hummed in satisfaction when the taste of her burst across my taste buds. I feasted on her pussy, and I was thrilled when she crooked her neck to watch and was elated when she began to clap her ass against my face as I lapped up her juices. I shoved her further down and attacked her unyielding clit. One harsh, powerful suck had her pleading for me to stop but then begging for me to continue.

"Ms. Caldwell... I think you're ready to take me," I rasped as I stroked myself. Victoria reared back from her kneeling position and hungrily kissed me. I cupped one of her breasts from behind and tugged on the dark, turgid nipple. I hissed when she ended the kiss by sucking her arousal off my tongue and biting my lip firmly before relinquishing control to me again. She assumed the position without being told, and I was about to enter her pulsing pussy when I paused. "Safe word, Ms. Caldwell?"

"Stapler. Now fuck me already," she demanded.

Why does she always have to be so difficult?

I gripped the back of her neck, shoved her face into the tiny pillow we acquired from the wreckage, and thrust inside of her. I closed my eyes and blocked out her gratifying cries, giving both of us time to adjust. She pushed back on my dick, and I pressed my hand out to put space between us.

"What's the matter, Knox?" she whispered.

"I need a moment."

"Knox, baby. I need you to move. I need you to move, baby. You dropped eight glorious inches of dick in me. You can't leave me hanging like this," she whined.

"Nine."

"What?" she asked, exasperated from her orgasm denial.

"Nine inches," I corrected.

"Eight inches, nine inches, same difference."

Victoria

"There's a difference," Knox said as if he needed to defend his manhood. I didn't give a damn about that extra inch. I would get wrecked either way.

"Maybe it was you who needed a safe word," I taunted as I stood on my hands and knees with my pussy stretched around him. Knox pulled out, and I nearly cursed when he thrust back into me with so much force that I almost fell on my face. He plunged into me like a madman, and the sound of my ass clapping crashed louder than the ocean's waves. I tried to create a little bit of distance between us, but he saw to it that I'd take every inch of that nine-inch dick. He was giving me too much, too fast. I threw my hand back and pushed against his abdomen. I cried out when he wrenched my arm back and stuck my fingers in his mouth while he drilled away.

"Too much, baby?" he murmured tauntingly around my

fingers. "Just say the word," he mumbled as he continued to break my back in. Knox was fucking me viciously as if he was told he could have one last meal before walking the Green Mile, and I was that meal. He spat my fingers out, flipped me onto my back, and hooked my legs around his hips. With each pump, he knocked a little gust of air out of me. I quickly realized that breathing was overrated when he slid his hands beneath my ass and lifted me off the mat. My mouth gaped in a silent scream as he punished my g-spot. My fingernails scratched down his neck and back as I scrambled for purchase. I needed something to anchor me as Knox brought me to the finish line. I buried my face into his neck and wailed as he coaxed my second orgasm of the night out of me.

My breath hitched when I felt his cum shoot inside of me as my pussy still spasmed around him. Like the greedy bitch she was, she milked him for every drop. I caught my breath as he peppered kisses on my face while still inside me.

"I want a raise when we return home," I teased.

He laughed. "That depends on your performance review, Ms. Caldwell."

"You got me hunching in a hut, and I'm pretty sure I have sand in my ass crack. I'm getting that raise."

His chest rumbled with laughter. "And if I don't?"

"I will be on the news in a darkened room wearing a hoodie with a voice changer, telling my story."

He pulled out and rolled us over until I was on top. I lay on his chest and lived in the moment.

"How about instead of a raise, I'll let you come over to my place and raid your side of the closet?"

Shit. I had forgotten that this man bought me an entire wardrobe, shoes, and jewelry.

"I find your terms acceptable, Mr. Ramsey."

"Good. Now, let's eat. I've worked up an appetite."

"Sorry to burst your bubble, but we can't eat that shark."

"Why not?" he asked incredulously.

"It wasn't bled in time. Sharks have a lot of urea and ammonia. They have to be bled immediately after catching them." Knox sighed heavily. "It's the thought that counts, though. If it makes you feel better, I can do a mean reverse cowgirl."

13

Caftan

Knox

A soft wind blew through the trees, stirring Victoria. I smiled as I looked down at her. Her leg was thrown over my hip, and her head rested on my shoulder with her eyes closed.

I'm in fucking paradise.

We rocked softly in a hammock that we cobbled together out of scraps—some vines, rope, and the seat belts we scavenged from the plane. I was surprised it could hold both of us, but there we were, swaying as if we didn't have a care in the world.

Her hair smelled like her coconut conditioner, and despite how hot it was, I couldn't help but hold her tighter. She heaved a satisfied sigh and ran her hand up and down my well-defined abs. I was astounded and mesmerized that she was still the epitome of beauty after everything—plane crash, mosquitoes, lack of food and basic human necessities, and harsh sun.

"I think it's been six weeks," I murmured.

Her long lashes fluttered, and in the next second, she stared up at me with her gorgeous eyes.

"Six weeks? That's it? It feels like it's been a hell of a lot longer than that. It feels like forever," she said softly before closing her eyes again. "This almost feels like a vacation," she admitted.

"An extended vacation," I chuckled.

"Don't get me wrong—I still miss hot water, my food delivery app, and Wi-Fi, but I think I'm starting to get to that point of acceptance, you know?"

I nodded. I never considered myself an optimist or a pessimist, but a realist. And the reality was that we hadn't seen a single helicopter, plane, cruise, or cargo ship since our arrival.

"I'm offended."

"How so?" she asked with uncertainty.

"I'm your food delivery app."

She snorted, and I grinned. I knew she was about to follow up with a slick comment.

"Knox, leave me alone. There is a big difference between you bringing me a damn turtle and a twenty-piece lemon pepper wing, all flats with bleu cheese."

"That turtle was delicious," I insisted.

"It was aight by stranded-on-an-island standards, but we're not gonna pretend that eating a turtle is better than wings."

"I wouldn't dream of it, but there are things I wish as well."

"Like what?"

"Like the coffee you make me every morning."

"I spit in it every morning."

I sighed and tightened my arms around her. "I know...that's what makes it so delicious."

"You're disgusting. I never spat in your coffee, weirdo."

"My day will come," I said hopefully.

"We should probably get out of the sun because you're clearly having a heat stroke.

"Relax," I said, laughing, pulling her back down to me. "I'm joking." It took me a struggling minute, but I'd finally gotten her settled down. We lay there in silence for several minutes before I finally said something. "Your friends and family must be worried sick about you," I murmured.

Victoria scoffed. It was a mixture of a laugh and a disbelieving snort. "The person I spent most of my time with is right here with me." I smiled at that before I realized what it meant. Victoria's relationships probably suffered because of me and my attempts to consume every single waking moment of her life. "I'm sure my sisters are having a field day doing interviews, sobbing, and telling lies on camera about how close we were and how much they missed me. Hell, I wouldn't be surprised if they started a GoFundMe and started cashing in on my disappearance," she said matter-of-factly.

It's the certainty in that statement that makes it so sad.

"What about you?" she asked, hiking her leg up higher on my hip. "What about your family and friends?"

"Oh, you know, the one person I spent most of my time with is right here with me," I joked, pulling a soft chuckle from her.

"Fair enough, but answer the question."

I looked up through the canopy of palm trees and considered what I'd tell her. There wasn't much to tell.

"I don't know. My father passed away a few years ago. I wouldn't say we got along, but then again, I wouldn't say we didn't. We just... existed."

"And your mother?"

113

"She is alive and well, and is a bossy pain in the ass. Unfortunately, we don't see each other often."

"Does she not live nearby?"

"She's an hour away."

Victoria pursed her lip and pushed herself up. That inch of space between us made me anxious. I felt like a fool when I realized she was repositioning so that we could be nose-to-nose.

"And you don't see each other often?" she whispered as if we were telling secrets that should be taken to the grave. Shockingly, it made me want to open up more.

"What can I say? Work got in the way. Finding work-life balance is hard when you're at the top."

"You probably should've paid attention when viewing the work-life balance module—"

"Fuck the modules," I interrupted. Victoria snickered at my disdain for the stupid training videos.

I felt her fingers gently caress my face, and just like that, I was bewitched by her all over again. The tender moments between us had increased since sleeping together. Every morning began with sensual wake-up kisses that eventually led to passionate love-making. We held hands on our daily trip to the falls and languidly washed each other with no sense of hurry. Despite the sex, the physical gratification, and the lessening of threats against my life, the best thing Victoria gave me was a warm, welcoming smile when I returned from fishing. I felt as if I redeemed myself in her eyes—that she'd truly forgiven me for intentionally acting like an ass towards her.

I'd been doing some deep self-reflection during my daily alone time, and it took a few sessions for me to realize that I didn't purposely get under Victoria's skin because I loved her feisty reaction.

Don't get me wrong, I love it when we engage in intense banter, but...

I purposely mistreated her because I was insecure. I thought there was no way she'd consider me anything but her domineering middle-aged boss—nothing more, nothing less. So, instead of being a gentleman and asking her out, despite some outdated fraternization policy, I was a dick because I feared rejection.

"Do you think we're going home?" Victoria asked.

"Do you want me to tell you the truth or a lie?"

She smiled weakly. "Lie to me, Knox."

"A few more months, and we'll be back in civilization."

She laughed and buried herself back into my embrace.

"I wonder what life will be like when we return," she mused thoughtfully.

"Hectic. There will be constant requests for interviews from the media. The deceased crew members' families will try to sue me."

"For what?" she questioned, voice rising an octave from disbelief.

"A fucking money grab, what else?"

"You're right. Would you settle to get it over with?"

"Absolutely. It would probably cost less for me to settle than to have my lawyer fight a class action lawsuit."

"That's fucked up. I can't wait to get my settlement check."

"Seriously?" I groaned, rolling out of the hammock. She laughed and followed suit.

"I'm going to be the *first* one in line for my check for emotional distress—not because you forced me on this trip and the plane crashed, but because I'm subjected to seeing you walk around in my caftan dress. Take that shit off, Knox."

"Sorry, no can do. It feels so soft. Plus, I can let my dick and balls breathe without being obscene."

Victoria

"I have a question," I said, handing Knox a half-melted candy bar for his dessert after we indulged in a dinner of fruit and turtle soup: turtle meat floating in a seaweed and coconut milk broth.

"I might have an answer."

"I have two questions, actually."

"Hit me."

"First, why the hell do you have my bonnet on?"

"To protect my curls. Next question."

This man gets on my everlasting nerves. He has the gall to be so nonchalant when he's dressed like someone's Big Mama.

"Your hair is getting a little hang time, and now you're acting brand new."

"A little? I can put it in a ponytail now. As you would say, you're hating."

"Knox Sharkeisha Ramsey, ain't nobody hating on you."

"Hey. I kinda like that," he said, chuckling at my diss.

"You would," I huffed, staring into the fire.

"It has a nice little ring to it."

"When are you going to tell me your middle name?"

"When we're rescued," he answered honestly.

Okay...probably never.

"Who hurt you?"

"Excuse me?" he asked. His brow raised to the top of his

head, and he paused, licking the chocolate wrapper.

"I don't believe the workaholic bit, and that's why you're a forever bachelor. Somebody hurt you."

He remained silent but resumed his licking activities. I looked away briefly.

This man is licking this wrapper in the same reverent way he licks my cat.

"You first," he said, catching me off guard.

"Excuse me?" It was my turn to question him in disbelief.

"I don't believe the overworked executive assistant bit. You're a very intelligent and attractive woman with a heart of gold, Victoria. You could have any man you desire."

"And you're a wealthy, handsome man with a heart of coal. You could have any woman you desire," I rebutted.

He snickered. "You forgot intelligent."

"I didn't forget. That was intentional."

"I have the woman I desire," he answered casually, not realizing that he was making my heart do illegal Simone Biles moves in my chest.

"Anyway, what's your story? What's her name?"

"You first."

"I asked first," I argued back.

"I have to go last for dramatic effect."

"Why do you always have to be so fucking difficult? Damn," I muttered. "His name was Desmond Banks—"

"Desmond Banks? Why does that name sound familiar?" Knox asked, narrowing his eyes as he attempted to pinpoint why his name was ringing a bell.

"He was my high school sweetheart, and we dated throughout college. He played football and was drafted to—"

"The New York Mariners!" Knox exclaimed.

"Gold star for you," I said with a weak smile. "But anyway, we had this long ass history together." I fell back on the blanket I was sitting on and propped myself up on my elbow, making myself comfortable for our trauma dump session. "He sold me this dream and told me that we'd live in a big ass house on a hill, drive luxury cars, and jet set around the world. It all sounded good to me, but I was a fool. I should've known better when his version of "the dream" only included materialistic things. He never mentioned marriage or children or shit like that; that should've been an eye-opener, but I was young, dumb, and in love."

"What happened?" Knox asked softly, looking like he was on the edge of his seat.

"The NFL draft was coming up, and we knew he was a shoo-in, but it was also around the time of my mom's surgery—same day, actually. I had a choice—be there for my mother or be there for my man. I chose my mother, and as my reward, I watched my man on draft day, sitting on the couch, with his tutor beside him."

"Shit," Knox whispered. "He left you for a white girl."

I collapsed against the blanket and laughed until I almost threw up my lungs. "Wh-what do you know about that?" I asked, still laughing.

"It's not hard to put two and two together. I've seen those NFL draft couches."

I pulled myself back up and crossed my legs. "Yeah... well... it is what it is. Desmond gets the call, and he, Kendall, and his goofy ass mama jump off the couch in celebration."

"Uh-oh, I hear some animosity there with his mother."

I rolled my eyes. "Desmond was a huge mama's boy, and she was always in his ear, and his mother could do no wrong

118

in his eyes, even when she was dead ass wrong. She stayed in our business and made it seem like whatever I did for him wasn't good enough. I remember one time she came over to his place on a Sunday, and I had spent all day meal-prepping for him for the week and made his Sunday dinner. She came breezing in with a Sunday feast that rivaled any Thanksgiving dinner and bitched and complained about the food I made for her "precious baby" and how I needed to step my game up, not taking into account that her "precious baby" was a fucking athlete and didn't need to be eating soul food every time he turned around."

"It wouldn't have ever worked out," Knox mumbled.

"No, it wouldn't have, but I swallowed down my pride because I was still holding out for that fucking house on the hill. But back to draft day. They're all hugging, kissing, praising Jesus—the whole nine yards. My dodo bird self sat there beside my mother in the hospital room and cried. And that's not the worst fucking part. For a split second, I hated that I chose my mother. I never felt so fucking low in my entire life. That no-good, cheating ass son-of-a-bitch was on live TV proposing to his tutor from the spring semester with his trifling ass mama jumping in the background like Drew Carey invited her down to play *Plinko!* and all I could think about was that it should've been me."

"I'm sorry, Victoria."

"You don't have to feel sorry for me, Knox. The ancestors got him back. As you very well know, he blew his knee out in his first game and never stepped on another football field again."

"Serves him right."

"His fiancée left him, too."

"Of course. She was only there for the check," he co-signed.

"I thought him blowing out his knee was the icing on the cake, but the sweetest revenge was when he lost everything and tried spinning the block."

"Spinning the block? What does that mean?"

"He tried to come back."

"Fuck that," Knox exclaimed, rightfully offended for both of us.

"Mhm. He tried limping right back into my life, telling me he made a mistake, and I always held him down, and we were always meant to be together, blah, blah, blah. I told that boy to kick rocks and to make sure he got back home before the streetlights came on unless he wanted to see his mama waiting on the stoop with a belt in her hand."

"That sounds satisfying," Knox said with an appreciative hum.

"It was."

"And you never dated after that?" he asked curiously.

"I dated here and there, but nothing serious. Truthfully, dating wasn't high on my priority list, and then I started working for your bitch ass, and that left no room for dating," I explained.

"If it makes you feel better. My fiancée attempted to murder me."

14

Take a Hike

Knox

I chuckled when Victoria's eyes bulged from her head in shock.

"I'm sorry... what?"

I snatched off her bonnet that I was wearing just to fuck with her and motioned for her to join me on the other side of the fire. Seconds later, I held my island wife in my arms and buried my face in her neck.

"Her name was Naomi Lereaux."

"Damn, Knox. She had one of those soap opera names. That should've told you everything you needed to know," she said, pushing my face away.

"It should've," I muttered. "But as you said, I was young, dumb, and in love."

"How old were you?"

"Thirty-four."

Victoria snorted. "You were old enough to know better."

I shrugged. "I heard that men's brains don't fully develop until age 35."

"It's 25, and you know it."

"I tried."

"You did," she replied, patting me sympathetically on the back of the hand.

"Her real name was Lucy McGill, and she originally hailed from some butt fuck town in Louisiana but claimed she was from New Orleans."

"How did you two meet?"

I sighed. "My mother."

"Oops. That explains why you keep your mother at arm's length. It's not her fault, Knox. Or was it? Was she in on the plan?"

I shook my head. "No, she wasn't in on Naomi's plan." I sighed again.

"You don't have to keep going if you don't want to," Victoria said reassuringly, picking up on how difficult it was for me to get the words out.

"No, I'm fine. Naomi targeted me specifically. I was a young, rich bachelor making a splash in the industry at the time. I was on the cover of *Forbes* and *Entrepreneur* for the successful launch of our company. I was giving interview after interview on various talk shows—my face was everywhere."

"Oh, my God," Victoria moaned, covering her face with her hands.

"What?"

"I was nine then, and now I remember seeing you on the news."

"Fate is so fickle. You were a child and didn't know you were watching your future husband on TV."

122

"I don't care what you say, Naomi's innocent. You set her up."

I laughed. "Would it kill you to be on my side for just once?"

"I'm always on your side, Knox. I've done shit for you that you don't even know about."

"Like what?" I pressed.

"Hmmmm. Do you recall that board meeting when Mr. Forsythe was chewing your ass out and had to call an end to the meeting early?"

"I had a migraine for two days because of that spiteful bastard," I hissed.

"Yeah, well, I didn't like how he was disrespecting you, so I doused his coffee with laxatives every time I fixed it."

"That is the kind of commitment that gets you raises."

"I also didn't like how he called me 'gal,' so Mr. Forsythe was getting got regardless."

"Victoria, I want you to know that you always held me down, and we were always meant to—stop hitting me!" I laughed when she stormed away to our home away from home. I doused the fire and followed after her. "You have to admit it was a little funny," I teased, crawling into the hut with her.

"It was hilarious, Knox Desmond Ramsey," she drawled. I couldn't see it, but I knew she rolled her eyes. "Hurry up and tell me how this woman almost killed your ass so I can go to bed."

"Death by stapler."

"Really?" she asked skeptically.

"No, she hired a professional hitman."

"For real?" she asked, yawning that time around. I only had five minutes until she passed out. I had to make this quick.

"Long story short, Naomi Lereaux was a black widow. I

would've been her fourth husband that she killed."

"That's wild," Victoria whispered, snuggling closer to me.

"Indeed. With each victim, she had a new identity with a different backstory. She stalked her victims extensively."

"How extensively?"

"She stalked me and my mother for a little over a year before she initiated her plan."

"A year? She was committed."

"And meticulous. She had my mother's schedule memorized and knew everything about her and her hobbies. She knew my mother's favorite cafe, which she frequented and visited every Thursday for a coffee and a chocolate croissant. She knew that my mother enjoyed volunteering at the local animal shelter on the weekends and that she played bridge at the country club on Tuesdays with her friends. It was easy for her to "randomly" meet my mother and strike up a conversation with her.

"My mother believed they had so much in common and that she'd made a new friend. I'd have Sunday dinner with my mother, and she'd be so chatty about her new friend Naomi, who was around my age, single, and into traveling. I was dismissive because my mother had a nasty habit of always trying to hook me up with someone. She decided to take matters into her own hands and invited Naomi for Sunday night dinner one evening. And I was a fucking goner as soon as I met her. She was gorgeous, brilliant, humorous, and I loved watching her interact with my mother and how happy she made her."

"Get to the good part where she tried to kill you," Victoria mumbled sleepily.

"Be patient. I'm getting there," I replied, covering us with a blanket. "Six months later, I was engaged to my at-the-time love of my life and looking forward to spending the rest of our lives together. I came home early one day, hoping to surprise her with flowers and her favorite chocolates from a downtown chocolatier. I stopped outside the bedroom when I heard her on the phone. I wasn't one to eavesdrop—"

"You're a damn lie about that eavesdropping, but please continue."

"As I was saying, I wasn't one to eavesdrop, but she sounded distressed—enraged. She spoke in a tone I'd never heard her use before—a tone I never thought she was capable of. It was dark and sinister—a far cry from her soft, wispy voice. Then I overheard her finalizing her plans with the hitman for my demise."

"How did she plan on having you taken out?"

"She knew I was a fan of hiking, and that was one of the only hobbies we didn't share."

"Let me guess. For the honeymoon, she wanted to go somewhere where you could hike while she stayed behind at your hotel or residence. The hitman would push you off a cliff, and later, she'd be frantically calling the authorities to report that her husband went hiking and never returned. They'd find your mangled body at the bottom, and Mrs. Naomi Ramsey would be a very wealthy woman."

"It's almost as if you planned my expiration with her."

"I'm not that creative or patient."

"I know. Your PowerPoints aren't the most eye-catching."

"Fuck you. My PowerPoints are the shit."

"I agree. They're shit." I continued my story before she could argue. "I contacted the authorities, informed them of what I overheard, *and* hired a private investigator. A few weeks later, Naomi was arrested, and I was heavily abusing alcohol to try to mend a broken heart. Despite what you may believe, I don't have mommy issues. My mother took the news harshly. She blamed herself for introducing me to Naomi. I tried to explain to her that Naomi would've found a way to get near me whether she introduced her to me or not, but...my mother had always been the self-deprecating type. Naomi's betrayal spiraled her into a deep depression. Eventually, she snapped out of it, but I know she still feels guilty for being unable to see through Naomi's carefully constructed plot. After all these years, she still won't let the shit go."

"Did you swear off love after Naomi?"

"For a long time, I did. I knew my situation wasn't typical, but I was all in, you know?"

"Did you change your stance on love?"

"I did. Last year, I interviewed a young woman for the executive assistant position. I told myself, this woman will stab me in the face instead of the back."

"I don't even have anything to say to that. Goodnight, Knox."

I chuckled and pulled her closer to me. "Goodnight, Victoria."

A few minutes had passed of me rubbing her hip and ass when I felt the need to address something with her.

"Victoria?"

"What's good, Knox?"

"I-I can give you the house on the hill, the luxury cars, and the trips around the world," I said softly as we lay beside each other.

"I don't want those things anymore," she whispered in the dark. "Why would I want that when I have a condo with a million-dollar view?"

15

Trifling

Knox

You can do it. Just ask her. The worst thing that can happen is she tells me, " No, get out of my face and go sit down somewhere, Knox Amadeus Ramsey." That's not my middle name, but to be fair, pre-crash Victoria would tell me that, but Island Wife Victoria is calmer and more agreeable.

"Are you constipated, Knox?" Victoria asked, pulling me away from my intrusive thoughts. "Because if you are, you'd better eat a mango. You'll be squatting over a hole by lunch."

"No, I'm not constipated. Why do you ask?"

She squinted up at me from her palm fronds-woven yoga mat and assessed me further.

"It's your face."

"What's wrong with my handsome face?"

She snorted. "I didn't say all of that."

"What's understood doesn't have to be said."

She shook her head with a small smile. "The sun hasn't even

risen yet, and you're already on your bullshit."

"My bullshit is 24/7, baby." Victoria fell back on her mat and clutched her stomach while she laughed. I plopped down beside her and patiently waited for the giggle factory to hang up their hard hats and punch their time cards to end their shift. "Okay, that's enough," I insisted, straddling her. I groaned when she ran her hands up my thighs beneath the caftan, giving them a tight squeeze. "That's sexual harassment, Ms. Caldwell."

"Shhhh. No one has to know," she whispered, reaching up to caress my bearded cheek. "It can be our little secret. I'll give you whatever you want as long as you say you'll be mine. Name your price, Mr. Ramsey," she said teasingly.

"You'd make an excellent CEO. You have the whole preying on the vulnerable employee thing down."

"Is that what I was to you?" she questioned as her hands continued to roam.

"Everyone comes with vulnerabilities."

She hummed contemplatively. "True. What's your price, Knox? I know you have a son at home, crying all alone on the bedroom floor cause he's hungry, and the only way to feed him is to sleep with your boss for a little bit of money."

I squinted at her skeptically.

Isn't that from a song?

It took a few seconds for me to place the lyrics.

She's an idiot.

"No, his father is not gone and smoking crack. I want you to go on a date with me."

Victoria's brows tilted in confusion. "Like when we're rescued?"

"No, this afternoon. I found this place the other day and

want to show it to you. I know we don't have basic amenities like running hot water and electricity; hell, we shit in holes and have to dive to the depths of the ocean for food, but you still deserve to be treated. We may not be dining on Wagyu steak tonight. Still, I can promise you lobsters fresh from the ocean without the sky-high market price and some leftover bourbon. What do you say? Will you go out with me?"

My heart thumped against my rib cage as I waited for her response. She chewed her lip thoughtfully as she considered my offer.

I don't think I'll recover if I get turned down on a deserted island.

"I have one condition," she said.

"What is it?"

"Please ditch the caftan for our date." I grinned and stood to my feet, ripping the comfy dress over my head. "Oh, my God. You're such a child," she groaned as I did a little naked celebratory dance.

"Don't look away, Tori. Feast your eyes on perfection."

"You better feast your eyes on some pants and a shirt if you want to go out with me," she insisted.

"Fine. You win."

"When do I have to be ready?"

"Be ready in two hours. We'll skip breakfast and have an early lunch. We have a little bit of a hike to get to our destination."

"I'll be ready," she confirmed.

* * *

I buttoned up the dress shirt that I wore when we crashed and rolled the sleeves up. The shirt was a few sizes too big

129

and seemed to hang off of me unnaturally, but it would do. I tucked it into my dress pants, which were also ill-fitting, and stretched out the waistband to measure the size difference. There were several noticeable inches between my waist and the stretch of the fabric. If I had to guess, I had lost about 40 pounds since arriving on the island, and my body fat was now in the single digits. I was what you would call "sinewy."

Sinewy and sunburnt.

We'd been on the island three months, and were eating decently now that we'd gotten the lay of the land and the ocean. We'd rigged together lobster traps, discovered mango on the far right of the island, and I'd caught another shark, but that time, I bled it immediately, and we ate like royalty that night. Food scarcity was no longer an issue—the land, the ocean, and Victoria's suitcase snacks provided for us abundantly.

"Knox?" Victoria shouted in the distance.

Shit. She's ready.

I rushed through dressing, tightened my belt around my waist, and ran my fingers through my hair before leaving the tree line with the flowers I gathered for her. My heart kick-started when I found her standing in the distance. She smiled at me warmly and waved, and all I could think of was how radiant she was in her white sundress.

I finally closed the distance between us and chaotically shoved the flowers at her. As she took a moment to inhale the makeshift bouquet, I spent my time committing her luminescent vision to memory. She wore the bulk of her braids piled high with a few curled tendrils framing her face. She wore light makeup—eyeliner, mascara, and a clear lip gloss that made her lips look more plump and suckable than ever.

I felt myself falling, and by the time I hit the sand, it was too late.

"Ummmmm, Knox? What the fuck are you doing?"

"I'm tying my shoes. What the hell does it look like I'm doing?"

"You're not wearing shoes," she whispered.

Who has heat stroke now? Probably both of us, if I'm being honest, because I don't know what compelled me to drop to one knee and propose to my volatile executive assistant.

"Victoria Diamond Caldwell."

Her mouth gaped. "That's *not* my middle name!" she hissed. I nearly toppled over into the sand from laughter.

Sure.

"Now you know how I feel."

"I never gave you a stripper middle name, though," she protested.

"You did call me Sharkeisha that one time."

"I mean, it fits if you think about it. You are a shark killer."

"That I am."

"Are you seriously proposing to me?"

"That I am."

Victoria's brows raised to the top of her forehead, and she folded her arms over her chest. "What's the matter?"

"Where's the ring?"

"The ring? Victoria, we're on a fucking island. Where the hell do you think I'm supposed to get an engagement ring?"

"I don't know, but you could've put a little effort into this proposal. You could've whittled me a ring out of wood, bamboo, or something. Hell, you could've intertwined some palm fronds together. Shit, if you really wanted me to be your wife, you could've hunted down an oyster and snatched me a

131

pearl out of it."

Do I really want to tie myself to this woman for the rest of my life?

I tuned back in when she called me a brokie and made up my mind.

"Victoria Druscilla Caldwell—"

"Asshole," she huffed under her breath.

"I have full function of my knees, and my mother isn't waiting for me on the stoop after the street lights came on with a belt in her hand. Will you marry me?"

Victoria's mouth gaped in abject horror.

"That has to be *the* most trifling proposal I've ever heard."

"That's the only proposal you've ever heard." She squeaked and slapped a hand over her mouth. I smirked.

I love getting under her skin. She makes it so easy.

"And probably the only one you'll ever get."

She blew a raspberry and waved me off with your hand. "Watch, Knox. I'll leave this island and find the man of my dreams."

"Still me," I reminded her.

"I said the man of my dreams, not the man of my nightmare."

"Future Mrs. Knox Ramsey, can you just say yes already? The sand is burning my knee through these pants."

"Yeah, I guess I'll marry you. I have the perfect idea for a honeymoon."

"Oh, yeah? What's that?" I asked, rising to my feet.

"Let's go hiking. It will—"

"No," I responded immediately as I trudged towards her suitcase. I unzipped it and selected a piece of fabric and a hair clamp.

"What are you doing?" she shrieked when I ripped the fabric

in half.

"I'm being innovative and making you a veil."

"You ripped my bathing suit cover-up," she accused. I shrugged.

"So? What do you need to cover up for? I've seen everything multiple times. Turn around." She complied, but not without a few under-the-breath grumbles that I knew she wanted me to hear. "Can you shut up already? Damn," I said as I fashioned the makeshift veil in her hair. I spun her around and flipped the veil over her face to see if it would produce the desired effect, and it did.

"Knox...we can have a painful marriage or a pleasurable marriage. It's your choice."

I flipped the veil back to reveal her grumpy face.

"What if I want a little bit of both?" I teased. She was about to respond when I cut her off with an aggressive kiss. I picked up the bouquet I made for our date, shoved it in her hands, and dragged her to our "wedding venue" caveman style.

* * *

We were silent as we trudged through the jungle to the special place I'd discovered. I threw sideways glances at Victoria as we journeyed, trying to get a read on her, but she was a blank canvas. I wanted to ask her what she was thinking, but fear held me back. The last thing I wanted to hear was that she wasn't nervous or worried about our island wedding because none of it was real. It might be a case of escapism for her—a blip of excitement to break up the monotony of wake, fuck, fish, wash, fuck, and repeat. But it was real to me.

We may not be making vows in a church before God, but one

thing I've learned since being stranded on this island is that God is everywhere.

"You're quiet—too quiet," she said suspiciously.

"I could say the same for yourself," I answered, guiding her off the familiar path that carried impressions of our feet from continuous travel. "Care to share?"

"I'm thinking of my vows."

Well...that was unexpected.

"I see. I'm expecting something along the lines of, 'Knox Frederick Ramsey, I'm only marrying you because you're the last man on the planet.'"

She laughed and bumped her shoulder into mine. "Damn... now I have to start from scratch."

"I'm sorry I stole your thunder." I laughed.

Thunder erupted in the distance as if I had just pronounced gloom and doom on our nuptials. We were further inland, but I could still smell the sharp, salty scent of the ocean. It had stormed quite a few times since our arrival, and I welcomed it most times. It was another chance to cuddle with the woman I loved.

"Do you think it's going to rain?"

I scanned the sky, but I couldn't see far out due to the vegetation. "Probably. Let's get a move on."

Another thirty minutes of walking led us to a cave.

"Yeaaaah, I'm not doing this," Victoria declared.

"What? Why not?"

"I watched *The Descent*. I don't do caves."

"Victoria, there's nothing harmful in this cave. Do you trust me?"

We gazed at each other while I waited for her response.

Please say yes.

134

"I trust you with my life, Knox," she whispered.

That's a better response than I expected.

"Good, because we're kicking it up a notch. Close your eyes."

I was relieved when she obeyed without giving me hell. I led her through the cave, and reaching the beautiful paradise on the other side only took a few minutes.

"Hey, Batman. Can I open my eyes yet?" she asked, her voice filled with anticipation.

"You may."

She opened her eyes and her feet propelled her forward, but not before she glanced back at me. I nodded in encouragement. The gasp that left her lips was worth more than gold.

"Is... is this—"

"It's a bird sanctuary."

"There have to be at least fifteen different species here," she said in awe as she ventured further into the birds' personal oasis.

"Go explore, but don't go too far," I warned. Victoria was gone in the blink of an eye. I shoved my hands in my pockets and watched her as she cautiously tiptoed around the storks wading in a pool of water, not wanting to invade their personal space as much as possible. My attention was distracted from her when a flock of vibrant-colored parrots flew above and perched on a nearby tree.

Thunder boomed again, but that time, it was closer.

"Victoria, I don't mean to rush you, sweetheart, but I think it'll rain sooner than we thought."

"I don't hate you. I do!" she shouted from a distance, not giving me the time of day now that she was surrounded by colorful chicken nuggets with wings.

God, what I would give to have a fucking chicken nugget.

"While I appreciate your efficiency—"

"Make sure you put that in my performance review," she joked as she returned to me with the veil over her face. I smiled briefly.

"While I appreciate your efficiency, that is the most trifling wedding vow I've ever heard."

"It's the *only* wedding vows you've ever heard."

16

For Better or For Worse

Victoria

"Are you sure you want to do this right now?" I asked. The threatening thunderclouds made me fear we should seek shelter instead of exchanging nuptials.

"There's no time like the present," Knox said, corralling me to the altar, which was a tree with hanging vines and pink flowers. "Where is your bouquet?"

"Ummmm… see… what happened was—"

"I swear to God, if you say a stork took it, I'll scream."

I twisted my lips and waited for Knox to proceed with our sham of a wedding.

It's not a sham. Once Knox says, "I do," we're locked in for life.

"No response?"

I shrugged. "I'd rather you didn't scare off the birds with your screaming," I mumbled as I assessed the sky that was darkening with every passing second. "The only screaming I want to hear from you is screams of ecstasy. Do you want to say your vows first, or do you want me to go first?"

"Ladies first," he insisted, grabbing my hands and wrapping those rough, calloused fingers around mine.

Here goes nothing....

"I'd always fantasized about becoming Mrs. Ramsey." Knox's brow quirked in surprise until his lips slid into a satisfied smile. I refrained from rolling my eyes when his chest puffed out.

Idiot.

"Yes, Mrs. Gordon Ramsay has a lovely ring to it."

His jaw dropped, and I snickered until his shock was replaced by genuine amusement. "I think Mrs. Knox Ramsey is more fitting. Plus, I think your marriage would fail immediately."

"Why?" I asked with a curious head tilt.

"Can you imagine the carnage if that man slammed two slices of bread against your ears and forced you to call yourself an idiot sandwich?"

I puffed my cheeks out and blew a raspberry. "When you're right, you're right."

"Thank you. Proceed."

"Becoming Mrs. Knox Ramsey was never on my vision board, and after suffering heartbreak, I told myself that when it came to my future husband, I would never settle for less than what I deserved. I envisioned a man who was hardworking, loyal, intelligent, patient, respectful, accepting of my flaws, supportive, communicative, and a provider." I flipped his palms over, and my throat tightened from the surge of emotions that broke through like a rushing river breaking through a collapsing dam. I sucked my bottom lip in between my teeth when translucent drops speckled his open palms.

"Fuck, I'm going soft," I whispered as Knox wiped away my tears with his thumbs.

"Thank God," he murmured, making me chuckle. He kissed me before releasing me. I scooped his hands up again and picked up where I had left off.

"I remember going home one night, annoyed as fuck because you kept bitching throughout the evening about a callus you developed from playing tennis. Since then, the callouses have multiplied, not because of tennis but because of your determination to provide for and protect us as we face the challenges of the island and the uncertainty of our future. We don't know what tomorrow may bring, but I vow to stand by your side and be your companion and confidant as we build a life of tenderness and joy. We may not have modern amenities like TV, Wi-Fi, and food delivery apps, but we have each other. And as the song goes, I think I like this little life. The island may be our forever home, and because my birth control is nearly toast, it might be where we raise a family."

"You want children with me?"

I shook my head solemnly. "Not on an island without the intervention of modern medicine."

"But if we were home, you would?"

"I'd be open to the idea. Can I finish my vows? I was on a roll, and now I've lost my train of thought."

"I apologize. Please continue," Knox said, looking every bit satisfied with himself.

"In closing, you're not the man you used to be. You used to be the first thing I thought about when I opened my eyes, but for the wrong reason. You're still the first thing I think about when I wake, but for all the right ones because I know that each new day with you brings affection, comfort, healing, acceptance, appreciation, and laughter. You've earned my forgiveness, respect, loyalty…and my love. I can't believe I'm saying this, but… thank you, Knox."

"For what?"

"For being an overbearing, possessive asshole and canceling my flight to Miami."

Knox

Lightning streaked across the sky, and the resounding thunder nearly drowned out Victoria's love confession. But I refused to allow her declaration of love to be lost amongst the elements.

She loves me. This is all I ever wanted from Victoria, but why does her love feel circumstantial and that she loves me by default because she has no one else to choose from?

"Thank you, Knox."

"For what?" I asked dubiously.

"For being an overbearing, possessive asshole and canceling my flight to Miami."

I cleared my throat. "No thanks are required. There was no way I'd allow my future wife to embarrass my family name by twerking on tabletops."

"Hubby, you prance around in a caftan with your fucking dick print showing, and you think I'm embarrassing the family name?"

I grinned smugly and prepared to be punched in the gut. "You sound jealous. Is it the caftan or the dick?"

She snorted and rolled her eyes. "The ceremony has not been completed. I can still walk away from you as a single woman."

Victoria's threat cracked open the sky, forcing us to run to the cave for cover. I fell against the cavern wall and laughed as she sputtered and fought with the makeshift veil that clung to her face. She eventually yanked it off and threw it spitefully on the ground. My eyes wandered down her body while she cursed the former swimsuit cover to Hell. The white sundress embraced her now slender frame, showing off her tightened nipples and the gentle swell of her hips.

"Victoria," I said suddenly.

"What's up, Knox Berry Farm?" she asked, squeezing water from her braids.

It's Knott's Berry Farm....

"Love makes you do crazy things sometimes, you know that?"

"Oh? Is that why Naomi Lereaux wanted to ice you because she loved you?"

I barked out a laugh and pushed myself off the wall. "No, there was no love there," I said, extending a hand to her. She accepted it and allowed me to pull her into an embrace. "Love makes you do crazy things like planning a romantic getaway for you and your executive assistant under the guise of a business trip."

"Mmmm," Victoria contentedly hummed when I squeezed her ass. I slowly inched her skirt up her hips and was relieved she wasn't wearing panties.

"I may not have been on your vision board, but you were on mine as soon as you entered my office. I knew I wanted you, and I'd have you by any means necessary," I admitted as I slowly eased two fingers into her. She was warm and wet, and her arousal was leaking down my fingers in no time as I prepped her to take me. "While you were preoccupied hating every fiber of my being, I was busy loving every part

141

of you—every scowl, every satisfied smirk when you put me in my place, every accidental brush of the fingers when you handed me documents." My thumb brushed against her clit, and she nearly crumbled. "Not yet, baby," I whispered against her lips as my taunting caresses slowed. "I was so unreasonably enamored with you that seeing your name scrawled on documents angered me." Victoria's brow tilted in confusion through the lust. "I'd see your last name and wanted to scratch it out and write mine there instead."

"Jesus, Knox. You need help," she moaned, burying her face into my neck.

"I disagree. You said I'm a changed man," I said, picking her up. Her legs and arms secured around me, and I didn't hesitate to drop my pants.

"I...I...mmm, I take it back," she whimpered when I buried myself into her.

"I don't give a fuck, Victoria. You can take it back," I replied, thrusting deeply until her nails dug into my shoulders. "I'll just spend the rest of my life proving it to you."

I paused my vows temporarily to get a couple of strokes in and savor how she fit me like a fucking glove. We simultaneously groaned in disappointment when I pulled out, but I had a sudden urge to see my soon-to-be wife bent over with her ass slapping against my pelvis.

Seconds passed, and Victoria's speech slurred as I drilled into her from behind. One of her hands grasped the side of my thigh, and her other gripped the moist cavern wall. Her hand slipped down the wall, and in a flash, I was there, catching her wrist and slapping her hand back against the wall. I pressed my palm against the back of her hand for support.

Because there's no way I'll ever let my wife fall.

142

"It doesn't matter if we're on the island or off the island—I will always love... cherish... protect... and provide for you," I said between thrusts. "If you want an addition to our condo with the million-dollar view, then I'll build it. If you want a papaya from the tallest tree on the island, then I'll climb it. If you want a lobster with claws bigger than your fucking head, then I'll dive to the depths of the sea to catch it. My love for you may be viewed by most as unhealthy, chaotic, and obsessive, but you made me this way." Victoria tapped on my thigh rapidly, alerting me that she'd be gushing on me any minute and that I needed to wrap my vows up.

"In closing, I know when the jet crashed that you probably wished you were with anyone but me, but for me, it was always you. I take you to be my wedded wife, to have and to hold from this day forward, for better, for worse, for richer, for poorer, in sickness and in health, to love and to cherish, until death do us part."

Victoria's pleasured wails reverberated off the walls. Her pussy strangled, and I was trying to hold out until she finished, but her orgasm was endless.

Come on, Knox. You have to pull out.

I used the last shred of my self-control and common sense and pulled out. My cum jetted across Victoria's ass and back, blending naturally with the fabric of her sundress.

"I do," Victoria responded as she tried to catch her breath.

"As you should," I said boastfully.

"I know you said you'd tell me your middle name if we were rescued, but as your island wife, I think I should know," she said. She pulled herself up and slipped her soiled dress off, leaving her as naked as the day she was born and making my dick stand to attention again.

"I suppose it's only fair. We'll consider it a wedding present. My middle name is Giovanni."

"Giovanni?" she squealed. "I didn't know you were Italian."

"On my mother's side."

"Uh-uh. I need you to spend more time with your mother when we're rescued because I need her to become my pasta plug. Can I call you Gio?"

"You can call me anything you want as long as it's not That Man Over There."

"Giovanni," she mumbled to herself as she scanned me analytically. "Mhm. I can see it now. I was way off with Sharkeisha."

"No shit. Let's go, Wife. The rain stopped. I'll make dinner tonight. What do you want?" I asked, cleaning my cum off her.

"I want you to swim to the ocean's depths and grab me one of those Krakens."

I rolled my eyes.

Let me get right on that.

"Will you settle for an octopus?"

"An octopus will suffice."

17

Morning Mango

Knox

My dick hardened as soon as a burst of air breezed over it, courtesy of my wife ripping my caftan over my hips. She blew on my shaft, and I fought not to tremble from her teasing. Relentless taunting was guaranteed to follow. A prolonged groan escaped me as soon as she sank her mouth on me. That wicked tongue of hers wrapped around me lewdly before her head began bobbing up and down with enthusiasm.

"You're so good at that, baby," I rasped. "Too good," I added. She responded by slurping me down until my eyes rolled into the back of my head and my cum leaked from her luscious lips.

"Good morning," she murmured, kissing my lips.

"Good morning. You just earned yourself an extra crab."

"Gio, I'm not out here sucking dick for crab," she huffed. "What kind of ghetto shit is that?"

"Okay... okay... what about lobster?" I suggested lazily.

"What?" she asked, narrowing her eyes at me as if I said something truly absurd.

"You know, like that pasta and lobster song—something about sending $850.00."

"Oh, my God. I want an annulment," she said, snickering as she left the hut.

"You said until death do us part," I reminded her, following her out of our makeshift home.

"*Correction—you* said that in *your* vows. I didn't say that shit."

"It was implied," I said, accepting the stainless carafe from her after she drank from it. I choked on the water when she mumbled that she would imply her foot up my ass.

This is why I love her. There's never a dull moment.

"I'm joking, Victoria. I do not wish to demean or objectify you. I apologize."

"I'll accept your apology in orgasms," she said, grabbing her bag for the falls and slinging it onto her back.

"I will be happy to oblige. We should get going before the sun comes up," I mentioned, nodding at the horizon that had yet to turn pink from the first morning rays. According to my calculations, it was mid-September at the latest, and the mornings were no longer sticky and humid like they were during the summer; however, the temperature still managed to fall between the high to mid-eighties during the day and low seventies at night.

We arrived at the falls in record time and didn't hesitate to strip our clothes off and discard them on the nearest rock.

"What's for breakfast?" I asked, offering my hand to help her into the water.

"Take a wild guess."

"Either papaya, mango, or the strange fruit we've yet to identify."

Victoria smiled and produced a plump mango from behind her back. I sighed begrudgingly as we eased into the crisp water.

"What's the matter?"

"Bacon."

"I could throat punch you right now," Victoria whined as she wrapped her arms and legs around me.

"I know. I want to throat punch myself just for thinking about it," I murmured into her neck as I shuffled away from the shore. Lately, our mornings have become more intimate. We spent the early morning hours in each other's embrace, feeding each other sweet fruits and nibbling at each other's lips, savoring the fruit's robust nectar.

"I wish we were on one of those islands that had wild pigs," Victoria said with a sigh as she sliced the mango open with her thumbnail.

"I don't. The last thing we'd need is to take a tusk to the side.

"Amen to that," she agreed as she leisurely peeled back the skin.

"Pick up the pace, Mrs. Ramsey."

"Keep playing, Mr. Ramsey, and I'll devour this mango in front of you."

"I'd drown you first," I insisted. Victoria mumbled something under her breath that sounded like, "Try it if you want to," but I couldn't be 100% sure.

I watched as she customarily took the first bite. As a husband, I had to ensure that my wife was fed before I was. If I thought about it, that was the dynamic Victoria and I shared long before we crashed on the island. Every breakfast, lunch, or dinner meeting, I always waited to eat until after she took a couple of bites. She caught onto my behavior and once accused me of using her as a food taster to ensure no nefarious characters with ill intentions poisoned my food. That led to a thirty-minute tirade about corporate employees being just a number and disposable. I could've ignored her while she rambled on, but instead, I indulged her and fed into the madness with some words of affirmation.

My dick swelled between us when Victoria moaned around the first bite. The juices from the mango dribbled from her lips and down her chin. Without hesitation, I leaned in to lick up the remnants of the nectar. My bite was long forgotten as soon as our lips locked. Her lips were gratifyingly sweet, and if her lips alone could sustain me, I'd only eat and drink her.

I pathetically groaned when she pulled away.

"Eat," she insisted, shoving the mango in my face. I rolled my eyes and took a bite out of the fruit.

I don't know why she must be so stubborn. She's only prolonging the inevitable—my face between her thighs.

* * *

"Holy shit! What is that?!" I exclaimed, snatching Victoria away from the tree and shoving her behind me.

I'm ashamed to admit it, but I squealed.

"That, my dear husband, would be a coconut crab."

"Okay, where did that alien motherfucker come from?"

"Coconut crabs are nocturnal and usually stay in burrows. That's why we've never run into them before until now."

"Can we eat it?" I asked, looking to my wife for guidance.

She shrugged.

Come on, Tori Montana. I need you to be sure.

"Theoretically, you can eat them; however, I wouldn't. That crab shouldn't be out this time of day. It might be defective. I wouldn't fuck with them, period. They have the strongest grip strength of all pincer-possessing animals."

"Have I ever told you how sexy your brain is?" I asked, squatting slowly to pick up a large rock.

"Not nearly enough. Knox, leave the crab alone."

"Victoria, look how big the claws are. There is meat galore in them."

"Yeah, well, I'd rather you keep all your fingers." I edged forward slowly and repeatedly clicked my tongue as if calling a kitten, trying to coax it down the tree. "Are you pspspspsing a crab?"

"Shhhh," I whispered as I neared the tree. "Fuck!" I yelled, jumping back as a sharp pain radiated through my leg. I reared back in shock from the sight of the black snake that slithered away with what appeared to be a satisfied smile on its face.

"Knox? What's going on?" Victoria asked softly.

"Stay back," I demanded with my hand raised, stopping her in her tracks. I'd only been bitten for a few seconds, and already my leg was red and inflamed. Worse than that, the pain was unbearable.

"A snake bit me," I replied through clenched teeth. Victoria's brown eyes shone in concern as she gave my leg a once-over.

"D-did you see it? Did you see the color or any markings?"

"It… it was black… that's all I know."

Victoria sucked in a deep, shaky breath and ran her fingers through her braids. She had her crisis face on—the same face she'd wear in my office when shit would unexpectedly hit the fan and we needed a resolution stat.

"Okay. Don't panic. If you start panicking, then the venom will spread quicker."

"Not panicking," I said, trying to keep my face expressionless.

"This wouldn't have happened if you had listened to me," she insisted.

"I love you, darling, but do you really think this is the time to say you told me so?"

"We need a tourniquet," she mumbled. I watched Victoria leap into action, ripping a lengthy vine off a nearby tree. She returned shortly and tied the tourniquet so tightly that tears welled in my eyes.

"What happened to sucking the venom out?"

"A myth. We need to return to camp. We're not far. We should get there in ten minutes."

"Camp is closer than that."

"We can't get your heart rate up. We need to take our time."

As we continued our trek to the camp, each step became more excruciating than the one before. An unparalleled burning and itching sensation now accompanied the swelling and redness—the pain had increased tenfold.

"Come on, Knox. We're almost there," Victoria encouraged as we crested the tree line. She slung one of my arms over her shoulder and pressed forward when my steps became less solid. My head was swimming, and each step seemed to zap away my energy. My eyes caught sight of our hut, and my vision swam.

I...I need to lie down.

I staggered and eventually collapsed to my knees before falling onto my back. As I began to lose consciousness, all I could think about was how I let Victoria down.

18

Silver-Capped Teeth Behavior

Victoria

He's not getting better.

My eyes stung from unshed tears. They burned and eventually spilled over, landing on his pallid face. It'd only been twenty-four hours since he was bitten, and with every passing minute, Knox slipped further and further away. His breathing was more labored than the breath before, and his soft groans of pain made my chest fiercely ache.

I pressed my ear against his chest, and I was both relieved to feel it heave and terrified.

He's alive... but for how much longer?

I'd done everything for him that I could. I immobilized his leg with bandages and a splint and tried to keep him as comfortable as possible.

At this point, it's in God's hands. But what if he dies? He can't die here. He can't leave me alone....

I shook my head, attempting to clear away the dreadful

thoughts as if my mind were an Etch-a-Sketch. I wished that were true. I wished I could shake away the moment my world came crashing down—the moment Knox yelped in shock, the moment I witnessed his leg inflame before my eyes, and the moment I realized he'd die if I didn't get him off that fucking island.

I'd never envisioned us being apart. I planned for everything, but for some reason, Knox's death never even crossed my mind.

What am I going to do? How can I live without him? If he's not here to hug me and lie with me in the hammock? Then what? Who's going to cup my face and shake their head good-naturedly when I drink too much water before bed and have to wiggle out of his grasp to relieve myself? Who's going to love me the way he does?

I closed my eyes and attempted to make peace with myself, Knox's impending death, and my future.

We're going to die here. Him first, and soon, I will, too. Knox did say, until death do us part. This would be poetic if it weren't so damn predictable.

"Tori…Montana," Knox wheezed.

"Shut up and save your strength," I said, wiping away tears.

"I'm… sorry… should… have listened… to you."

"You should've."

He chuckled for a few seconds before groaning pitifully.

"You're meaner… than… a snake."

"You knew that when you married me."

"I did. You're rich now."

"What do you mean?"

"You… in my will."

My eyes widened in disbelief.

153

Surely this man wasn't that obsessed with me that he put me in his will? Never mind, we're talking about Knox Giovanni Ramsey. Of course, he did.

"And you're a… liar," he heaved.

"What did I lie about?"

"Your middle name."

I sucked my teeth and looked away from him, staring out at the calm waves. "I don't know why my mom gave me that stripper ass name."

"She knew you could… stand pressure."

"Mmmm," I hummed, leaning back on my hands.

"You're gonna make it back… be rich."

I shook my head.

"I'm not going back without you."

"You have to." I shook my head solemnly. "I love you, Tori."

"Even on your deathbed, you're a cruel motherfucker," I hissed, stroking his hand.

"Be nice to me. I'm dying."

I glanced back at him and could see the resolve on his face. He'd already made peace with the fact that today would probably be his last night on the island.

"Take him and leave."

I jumped to my feet and left the hut. The voice in my head couldn't be any clearer. I never understood what people meant when they said God spoke to them, but this had to be it.

Or I'm dehydrated. Either way, we're leaving.

I busied myself filling the raft with supplies and dragging it as close as I could to the hut.

"What?"

"We're getting out of here."

"Tor—"

"We're getting out of here," I repeated in a tone that left no room for argument. Twenty minutes later, I'd managed to wrangle Knox into the raft with as much water as I could carry and a few days of food. "Say bye," I said as I shoved us into the water. I popped his hand when he gave the island a shaky middle finger.

Badass. That's why he's dying now.

"Can't... hit... a... dead person."

"You're dead but perpetrating silver-capped teeth behavior. Right. Stop talking. Close your eyes and get some rest."

* * *

I'd lost the feeling in my arms long ago, but none of that mattered. I ignored every ache, stab, cramp, and sear of pain and kept paddling because I had no choice. I had a dying husband on my hands, and I knew he'd do whatever he could to save me. Knox's crazy tail self probably would swim down to Atlantis and annoy those merfolk into helping us. They'd help just to get rid of our asses.

I paused to check on him. He'd been quiet for a minute.

"Still alive," he whispered as I felt for his pulse.

"Be silent."

To my dismay, his pulse was weak, barely a noticeable thump against my finger, and despite his deep tan, all color had fled him.

"Make me laugh."

"Why?" I croaked.

"I like... laughing with you."

155

I smiled wryly and set the paddle aside to give myself a little reprieve.

"Do you remember that time I came to work and I was walking around a few days with a limp, and you couldn't figure out why?" He nodded. "I tried to make a voodoo doll of you and ended up missing and stabbing myself in the leg with the needle."

I smiled when Knox's chest shot up and down as he struggled to breathe and laugh. "That... that... was your—"

"Yeah, it was my second day of work."

"That's what... you get." My brows pinched when he started coughing between his words. "Another."

I wasn't in the mood to laugh any longer—not when his time was ticking down.

But this is what he wants.

"Once, you received a letter at work from this woman who was a fan of yours. She professed her undying love for you and eagerly awaited a response."

"You didn't," he said, voice rattling in his throat.

"I responded as you and very politely told her you were gay and it would never happen. I forged your signature and everything."

He grinned painfully. "I get it. You... wanted to mark... your territory," he said, reaching his hand out.

"Yeah. Something like that," I whispered, grabbing his hand. Knox's eyes welled with tears, and that's when I knew I could quit rowing. "I know your stubborn ass is holding on for me." He nodded weakly. "Well... I think this is your stop." He opened his arms for me, and I leaned down to embrace him.

"I love you," he said, kissing my temple.

"I love you, too, Gio, and before you waste your last breath, I'm not just saying that because you're dying."

"Good."

Seconds later, I popped my head up like a prairie dog when I heard something in the distance. Knox tried to speak. "Shut the hell up," I hissed. "Do you hear that?" I asked, looking to him for affirmation that I wasn't going crazy. He nodded, and for the first time since he'd been bitten, there was hope in his eyes. I heard the whirring of what sounded like a helicopter. And then I saw it in the distance.

A helicopter. It's a fucking helicopter!

"Knox, baby. I know you were about to be ushered to the Gates of Hell, but I need you to hang on a little bit longer," I said. I snapped myself into my orange life vest and started paddling towards the helicopter with everything I had.

The waves began to rock our raft violently as the helicopter approached. I stopped paddling and started waving it in the air and shouting as if the occupants could hear me over the blades' chopping.

My heart sank in my chest when the helicopter passed over us, but I was determined not to give up.

"You see all this orange down here! Get your ass back here!" I shouted as I followed the helicopter. "Y'all bitches colorblind or something?!"

"I-I wouldn't... turn around... either."

"You're real chatty for someone who was about to be shark bait a few moments ago."

My heart kicked into high gear when the helicopter turned around, and I could see it lowering from a distance. I waved, shouted, and cried as it grew closer, and I never thought the most beautiful thing I'd ever witness was a man in uniform propelling down towards us.

"Gio... they're wearing military uniforms. We... we're going home, baby," I cried. "Did you hear me? We're—Knox?" I dropped to the raft and shook him. "Knox! We're going home!" I yelled in his face. I pressed my ear to his chest, but I couldn't hear his heart, nor could I feel anything when I checked his pulse. "I knew you were a sick bastard," I spat as I started compressions. "Y-you waited good until we were saved to die on me, you stupid son-of-a-bitch!"

"Ma'am, I'm Officer Grimes with the United States Coast Guard—"

"Fuck the introductions! He was bitten by a venomous snake approximately 36 hours ago. Send one of those damn baskets down and get him to your ship or base!"

The following two minutes were a blur. I continued compressions, and Officer Grimes radioed for them to send down the defibrillator. I was sobbing uncontrollably as another officer wrestled me out of the raft, and we were hoisted into the air.

"My husband! You have to save him!"

"Officer Grimes is working on him, ma'am. Calm down."

The radio on the officer's shoulder crackled. "We have a heartbeat," Officer Grimes' voice rang through the radio. I glanced down at the raft, and I knew everything would be all right when Knox's arm raised, and he flipped me off.

Suddenly, I felt weightless as darkness clouded my vision.

I did it... I fucking did it.

19

Heifers

Victoria

"Oh, my God, Victoria. It's so good to hear your voice. We...we thought—take this phone. I can't even talk right now," Alyssa said. I laughed as I pictured over-the-top Alyssa wiping away tears and shoving her cell phone to Brittney.

"We're so glad they found you, sis," Brittney said, voice as soothing as ever.

"Me too."

"What happened?"

I spent the next thirty minutes giving my friends an island recap.

"You better sue that aviation company!" Alyssa shouted from the background.

"And will!" I insisted.

"Girl, I just knew that man kidnapped you and had you human trafficked or something. Trust and believe we were on social media 24/7 and stayed on necks trying to raise awareness to find you," Brittney expressed.

"We even posted a $50,000 reward to find you," Alyssa added.

Fifty bands? My friends love my ass!

"Y'all are real ones, but I need y'all to get on social media and clear Knox's name."

"We'll clear the air, but he's still an asshole for canceling your trip and forcing you to go with him. This wouldn't have ever happened if he hadn't been a creep!"

"I agree, but I'm over that. This whole experience has been… eye-opening. I've fallen in love, learned more about myself, and will never take life for granted. I feel like I can take anything on."

"That's… that's amazing, Victoria," Alyssa commented.

"But how do you know you're not going through Stockholm Syndrome or something? How do you know your love for Knox isn't out of convenience—last man on Earth kind of thing?" Brittney asked.

I sighed before answering. "Because I pictured what my life would look like without him, and I didn't like what I saw."

The line fell silent, and I waited for their response.

"Stockholm Syndrome," they both chimed before breaking into a fit of giggles.

"All right. You've had your laugh, but I need to know how my mom is doing."

My heart squeezed when I received the dreaded silence. I braced myself to receive the news that my mother had passed. I'd be devastated that I didn't have a chance to say goodbye, but relieved that she was no longer suffering.

"Your mom is doing fine. We check on her a couple of times a week to make sure she has everything. But we have to tell you something."

"Alyssa, quit being so damn dramatic and spit it out," I sternly demanded, tired of their pussyfooting around.

"Your mother was discharged from the nursing home and sent to another one," Alyssa answered.

"D-discharged? Why?"

"I spoke to the business manager at the facility, and she explained that the payments had stopped coming in. They discharged her to a hospital, and then from there, she was sent to a nursing home on the other side of the city."

The payments stopped coming in? How?

"Back up, back up. How did the payments stop coming in when I had 100k deposited into my account before we crashed? Her rent was set up on autopay."

"I don't know, sis. All I was told was that the payments started rejecting a month after your disappearance."

"This is some fucking bullshit! Is she at least at a decent facility?"

"Personally, I wouldn't put my mother there. It's a little dingy, and the staff always have funky ass attitudes," Brittney admitted.

"What about my sisters? Have you spoken to them?"

"Those heifers haven't answered any of our calls. We were trying to see if they would help us transfer your mother back to the facility, but they have been radio silent."

"Which is crazy because those bitches started a GoFundMe for you and made off with some serious money," Alyssa mentioned.

I snorted. "Of fucking course."

There was a knock on the door jamb, and Dr. Hubbard entered.

"Hey, guys. I hate to cut this reunion short, but the doctor is back, and I'm fully prepared for him to tell me I'm 29% octopus now."

"You're stupid," Alyssa said, laughing.

"I know, but thank y'all for coming through for my mother."

"We wished we could do more," Brittney added.

"You did enough."

We took another two minutes to say our goodbyes, and I made a mental note to call my bank to see what was going on.

"I want to see my husband."

"I know," Dr. Hubbard murmured as he retrieved a flashlight pen from his coat. I knew the man was sick of me asking for Knox, but That Man Over There was bitten by a venomous snake and died.

"Are you in pain anywhere?"

"No."

"Hold your head still and follow my pen with your eyes."

I was relieved many seconds later when he tucked the flashlight pen into his coat.

"Dr. Hubbard, I have Ms. Caldwell's blood work," a nurse announced as she entered the examination room.

"Mrs. Ramsey," I corrected firmly.

"I'm so sorry. I didn't mean to offend," she apologized quickly.

I'm not upset in the least bit, but I think, after everything, I deserve the title.

"Perfect. Let's see what we're working with." Dr. Hubbard said, humming to himself as he reviewed my results on a tablet. "Well, *Mrs. Ramsey*, except for slight dehydration and malnourishment, your labs are perfect."

"No babies, right?"

"Nope. No pregnancy."

Thank God. I need to get my life back in order before I go down that route. Wait a minute. I might be getting ahead of myself. Does he even want children? We joked about it, but Knox's near-death experience might turn him into one of those live-to-the-fullest types of people who want to explore the world and strike everything off their bucket list, and children might not be on that bucket list.

"What was your diet like on the island?"

"Pescatarian—shrimp, crab, fish, shark, lobster, octopus, oysters—a sea urchin once, but that didn't blow over so well when I was stung."

"Allergic reaction?"

"Not enough to worry—slight burning and a little swelling; that's all."

"What else sustained you on the island?"

"Seaweed, coconut, nuts, and fruits—oh, I almost forgot, once we ate some parrot hatchlings. And when Knox recovered my suitcase from the ocean, we had snacks I'd packed."

He nodded. "You had a colorful diet while on the island, but you're nearly underweight. I'm sure that'll change when you return home and reintroduce fats, carbs, and sweets into your diet. However, it'd be ill-advised to get off the ship and have a triple cheeseburger and French fries for your first meal. After three months without these foods, you might be more prone to stomach issues like indigestion."

"Honestly, this is the healthiest I've been since high school, and I don't plan on putting all that weight back on. A triple cheeseburger doesn't sound appealing in the least bit."

The pager at Dr. Hubbard's waist went off, alerting him to what I hoped was an update on Knox. I was on pins and needles while I waited for his response.

"Good news, Mrs. Ramsey. Mr. Ramsey is stable. Given the severity of the bite, I'm shocked he survived. You can visit him briefly."

"Is he conscious?"

"He's sedated, but we will bring him out of sedation once he gets some more rest. You ready?" I hopped off the examination table like my ass was on fire and followed closely as he led me further into the medical bay to Knox. "I'll come back and get you in thirty minutes. From there, you'll be escorted to a bunk room we prepared for you, where your dinner will be waiting."

"Thank you," I murmured as I stared down at Knox's sleeping face. "Dr. Hubbard, is Knox in the clear?"

"Again, he's stable but is responding positively to the antivenom and IV fluids."

"In your professional opinion, was his heart going out a one-off?"

"Mr. Ramsey's labs were all over the place due to the toxins; however, when we get him to baseline, he'll be in excellent health for his age. I can't predict the future, but the heart issue was directly related to the bite."

I nodded and gently grabbed one of Knox's hands. "I have a few more questions. Is that okay?"

"Absolutely."

"How's his leg?"

"There was some tissue and muscle breakdown; however, we intervened before necrosis set in."

"Meaning?"

"He'll need wound care for a few weeks to ensure it doesn't become infected. I'd suggest he use a cane or crutches during this time, but based on my brief interaction with Mr. Ramsey,

I doubt he'll be compliant."

I smiled softly. "You'd be right. So, after a few weeks…"

"He should ambulate fine without assistance."

All the air whooshed out of my lungs.

Thank you, Jesus.

"Any other questions for me?"

"Can a pair of scissors be dropped off at my bunk room?" His brow raised as he considered my request. "My braids," I responded quickly.

"Right," he said, blushing slightly. "I'll leave you to it—thirty minutes, Mrs. Ramsey. I know you want to remain by your husband's side, but he'd want you to take time to care for yourself."

"I hear you, Doc. I won't give you any issues."

Dr. Hubbard had barely left when I ripped back the cover and carefully climbed into bed with Knox.

"Listen good, Gio. I don't want any shit out of you when we get back. You don't have to use the crutches, but we can get you a sweet-ass pimp cane or something."

I rattled on with my demands until my fatigue finally caught up with me.

20

Stinky Sock Puppets

Knox

The beeping sound interrupting my sleep was irritating until I realized that hearing it was a blessing. Relief washed over me. The beeping had quickly gone from an irritant to music to my fucking ears.

"Mr. Ramsey, can you open your eyes for me?" a man asked. As much as I hated to admit it, I felt frail, and the thought of opening my eyes seemed insurmountable. "Mr. Ramsey, your wife is eager to see you."

My wife.

And just like that, my eyes were opened, frantically searching for the woman I loved.

"Somehow, I knew that would work," the man, who I assumed was the doctor, commented.

"Where—"

"She's resting; trust me, she didn't want to leave your side. We had to drag her out of here kicking and screaming."

"Did—" I paused to swallow around the dryness in my throat, "Did she threaten you with her stapler?"

"No, but she called me a motherfucker nine times."

"That's my woman," I said wistfully. "Is she injured? Has she eaten? She's probably hangry. Once you get past the fifth motherfucker, she's hangry," I remarked quietly.

"She was fed."

"What did she eat?"

"Chicken noodle soup." I grimaced. "Is everything all right, Mr. Ramsey? Are you in pain?" he asked, raising the hospital bed. His cold stethoscope was on my chest before I could answer.

"I'm not in pain, but a fat, juicy steak sounds nice right about now."

The doctor smiled warmly. "That's not happening any time soon. All right, Mr. Ramsey, let's get down to it. I don't know if you remember, but I'm Dr. Hubbard. You and your hangry wife were rescued by the U.S. Coast Guard and brought to our vessel for triage and treatment. Once you are stable, you both will be transported to Guam, where you'll undergo a more thorough medical examination. From there, you'll be flown to our Pacific base in California for further evaluation and an intensive and rigorous interview with police, FAA, and possibly the NTSB. Then you'll be flown back home to New York."

I listened intently as Dr. Hubbard gave me the rundown on my health and what to expect during my recovery.

"Can you take me to my wife now?"

"I don't think that's a good idea, Mr. Ramsey. You should stay in bed," he worded cautiously.

"I should be dead, but here I am."

167

* * *

"How the hell is someone supposed to fit in these?" I complained.

I was appalled at the coffin-sized bunk the sailors were subjected to sleeping in. You'd think they'd make the people who serve our country more comfortable.

"Did you have permission to leave the medical bay?" Victoria asked groggily.

"Of course I did."

"After you strong-armed Dr. Hubbard, I'm assuming."

"You'd assume correctly. Scoot over and give me some room."

"Please return to your full-sized bed in the med bay. There is not enough room for both of us."

I ignored her and wedged myself in the small bunk behind her. I kissed her shoulder and wrapped my arms around her. "You feel that?"

"I guess your heart is working just fine," she commented, trying to put some distance between her and my erection digging into her ass.

"Mhm," I agreed, rubbing my hand up and down her hip.

"No strenuous activity for two weeks."

"That's what that crackpot doctor said, too, but there's nothing strenuous about it—just a little roll of the hips from King Dong, and you're gushing all over me."

I smiled when Victoria released a deep, regretful sigh.

"I never want to watch you die again," she murmured.

Okay, fun time is over; it's time to get serious.

"I hate that my recklessness nearly cost me my life and traumatized you in the process. But I want you to know that I

168

fought to stay with you every second. There were times when I said, 'This is it,' and I think I saw the light at the end of the tunnel a few times. It wasn't until I knew you were safe that I checked out."

"What was it like, Gio?"

I warmed like I did whenever she called me by my middle name.

"What was what like?"

"Dying?"

Emotion clogged my throat—strangling the words in a chokehold.

"It… it wasn't fun. For me, there wasn't a moment of enlightenment or peace, just misery and what-ifs or what could've been. What if I had been a gentleman to you from the start? We could've had a good life with kids, ferrets, and the whole nine yards."

"I fucking hate ferrets," she responded, sounding like she was on the cusp of sleep again.

"What's your beef with ferrets?"

"They sleep like the dead, they stink, and I don't like how they flop around. They're stinky sock puppets."

Stinky sock puppets?

"Okay, it's time for you to go to sleep."

"Mhm. I'll take the kids, not the ferrets."

"It'll be great, Tori. Nine months from now, we'll have a beautiful—"

"No, sir. I'm no one's baby mama. You're officially marrying me, and we'll see how a year of marriage post-island goes before we bring children into this world."

I chuckled into her back. "Is this because you doubt your feelings for me?"

"What are you asking?" she asked hesitantly.

"Are you with me out of default?"

She laughed softly. "What is with you people?"

"You people?" I asked with mock offense.

"Yes, *you people* who refuse to trust me with my own feelings. I spoke with my friends earlier, and they suspect I suffer from Stockholm Syndrome."

I shrugged. "I think it's a fair assumption. As a precaution, we should go to couples' therapy."

"You hate therapists."

"I do, but I love you more, and I don't want it to be a year from now and you look at your life and realize you made a mistake."

"You're not a mistake, Gio, but I hear you. You'll never find me arguing with a man who wants to go to therapy."

"Thank you, love. Were you able to check on your mother?"

"I did," she admitted. "While we were gone, she was discharged from the memory care facility for non-payment."

My brow tilted in confusion. "Non-payment?"

"After you paid me off, there was plenty of money available to cover her rent for nearly a year."

"Did you get in contact with the bank?"

"I did. Apparently, I initiated two wires of $50,000 to Faith and Hope from my online banking a month after we were stranded."

"Fuck," I said, sighing.

"The bank is launching an investigation, and I'm calling in a case for Adult Protective Services because their theft put our mother in a state of neglect when she was sent to some bummy-ass nursing home that couldn't meet her needs. Those bitches are going to the pen."

"Amen. I'm sorry, Victoria."

She rolled over in the bunk coffin and pinned those espresso-brown eyes on me. "Don't feel sorry for me. I came out on top, and those bitches are gonna pay for everything."

I kissed her, and my mind flashed back to every kiss we shared under the waterfall, the afternoons we spent huddled in the hammock—praying to get home and dreaming of A.C., ice-cold sodas, and countless hours of lovemaking.

I have a second chance at life, and I'm taking it.

I broke the kiss and stroked her face. "May I offer my assistance with having your mother transferred?"

"I can handle it."

"I know you can, Tori, but let me do this for you, and if not for you, then for your mother as a thanks for birthing and raising the most diabolical woman I've ever loved."

I thumbed away the tears that slipped from her lids.

"I'm so glad that shark didn't eat you," she whispered through tears. She pressed her face into my chest and wrapped her arms around me.

"Me too. But now that I think about it, why did I always suffer catastrophic injuries?"

"I was stung by a sea urchin," she reminded me.

I rolled my eyes.

"Big fucking deal," I murmured, feeling my lids grow heavy.

"Will you allow me to escort you back to the med bay now that you've properly harassed me? I'm no doctor, but I have a feeling you should be hooked up to an IV and a vital machine."

"Sure. Just give me one more minute," I answered sleepily.

"You're not going back, are you?"

"Not unless you come with me."

She groaned, and it was music to my ears.

"You better be glad I love you, Gio."
"I love you, too, Tori."

21

California Dreaming

Knox

"Oh, my God, Knox. You look...."

Doug Reynolds, my trusted attorney of fifteen years, smoothed his hand down his tie repeatedly as he tried and failed to find the words. Typically, the man was brutal, so it was intriguing to see the harsh man, tongue-tied and ill-prepared.

"Like a cracked leather handbag you found at the church bazaar with a five-dollar price tag; don't be shy," Victoria remarked, her weak attempt at trying to turn my trusted lawyer against me.

"I-I wouldn't say that," Doug sputtered, unable to meet my gaze. "You look like a survivor."

"Yikes," Victoria said, laughing as she entered the SUV that idled on the tarmac. I rolled my eyes and climbed in after her.

After we were rescued, Dr. Hubbard determined I was stable enough for transport after 48 hours. Victoria and I were transferred to Guam before being flown to Los Angeles via private jet. The jet had barely landed, and I was already ready to say, "fuck it all" and charter a flight back to the island with my mouthy bride.

Being rescued and returning to civilization should've felt like a relief. Like the end of a nightmare and the beginning of the sweetest dream. But the truth was that reality wouldn't wait for us to catch our breath. I had seen my first glimpse of the headlines of our rescue and didn't know whether to laugh or cry.

From Boardroom to Beach: Billionaire's Survival Raises Questions About Mental Fitness.

FAA Launches Probe into Jet Crash That Left Billionaire Stranded.

Knox Ramsey Undergoing Psychiatric Evaluation—Board Demands Clearance Before Return.

Victoria Caldwell: The Assistant Who Won't Leave—Is Knox Ramsey Being Silenced?

Is It Love or Leverage? Tabloid Sources Raise Elder Abuse Concerns in Ramsey Case.

That elder abuse claim really chapped my hide. I was 49 years young and could still run circles around Victoria.

I was overwhelmed.

The headlines were relentless with speculation regarding my mental and physical health, and Victoria was getting picked apart by the media. They were determined to unearth anything from her past that would paint her as the villain instead of my savior.

The FAA and police wanted answers I couldn't give them, and the board was digitally breathing down my neck. Getting bitten by a poisonous snake sounded a hell of a lot better than returning to a corner office that would feel more like a prison of glass and steel with million-dollar views.

Truthfully, I don't know if I have it in me any longer.

"Who is this?" I asked, motioning towards the bleach blonde in a pink pantsuit that reminded me of Barbie and chewing gum.

"This is Amelia Cranson. She is a publicist from Stratus PR Group," Doug explained.

I grunted.

"What happened to Blackwell Communications?"

"They couldn't handle the magnitude of your disappearance," he answered.

"And you're telling me this twenty-three-year-old can?"

Amelia smiled broadly, showing off perfect white teeth achieved by the occasional whitening and Invisalign.

"With all due respect, Mr. Ramsey, Ms. Caldwell began her career with you when she was only twenty-three."

"And did," Victoria piped up. I glared at her before returning my attention to the young woman.

"Now, look here, Polly Pocket."

Victoria snorted and tried to cover it with a cough, but it didn't work. Her shoulders shook with laughter, and I gave up when Amelia joined in. The SUV turned into the giggle factory as the women wiped tears from their eyes.

"P-Polly Pocket... that's a good one, Knox, but please behave," Victoria requested as she dabbed at her eyes with a tissue.

"I'm just calling it how I see it," I replied with a shrug.

"Wonderful. Since we're just 'calling it how you see it,' then you don't mind if I have a turn?"

"I don't mind at all," I answered confidently.

"Perfect. Here's what your return looks like from the outside, Mr. Ramsey. You're the CEO of a billion-dollar company who vanished for three months. You reappeared with your assistant, who is half your age, clinging to your arm, and somehow, it was already leaked that Ms. Caldwell is your "spiritual wife." You have not released a single public statement, opening up the media to control every aspect of the narrative. The board is whispering about keeping your VP in place permanently, and investors are questioning your mental fitness, leadership, and most of all, your judgment. The families of those who died in that crash want answers and are threatening lawsuits, claiming that your last-minute demands put the flight and employees at risk. The public wants answers, and the speculation grows with every silent second that passes. They want to know about the crash, Victoria, and whether you're capable of running Ramsey Acquisitions Group. I am here to salvage both of your images, and no pun intended, but I can't hold back the sharks forever. So... you can make your jokes and call me names, but I've heard it all before."

"No one has ever called you Polly Pocket before," Victoria interjected. Amelia smiled softly.

"No, that's a new one, but this isn't my first rodeo with dealing with assholes who undermine my intelligence and expertise." Amelia's gaze ticked towards me. "Let's make this very clear, Mr. Ramsey. I have nothing to prove, but you do."

"Oop," Victoria whispered, turning her attention to the window and the passing scenery of reporters and cameramen who clamored outside the airport gates, nearly busting their asses to get a picture of us through the tinted windows.

"I will always have a career because wealthy people like you can't even breathe wrong without the world coming down on your shoulders. My career is guaranteed; yours is not."

My head snapped towards Victoria, and I asked, "Are you going to let her talk to me like that?"

"Did she lie?"

"You're not the ride or die I thought you were," I responded playfully.

"You're right. I'm better than you ever imagined. Now, sit there and listen to the woman like you have some sense."

I sighed and dragged my hand over my face before giving Amelia my undivided attention.

"I apologize for being untoward and undermining you. I think the snake venom has my brain a little scrambled. I appreciate your diligence and look forward to what you have planned to salvage my reputation."

Amelia beamed.

"Apology accepted. We need to discuss your next steps. We have less than an hour before we reach UCLA Medical Center."

I held up a hand to pause.

"Wait. Why are we going to UCLA?"

Doug cleared his throat and took over.

"The board wants a full workup before you set foot in the building again."

"I have been medically cleared," I protested. I was tired of being poked by needles and evaluated like a lab rat. I wanted to go home. I wanted my bed. I wanted to see Victoria hydrated and moisturized while relaxing on the verandah with a coconut water.

"No offense, but you have not been medically cleared by doctors at one of the top-ranking hospitals in the U.S. The hospital's reputation would reassure shareholders and the media that your return is being handled with the utmost professionalism. You'll be assigned an executive liaison to manage every detail from scheduling to post-evaluation follow-ups. You'll undergo comprehensive testing: cardio-vascular, neurological, psychological, and trauma-related assessments. There is no way around this, Knox, so don't even fight me on this. The board needs to know you are of sound mind and judgment when you return."

"I'll say what Mr. Reynolds here is too afraid to tell you," Amelia chimed in as she tapped away at her phone screen. "The board is questioning your judgment because of Ms. Caldwell."

"I can personally attest that his judgment was skewed way before I entered the picture," Victoria drawled.

Amelia nodded.

"I believe you, but nothing screams midlife crisis like marry-ing a woman half your age and leaving her with generational wealth."

"And nothing screams insane like enticing your executive assistant with $100,000 to go on a vacation with you after calling her airline claiming to be her husband and canceling her flight," Doug added. "Thank God you used your personal funds to fund this little venture instead of company funds. We'd really have a mess on our hands then."

I sighed and grasped Victoria's hand—searching for that steady strength she always provides.

"What next?"

"We release a prepared statement before arriving at UCLA. You undergo all of the necessary tests and spend some time acclimating in California before returning to New York. You need to publicly declare your relationship with Victoria, and we need to get you and Victoria in front of a camera for an interview, but not before announcing your condolences for the lives lost, especially First Officer Lancaster."

My brows knitted in confusion.

"Who is First Officer Lancaster?"

"The co-pilot who perished," Doug advised.

"Co-pilot Josh?" Victoria questioned, just as confused as I was.

"Correct. First Officer Joshua Lancaster is the son of the CEO of Solara Dynamics."

"Solara Dynamics? The aerospace company?" I asked in disbelief.

"The one and only," Amelia confirmed.

"Hmph. I don't believe it. His father is the CEO of an aerospace company and couldn't locate us with satellites?"

"That part," Victoria mentioned. "Also, how weren't we located sooner? Doesn't the plane have a black box and tracking device?"

Doug cleared his throat again and fiddled with his tie.

"No," I whispered.

"The aircraft was equipped with both; however, neither of them were functional. The FAA has officially grounded the aviation company, and I doubt they will clear another flight."

"So why is Knox being sued again?" Victoria demanded.

"Knox is being named as a co-defendant in the lawsuit due to alleged duress that influenced the employees and the company. The lawsuit states that Knox has a history of chartering last-minute flights and has a reputation for being demanding, controlling, and creating high-stress environments."

"This is bullshit," I muttered.

"They didn't lie about that last part. You are demanding and controlling, and that is why I had a cry room at the office," Victoria said matter-of-factly.

"You knew this was coming," Reynolds stated, flipping open a leather-bound portfolio and handing it to me. I scanned the documents.

"You want me to settle for $1 million per life lost?"

"Five million is a drop in the bucket for you, Knox," Doug said, trying to reason with me.

"This is bullshit," I argued, snapping the folder shut.

"Settling will be freeing," Polly Pocket remarked. "It'll all go away, and you'll never have to look over your shoulder again, wondering if you'll be called to take the stand. You settle with the families now, they sign their NDAs, and you focus on healing. The settlement will never make it to the media."

I turned to Victoria and asked, "What do you think?"

She heaved a deep sigh and squeezed my hand before shooting me a look that had me folding like origami.

"I think these families woke up in the middle of the night with calls that their loved ones never made it to their final destination. They agonized for months, wondering if their loved ones were dead or alive, and now they have their answer. They're hurting, and we're thriving. If I could, I'd pay it and move on, but the decision is up to you."

I lifted her hand to my lips and kissed it.

"Pay the money, Reynolds," I said, not taking my eyes off the woman I fell in love with long before we crash landed in the middle of paradise.

"I'll get on that right away."

"Tell the driver to make a detour."

"Excuse me?" Doug and Amelia said simultaneously.

"I want to ensure that my wife is comfortable before I'm admitted to the hospital. Doug, book a suite—something with a panoramic view and an exquisite room service menu."

"No, Gio. I'm going with you," Victoria protested defiantly.

"Not this time, Tori. I want you to rest and relax before I return and be the biggest pain in the ass you've ever seen."

"How thoughtful," she replied, smirking as if she had won something.

"I've found a suite at The Marlowe Regent," Doug mentioned.

"Sounds expensive. Book it."

22

Reunited and it Feels so Good

Victoria

A small sigh and groan escaped me as I rolled over, reaching for Knox. He wasn't there, but the sounds of the Pacific rolling in from the open balcony startled me as much as his absence. For a moment, my body still thought it was dawn on the island. I had expected salt wind, sand in places it didn't belong, and Knox breathing down my neck and whining about having to trek to the waterfall. Instead, I lie on high-thread-count sheets and a memory foam mattress that should be illegal while wearing satin pajamas.

It felt like a dream, and I feared I'd snap out of it at any moment. We'd still be stranded, and Knox would still be suffering.

I stared at the ocean through the gauzy curtains and tried to breathe. On the island, everything was stripped down to survival, but here in California, the sheets smelled like citrus detergent instead of smoke. Breakfast promptly arrived at

8:00 AM under a silver dome on a rolling cart, and instead of hot sand between my toes, my feet were clad in hotel-provided slippers. We'd fallen in love on the island, and part of my heart was still there.

"Get it together, girl," I mumbled, reaching for the folded note on Knox's cold pillow.

Tori Montana,
   I'm running errands. You should worry. Kidding. Don't worry. I'll be back soon. Don't call me.
   -That Man Over There

I crumpled the note in my fist. The man was out running errands when he should have been peacefully recovering after three days of being poked and prodded like an animal.

I snatched my phone off the nightstand, impatiently ripping the charger from the base, and called him. My jaw tightened, and my fingers curled into the bedding when the call went straight to voicemail.

"This is Knox. I can't talk right now. If this is an emergency, call my assistant, Victoria. If you're Victoria, I told you not to call."

Heat rushed to my face.

"Unbelievable," I muttered, stabbing the screen to hang up. Somehow, I refrained from throwing my phone against the wall in frustration long enough to guide myself through a round of breathing exercises.

A sharp knock from room service interrupted me.

I climbed out of bed, tugged on a robe, and padded across the marble floor to open the door. My brows lifted in surprise when two hotel staffers greeted me and wheeled in two carts laden with silver domes.

"Good morning. This is... a little more than usual," I mentioned as they uncovered the domes revealing platters of eggs, smoked salmon, waffles, pastries, bagels, bacon, and fresh fruit. It was enough to feed at least six people, and I didn't miss the bottle of champagne chilling in an ice bucket.

"Compliments of Mr. Ramsey," one of them said with a polite bow, handing me an envelope.

"Thank you," I replied, tearing open the envelope and pulling out the note and a Black AMEX card.

No limit.
 -Gio

I shook my head, and a reluctant smile tugged at my lips.

"Yeah...you're Gio now."

I'd barely settled at the table and fixed a moderate plate when another knock echoed through the suite.

"Now what?" I muttered, setting the fork down and walking towards the door with my slippers slapping against the marble. I threw the door open and nearly fainted.

"Surprise!" Brittney squealed, wrapping me in her warm embrace. Alyssa followed, laughing through her tears and trying to wedge herself between me and Brittney.

My vision blurred as they squeezed the life out of me.

"Oh, my God. W-what are—how?" I asked, barely able to string a sentence together.

They both started talking at once.

"Knox flew us out on a private jet—"

"And he even slipped us some spending money, girl!"

I laughed, half crying and clutching them both as we

stumbled deeper into the suite.

"I-I can't believe you guys are here."

"We're here, and we're never letting you out of our sight again!" Alyssa proclaimed.

"For real. We're gonna have to get your ass microchipped," Brittney declared, finally releasing me. Alyssa gravitated towards the balcony and stood with her hands on her hips.

"Jesus… look at this view. I can't even imagine how much a room like this goes for."

"I don't even think about it," I replied, tugging her to the table.

Brittney let out a low whistle, mesmerized by the ocean. "Seriously, this feels like a movie."

"Let's eat before the food gets cold," I said, herding her to the table with Alyssa. We piled our plates—mine with fruit and salmon only because I didn't want to chance an upset stomach and be confined to the bathroom for the rest of the day. Alyssa popped the champagne with a grin, sending the cork ricocheting in the distance before expertly filling each flute. I took mine, and Brittney stood and cleared her throat theatrically.

"I need to get some things off my chest."

Alyssa sighed and downed her glass before refilling it.

"She's gonna get all sentimental and have all our asses crying," she complained.

"Girl, hush. Anyway… I have a few things to say, Victoria. First, you always looked fine as hell, but right now? You look like a Bond girl who survived a jungle apocalypse, and I'm obsessed with the hair—it suits you." She cleared her throat. "When we saw the news about your plane disappearing… I swear, I didn't breathe for three entire months. We didn't know where you were or what was happening to you, and as the months passed, I struggled with letting you go. I was edging closer and closer to acceptance that you weren't coming back, and it'll take a long time to recover from the guilt I feel. But here you are—always proving me wrong. You survived the improbable and clawed your way back." Alyssa sniffed, and Brittney powered through. "I hope you never forget that we're your people and we'll always ride for you, and those you love."

"Including Knox," Alyssa chimed in.

I could tell from the pinched expression on Brittney's face that she wasn't 100% sold on Knox. That woman could hold a grudge like a motherfucker.

"Including Knox," she said hesitantly. "Here's to survival, sisterhood, and to never letting go."

We raised our glasses, clinking them together in unison.

"It's my turn," Alyssa announced, rising from the table. "Victoria, you've always been the strong one—the fixer, the problem-solver, and the go-getter. And as much as these qualities are strengths, I also know they're burdens. You're back, but you need to take time to heal and figure out who this version of Victoria is. And yeah, we joke about microchipping you, but it's because losing you, even for a second, was like losing gravity. How can we orbit without the sun?"

Her voice cracked slightly, and I was dabbing at my eyes with a napkin that once held my silverware.

"Today, we celebrate you. Not because you're a survivor, but because you're a hero. We love you."

Another round of sobs ripped from us, and soon we were enveloped in a group hug that I never wanted to break. For a moment, we just existed as three women tangled in love and friendship, and an unshakeable bond. But eventually, I pulled away, wiping my face with the sleeve of my overpriced robe and clearing my throat.

"I should say something," I murmured, voice hoarse but firm. "You flew across the country for me. The least I can do is try to put my gratitude into words."

"Your speech won't come near mine, but you can try," Alyssa teased gently as she refilled flutes.

I shrugged.

"Maybe not. You are the best bullshitter out of the group."

Brittney snorted, and Alyssa rolled her eyes.

"Hey! I spoke from the heart!" she insisted.

"I know. I know. Here goes. I didn't plan to make a speech because I didn't plan on a surprise visit from my best friends. You showed up when I didn't even know how to ask. And I need you to know that I didn't survive that island because I'm strong or brave or whatever headline the tabloids will say about me. I survived because I kept thinking about the people who were worth coming back to." I paused and swallowed the lump in my throat. "I will never be able to repay you two for what you've done for me in my absence. You fought and advocated, not only for me, but for my mother. I prayed for y'all. I prayed for healing, peace, and that you clung to the memories we shared of last-minute cram sessions, late-night pizza runs, and avoidable hangovers. There were times on the island that I was scared, but it wasn't because I was fearful of dying; I was fearful of being alone. I can't go through life without my people. Thank you for reminding me that I'm loved and not alone."

My voice steadied as I raised my glass.

"So, here's to friendship that transcends blood, and love

that's never conditional." I clinked my glass against theirs. "To us."

* * *

The door clicked open just past midnight. I was curled up on the couch, surrounded by shopping bags and the faint scent of overpriced perfume. He limped towards me, his cane thudding against the floor. He paused, and his eyes scanned the sea of luxury shopping bags.

"So, this is what happens when I leave you unsupervised with my AMEX."

"You said—"

"I know what I said, woman," he interrupted, grabbing my wrist and lifting it towards his face for a closer look.

"Do you like it? Me and the girls got matching watches. Alyssa picked the brand, Brittney picked the color, and I signed the receipt."

"Rolex. Classy. Did you have fun?" he asked, voice low, warm, and inviting.

I nodded, suddenly shy. "I did. We laughed. We cried. And spent your money like it was Monopoly money. It was everything. Thank you for flying my friends out. It means the world to me."

He didn't say anything right away. Just reached into his jacket pocket and pulled out a small velvet box.

My breath caught.

"I was going to wait until it was the right time," he said, kneeling in front of me for the second time. "But then I walked in and saw you relaxed and glowing and knew I didn't want to waste the moment." He cracked open the box, and I gasped.

"This was the errand I was running all day. I scoured most of the jewelry stores in Los Angeles, looking for the perfect ring."

I couldn't take my eyes off the massive oval diamond that was nestled on a band of brilliant diamonds. It was bold, and if I was honest, terrifyingly beautiful.

"Victoria Diamond Caldwell, marry me. Not because we survived the worst, but because I want to build the best with you. And because I have functioning knees."

"Why are you like this?" I whispered through fresh tears.

"Because, despite what you tell yourself, you wouldn't want me any other way. Will you do me the honor of officially becoming Mrs. That Man Over There?"

23

Back to the Grind

Victoria

I loudly huffed for the umpteenth time, trying to grab Knox's attention, but he was lost in his own world. While in California, he'd gotten his hands on a new cell phone, tablet, and laptop and had been making business calls after business calls and answering emails left and right. He'd reverted to Knox Ramsey—the workaholic—as soon as electrical currents penetrated his brainwaves via his ears and fingertips.

I repeatedly tapped my foot against his knee, attempting to distract him from his call.

"Mhm...yes, that sounds doable. Mhm." He grabbed my stockinged foot and massaged it, shooting me an apologetic smile. "Okay, yes. Randy, something came up, and I have to go. Very well. My calendar is open—send me an invite."

He disconnected the call. "You're scowling. Why are you scowling?"

"I'm not scowling. I'm pouting," I corrected.

"Self-awareness is a beautiful thing, darling."

"You're working," I accused.

"Don't be unreasonable, Victoria. I'm trying to get our lives back on track."

I pulled my foot out of his lap and stared at the unique cane he had acquired from an antique shop in California. It was hand-carved with intricate designs and was fitted with a brass snake handle. Knox appreciated the irony and said it was only fitting that he got it.

"And I can appreciate that, Knox, but right now, I need you."

He swiveled his head to the bedroom at the back of the jet, and I rolled my eyes.

That's my bad. I should've been more specific.

"No strenuous activities," I reminded him.

"There's nothing strenuous about using my tongue."

"As wonderful as that sounds, I need you in a different way."

"How can I be of service?" he asked. I could tell he was trying to keep the concern out of his voice, but he couldn't hide it on his face.

"I'm scared shitless right now, and I don't know how you're not. I never thought I'd be on a plane again."

"You're nervous about flying, of course. I'm nervous, too."

"You don't seem like it. You're business as usual."

"Honestly, I was using business as a distraction. I don't want to be on this metal bird as much as you. The only thing that's keeping me from shitting a brick is knowing you're near. Actually, you're too far away. Come sit with me."

I smiled wryly. "You're clingy."

"Says the woman who climbed into the hospital bed with me and wouldn't leave my side."

"Don't flatter yourself. The bed was comfy," I replied, sitting beside him.

"Oh," he chuckled. "That's what it was. How silly of me."

"Mhm," I answered, leaning my head on his shoulder.

"If I haven't said it enough today, I'll say it again. I love your hair."

"Thank you," I whispered, running my fingers through the short curls. "It'll take some getting used to, but I'm enjoying the low maintenance." I smoothed the back of my hand across his cheek. "I'm glad you got rid of that beard."

"Really? I kind of miss it," he said, scrubbing his jawline. "I was thinking about growing it out again."

"Don't."

"Why not?"

"Because then I couldn't do this."

I kissed along his smooth jawline until his lips met mine. He deepened the kiss briefly, blessing me with a few flicks of his tongue before pulling away.

"A beard was a terrible idea. What was I thinking?"

"You weren't. How are things on the business front?"

He tutted under his breath. "I go on a three-month vacation and Blakenship slid in and ran the company as if I never left."

"Vacation?" I said, giggling at his optimism.

"It was paradise. I'm already considering going back. I miss my caftan already."

"*My* caftan," I reminded him.

"In my absence, the company's stock dipped slightly but is expected to bounce back. Global Solutions pulled out."

"Screw them. They were predatory at best."

"Amen to that," Knox agreed. "A few staff members had resigned. According to their exit surveys, they felt a little squirrelly about the management change, but who could blame them?"

I rubbed his chest, trying to soothe him. I didn't want him to work himself back up. "Why don't you retire?"

"Retire?" he asked incredulously. "It's too soon."

"It isn't."

"I have at least another decade in me."

"You don't need to work another decade."

He closed his eyes and massaged his lids with his thumb and forefinger before sighing. "Here is how it will go if I retire soon. Are you listening?"

"I am."

"I will annoy the absolute fuck out of you because I'll want to spend every waking moment with you and monopolize your time. I'll find new hobbies like ghost-hunting or something similar and try to rope you into joining me."

Ghost-hunting? Who does this man think I am? A Ghostbuster? Fuck that shit. My black ass doesn't mess with ghosts.

"Cue the part where you tell me you're not a Ghostbuster."

He gets stranded on an island with me for a few months and thinks he knows me.

"I—see—you're doing too much. The thought never even crossed my mind."

"Right," he remarked, failing to hide the smirk in his tone. "Whatever the case, retiring now is not an option, but you're free to enjoy your early retirement."

"I'm not retiring. I have to be there to keep you in line."

"I don't need a babysitter, Tori."

"I beg to differ. Plus, you're not replacing me with some slutty assistant."

"Why would I do that when I have one at home already?" he drawled, tapping away on his phone again.

"Call me Bernadine."

193

"Bernadine? Who's that?" he asked curiously.

"You haven't seen *Waiting to Exhale*?"

"No, I can't say that I have."

"You're so uncultured," I mumbled, wondering if I had the DVD lying around somewhere. "But can we be serious?"

"Being serious."

"I don't want you to turn into a workaholic again, where we're working into the night. We deserve a healthy work-life balance—arrive at 7:00, leave at 4:00."

He grabbed my hand and kissed my engagement ring. It was stunning, and I grew breathless every time the sun caught the magnificent oval diamond.

"I'm all for a healthy work-life balance; however, I can't make you any promises, at least not for the first couple of months while I try to get everything up and running again. I'm afraid the long nights are unavoidable."

"Is there any room for compromise?"

"We can leave early after lunch on Fridays."

I nodded as I considered his proposal. "Okay. I can get down with that," I agreed, smiling softly.

See? We can work together without cussing each other out.

"When are you returning to work?"

My slight smile quickly turned upside down when Knox checked his watch.

"Well…let's see. Our plane lands in two hours. We should finish the day at the office. How does that sound?"

"It sounds like you'll be upgraded from the stapler to a keyboard."

"I think it's a fantastic idea for us to return to the office today," Knox replied without skipping a beat. "I'm sure there is an HR module regarding workplace violence you need to

194

catch up on."

"And you're gonna be the star of the show."

"Victoria Lereaux," he muttered under his breath.

"I'm not going to the office. I need to see my mother. Which facility did you say she was transferred to again?"

"Only the best facility in Staten Island," he boasted before taking what I assumed was another work call.

Annoyed, I twisted my engagement ring around my finger as I stared out of the jet window. I wasn't an idiot. I knew Knox had a business to run, but was it selfish for me to want the man to myself for a few more weeks? I wasn't even sure I wanted my position back, but the thought of Knox finding another assistant was bothersome.

At work, we ran like a well-oiled toxic machine, and we fit together like that stubborn puzzle piece you had to bang into the puzzle with your fist to make it fit. It wasn't easy to imagine someone filling into my role and establishing the same rhythm we had. No onboarding packet or training manual could teach that because Knox and I ran on chemistry, trust, and respect that couldn't be replicated.

Knox didn't need someone efficient. He needed someone who could survive him.

And I had.

24

New York State of Mind

Knox

"I still can't believe you live on Staten Island," Victoria mused from beside me as the driver maneuvered the SUV off the bridge connecting the island to the New York boroughs.

"Why pay $30 million for a house in the city when I can commute a little further and get a better estate with acreage and privacy for a third of that?"

"Hey, you won't find me arguing. I'm just saying, you give off bachelor loft overlooking the New York skyline."

"And you give off—"

I paused to gauge her reaction.

Narrowed eyes, popped neck, screwed lips. She hit "The Trifecta" and isn't in the mood for my shenanigans. A wise man would tread carefully, but I've never been accused of being wise. I can't fuck for another week, so I might as well get my rocks off another way.

"—you live above Chinese restaurants so you can have easy access."

"It was a pizzeria, you dodo bird."

"That was my second guess," I replied with an easy grin.

"My college apartment was above Vince's Pizzeria. That Freshman Fifteen came out of nowhere," she explained. "It eventually turned into the Freshman Forty."

"It looked good on you," I complimented. "It certainly caught my attention."

My wife squinted at me suspiciously. "You're not one of those feeders, are you?"

"Feeders? What the hell is that?"

"You know those men who have fat fetishes and get with big women and feed them to their heart's content."

"First of all, you were never fat—you were thick, there's a difference. Secondly, I do enjoy feeding you, but not in *that* way. My mother often showed affection through her food—it's an Italian thing."

"That reminds me. I need to text your mother and remind her of her obligatory pasta drop," she mumbled as she rifled through her purse for her cell phone. "What should I request?"

"Her manicotti."

"Bet," she replied, tapping away at the screen.

"I'm returning to the office tomorrow to show my face and—"

"I don't approve of you scaring your employees with your face, but I can't stop you," she mumbled.

I chuckled softly while Doug squirmed in his seat from our unconventional dynamic.

"I scare them with my face? Do you know how many HR complaints I've had to squash because you are "unapproachable"?"

Victoria's brow raised to her hairline.

"How many?"

"Eight. Six from the same person."

"Uh-uh. Who was that?" she pressed.

I shrugged.

"The six complaints were submitted anonymously."

"Then how do you know it's the same person?"

"Because they misspelled your name every time."

"Imagine calling me unapproachable, but you're illiterate. Fire them."

"Are you asking me to abuse my power to satisfy your personal vendetta?"

"What's the point of being romantically involved with a CEO if he won't throw his weight around for you? I bet everything I have that whoever the anonymous reporter was was gunning for my job. They ripped that page straight out of the Hater Handbook."

"They did, my dear, but you emerged victorious. Not to change the subject, but when will you be returning to your apartment to collect your belongings?"

"I can handle that tomorrow while you're at the office. I'll get Brittney and Alyssa to help. I'll probably give them most of my belongings and donate the rest."

Relief washed over me when the SUV arrived at the gate surrounding my property.

Correction...our property.

The small creature comforts I once took for granted came flooding back as my home came into view. I missed the waterfall on the island, but nothing could beat the amazing feeling of four shower heads blasting nearly boiling water on you. I missed cuddling in our makeshift bed, but the thought of lying in my own bed again was enough to make me cry.

I was violently shaken from my commiseration by my wife.

"Oh, my God, Gio. Your house is amazing!" she gasped as the vehicle traveled the winding driveway.

"I told you this many times and invited you to see it."

I chuckled when she smacked her lips. "You weren't fooling me. You weren't inviting me to your house for some innocent home tour. You wanted to get me alone, ply me with expensive wine from your wine cellar—you have a wine cellar, right?"

"I do," I confirmed, still maintaining the smile on my face.

"You wanted to take advantage of me, Mr. Ramsey."

"Still do," I answered honestly. I leaned in and whispered in her ear. "You should be thanking God right now that I'm on light duty. Count your fucking days, Mrs. Ramsey."

I pulled away, leaving her stupefied.

"Keys," I demanded, holding my hand out to Doug. He patted his pockets until he found my spare keys in his jacket.

"I had a maid service perform a deep clean of your home, and the refrigerator and pantry are fully stocked," Doug mentioned, dropping the keys into my eager hand.

"Thank you, Doug. Expect a bonus for your exceptional work."

"Thank you, Knox. Enjoy your first night home."

I glanced at Victoria, and I relished the lust in her eyes.

"Don't worry, Doug. I will."

* * *

"This…is…gorgeous," Victoria whispered once we entered my lovely abode. Her heels clicked against the hardwood floors as she stared at the ceiling as if it were the Sistine Chapel.

I closed my eyes and settled against the door, breathing in the scent of fresh linen, citrus, lavender, and eucalyptus.

199

It was both familiar and unsettling—a vast difference to the smell of rain-soaked earth, salt air, coconuts, tropical flowers, and seaweed.

"You have an elevator?" Victoria screeched, bringing me back to reality. I smirked and pushed myself off the door. My cane thudded against the floor with each step as I searched for the missus, eventually finding her in the formal dining room, deep in thought.

"You seem troubled," I said, observing the tension in her posture.

"Not troubled… just… thinking."

"About?" I pressed, moving closer.

"Thanksgiving. My mom always made a big deal out of it. Even though she memorized most of the recipes, she'd crack open this old recipe book that was passed down to her and cook in the kitchen like she was a mad scientist. Every year, she'd try a different dessert recipe."

"What was the last one she attempted?"

"A fucking Baked Alaska."

I snorted at the randomness.

"It was a hot mess express. She had ice cream melting everywhere, but she enjoyed herself just as much as I enjoyed eating it."

"Do you have the recipe book?"

"I do. It's tucked away in my safe at my apartment."

"Maybe you should recreate it this Thanksgiving," I suggested.

A small smile tugged at the corner of her lips.

"I think I might."

"I look forward to it. I have a surprise for you in the guest house."

She narrowed her eyes suspiciously.

"What kind of surprise?"

"The kind you'll love," I replied, grabbing her hand and leading her to the backyard, past the outdoor kitchen and pool, to the guest house that was a mini replica of the main house. My stomach twisted in knots as we traveled down the stone pathway. I was worried about how Victoria would react. She was a wildcard sometimes, and the last thing I wanted to do was overstep again.

My hand landed on the doorknob, and I twisted it and pushed it open without another thought.

She froze.

Everything was in place. The living room had been stripped and rebuilt into a soft, sterile haven with wide walkways, low lighting, and a nurse station tucked discreetly into the corner. One bedroom had been converted into a caregiver suite, and the other into a fully equipped medical wing.

Victoria's mother lay in a hospital-grade bed, propped up with pillows. Gospel music played low from a speaker near the window next to the monitors that blinked quietly beside her. A cream buttery leather recliner for guests sat beside the bed.

"I had her transferred here this morning," I said quietly. "I wanted her close and safe."

Victoria's voice cracked.

"This... this is what you meant when you said she was transferred to the best facility on Staten Island." She turned to me and gazed at me with wide, shimmering eyes. "You did all this?"

I nodded.

"She deserves dignity, and you deserve peace."

Victoria slowly approached her, and her mother stirred when Victoria's fingers curled around her hand. Mrs. Caldwell smiled softly. Perhaps it was faint recognition, or just a motherly instinct that illness could never take away. Whatever it was, I was grateful.

"Hey, Mom. I'm back," she whispered, kissing the back of her mother's hand. Mrs. Caldwell opened her mouth to speak, but the words never came. The moment was touching—too touching, forcing me to excuse myself.

"Tori, I need to take a call."

She glanced back at me, tears trailing down her cheeks.

"I don't know what to say."

"You don't have to say anything. Just know that this is permanent. She's home now," I said before leaving the guest house.

I cleared my throat several times and dialed the number I knew by heart.

"Hello?"

"Ma... it's me... Giovanni."

* * *

I limped into the en suite bathroom with my cane and sighed at the beautiful sight before me—my wife soaking peacefully in a bubble bath.

I dragged the bench from what would be her vanity and positioned it in front of the claw-foot bathtub. I sat and watched her in silence, eyes roving over her exposed shoulders, slick from the bath oil I'd poured into the tub when I ran her bathwater. The top of her cleavage rose and fell rhythmically above the thick layer of bubbles, and I had the urge to reach beneath the suds and pinch her nipples.

Sensing my presence, Victoria briefly cracked an eye open before closing it.

"You know, usually I charge for this kind of thing."

I smiled and settled my chin on top of my cane. "And what kind of thing is that?"

"Letting old men watch me in a state of undress."

"You have a good eye for business," I remarked.

"Mhm," she hummed, shifting her legs beneath the water. My eyes were drawn to them like a cat chasing a laser pointer. "Did you need something, Gio?"

"I'm famished and thought that maybe you'd enjoy one of my famous handmade pizzas and a glass or two of wine before we settled for the evening."

"You make pizzas?" she asked skeptically, raising a brow.

"The pizza oven in the kitchen isn't for show."

"You can't make pizza better than Vince," she challenged playfully.

I scoffed and abandoned the bench. "You say that now, but I'll have you begging me to make pizzas every day. You'll gain that Freshman Forty in no time."

"Oh, you're funny."

"Thank you for recognizing one of my many talents," I said, retrieving her towel and quickly wrapping it around her body. I didn't need the temptation. "Just in case you've forgotten, your closet is there," I said, pointing toward the his and hers closet. "Your bed clothing is in the second drawer of the island. They might be a little ill-fitting, but I'm sure you'll find something that will work. Please stop by the cellar and select a bottle of wine before joining me in the kitchen."

She smiled genuinely as her feet hit the bathmat.

"You know you should see a therapist about buying all this shit for me when I wasn't even checking for you," she said, referring to my obsession with her. I snorted.

"I'm not crazy, my dear. I'm psychic."

25

Waiting to Exhale

Victoria

My feet padded down the spiral staircase that led to the wine cellar. I was immediately hit with various scents, notably berry, citrus, alcohol, and wood. Knox's wine cellar, along with the rest of the mansion, was insane. Hundreds of bottles tucked into wooden slots spanned the basement.

He boasted that all the wine was imported straight from Italy and proceeded to tell me about the best regions for wine, the types of grapes grown, and the ideal time to harvest. His spiel was a little long-winded for my taste, but I nodded, smiled, and responded positively as a supportive wife would.

Oh, word?

That's wild.

It gets him every time.

I randomly selected a bottle of Pinot Grigio and climbed the steps to the main level. Upon arriving, I paused to soak it all in again. Knox's home was perfect. It was a Tudor revival on nearly 1.5 acres that blended impeccably with old-world charm and modern amenities. It was more than spacious, with nine bedrooms, seven baths, an informal and formal living room, a dining room, an entertainment room, and a movie theater. The chef's kitchen was nothing I'd ever seen before. It showcased two top-of-the-line ovens, a six-burner gas range, a wine refrigerator, a commercial-sized stainless-steel refrigerator, an incredible 14-foot preparation island, and a dine-in nook overlooking a well-maintained garden. Our primary en suite bedroom had not one but two of the home's eight fireplaces, generous double walk-in closets, dual vanities, a glass-enclosed rainfall shower, and a decadent soaking tub that I wanted to live in.

The grounds were beautifully landscaped, which included a shimmering 48-foot pool with a beach entrance, a hot tub, and a full cabana bath. There was also an extensively covered outdoor kitchen, a gas fire pit, a private meditation garden, and a full basketball court.

Knox needs to hurry up and heal so I can break his ankles. He'll go from a cane to a walker real quick!

Lastly, the two-bedroom guest house for my mother was perfection.

Having my mom just steps away made everything feel lighter. I didn't have to worry if she was okay or if the staff at the facility was paying attention. She was receiving the best care from nurses who actually knew her name and what she needed. I could check on her anytime, sit with her, talk to her—even if she didn't remember who I was.

Knox didn't just move her here. He made sure she was safe, comfortable, and treated with dignity. That kind of effort said everything.

You can't convince me this man doesn't love me.

Knox glanced up briefly from the dough he kneaded at the kitchen island.

"I wasn't aware that my dress shirts were on your side of the closet," he commented before returning his attention to the pizza dough.

This man has a lot of nerve. I'm not going to let it slide.

"Oh, my God. I love wearing your dress shirt so much. It's so big and comfortable. I can let my lady bits breathe!" I exclaimed, reminding him of how he described the feeling of wearing my caftan. He smirked, rolling the dough into a ball before depositing it into a glass bowl. He placed a moist towel over the bowl before accepting the wine from me and sliding it into the cooler.

"I never knew you were such a spiteful woman."

"Spiteful, or am I just giving you a taste of your own medicine?"

He ignored my statement and reached for the bottle of wine. "Good choice. It'll pair nicely with the Margherita pizza."

"I'm shocked we're not having meat lovers pizza or something," I said, sliding onto a stool.

"As much as I bitch and moan about wanting a steak, I would rather not spend the next two days on the toilet."

"Amen," I mumbled. "Also, don't forget we have to do your wound care tonight."

"*We* don't have to do anything. I can do it myself," he protested.

"I won't fight you, Gio, but I'm leaving you if your leg falls off. My ride-or-die days are over."

He snorted, "Says the woman who paddled miles out to sea on a whim to save my life."

"It wasn't a whim. I told you that God spoke to me."

"Now, if you would only listen to me like you listen to him, then we'd get along beautifully."

I smiled genuinely. "I have two words for you, Gio. Coconut crab."

He barked out a laugh and limped to a drawer where he retrieved a rolling pin. "If you think about it, we might not have been found had I not disobeyed your orders."

I'll let him have that.

"Can I have your opinion on something, Gio?"

The pleased look on his face tickled me. He loved being needed by me, and I loved needing him.

"How can I be of assistance?"

"I want to do something special for my friends for holding it down while I was gone. What should I do?"

Knox snorted and mumbled under his breath.

"Spending over $100,000 on your friends wasn't enough?"

"Oh, wow. I didn't know I was dealing with a brokie," I teased.

"Cut your bullshit, woman."

"I will as soon as you give me an idea. I need to show my appreciation more."

He tilted his head to the side as he contemplated and dusted the rolling pin with flour.

"You should redo your Miami trip and go all out. I'll charter a jet, and the Knox Make-a-Wish Foundation will cover all expenses."

"Are you serious?"

"As serious as a snake bite," he replied with a charming smile.

"And you're not gonna follow me?"

"No."

"And you're not gonna blow up my phone every time I turn

around?"

"No."

"And you're not trying to get rid of me so you can work like a dog when I'm gone?"

"No, of course not," he answered with that stupid chuckle he does when he's lying.

"You are."

"I'm not. I just want you to have a nice week-long vacation in Miami with your gal pals. You can drink, party, and twerk on tabletops in style."

"I'm a spiritually married woman. I don't twerk on tables any longer."

He laughed warmly. "That was a test, and you passed. Get with your friends, pick a date, and I'll make all the arrangements."

I considered his offer.

A bougie week in Miami with my girls sounds fun as hell, but I don't know if I want to be away from Knox that long. Fuck it. I don't know if I can be away from him that long. The thought of him even going to the office without me drives me up the wall. Ya girl might have a little separation anxiety.

"I'll see," I said noncommittally.

"Good. The dough is proved."

"Already?"

"I used fast-rising yeast, and now that you're unofficially officially part of the family, I can let you in on all my pizza-making secrets."

* * *

"That's right, Bernadine! Tell him! Get your shit and get out!"

Knox yelled at the projector screen, pointing at the door. I side-eyed him and found the man sitting on the edge of his seat as Angela Bassett tore her trifling-ass husband's closet down. He glanced at me before returning his attention to the screen. "Can you believe that asshole? How can he do that to her after everything she's done? Fill the wagon up, Bernie!"

I smiled.

"Did you know that this scene was improvised?"

"Really?" he questioned, not taking his eyes off the screen.

"Yes, sir."

"That's fucking impressive. I know she won an Oscar for this scene alone."

"Nope!"

He paused the movie and turned in his seat to face me. "Don't piss me off, Victoria."

I shrugged with my palms up. "She didn't win an Oscar; however, she did win the NAACP Award for Best Lead Actress in a Motion Picture."

"Fucking bullshit," he muttered. I nearly dropped my slice of pizza when he jumped and yelled, "That's right! Burn… his…shit!"

"All right. I think that's enough culture for you tonight. Let's go to bed."

"But we're not finished."

"It's late. We can finish it tomorrow," I said, gathering our plates and glasses. Reluctantly, he followed me out of the theater and left to shower while I loaded the dishwasher. Once I finished, I had finally gotten around to sending a much-needed message to my sisters.

659-8774, 961-2130: I'm back, and we need to talk.

* * *

I breezed into our bedroom and was hit with the warm scent of Knox's body wash wafting from the en suite bathroom. It was a far cry from seawater, sweat, and unavoidable body odor.

"Take it easy on the pillows," he teased, limping out of the bathroom. I ignored him and launched another pillow across the room.

"All these damn pillows are annoying," I replied sleepily.

"I get it. I'm the only pillow you need," he said, helping me turn down the comforter.

And he's right.

"Sure. Did you take care of your wound?"

"I did, and you can stop asking me. Trust me, no one is more invested in keeping my leg than I am."

Oop! Well, shut my mouth!

"You're right, Gio."

"That's it? You're right, Gio?"

"What did you expect?" I asked, chucking the last pillow.

He snorted. "Well, I don't know, something snarky and threatening, I guess."

"I'm a changed wom—ohhhh, shit."

Knox stood there looking proud of himself. "Good, huh?"

"This has to be the *best* damn mattress I've ever slept on," I admitted. I giggled a little when Knox joined me. His pleasured groans were louder than mine.

"Damn...it's been too long."

"It sure as hell beats sleeping on the ground," I murmured. My head had barely hit the pillow, and I was already passing out. A chaste kiss pressed to my lips startled me back to consciousness. I returned Knox's affection before wishing him a good night.

I woke up several minutes later and was confused when *Waiting to Exhale* was playing on the TV.

"You know what?" I mumbled, pulling myself up. "I'm not marrying you."

"Why not?" he gasped.

"You've just proven you're disloyal and can't be trusted. You're one of those people who watches TV shows with your significant other and secretly watches ahead. Those are the most selfish people ever to exist."

"That's different. You've already seen this."

"It's not different," I said, taking the remote from him. I changed it to *YouTube*, selected a white noise station that would play ocean sounds, and tossed the remote into my nightstand drawer.

I settled down when Knox entangled his limbs with mine and was nearly asleep when he asked me, "So, who makes the better pizza? Me or Vince?"

26

Give it to me Straight

Knox

I woke up feeling like I had been sleeping on a cloud, but that euphoric feeling disappeared as soon as I rolled onto my side and realized the angel who should have been sharing the cloud with me was missing.

"Tori?" I called out, thinking she might be in the bathroom. I reached for my cell phone when she didn't answer and tried texting her, only to be interrupted by notification after notification from Instagram. I despised social media; however, Polly Pocket insisted that Victoria and I were "accessible" to the public in a poor attempt to control the narrative. Victoria and I didn't give a damn about the narrative. We were alive with all our faculties and in love. We didn't need to pander to the nosy masses who thought they knew our relationship better than we did. But here we were, posting pictures of homemade pizza and aged wine.

The comments were nonsensical, and I imagined I lost more

brain cells scrolling through the comment section than from the snake venom that nearly ended me. I gave up and swung my legs over the bed, planting my feet firmly on the hardwood floor. I winced when I put my full weight on my injured leg, but eventually made it out of bed.

I relieved myself before completing the remainder of my morning routine and found a suit that I'd picked up in California meticulously laid out for me with a coordinating dress shirt, tie, cuff links, watch, and dress shoes.

I boarded the elevator twenty minutes later with my cane and suit jacket before making my descent to Hell to come face-to-face with the devil.

"Good morning, my lovely wife," I said, greeting the she-devil who appeared to be putting her finishing touches on breakfast.

"Good morning, Gio. How did you sleep after waking up in the middle of the night and finishing the movie on your phone?" she asked sarcastically.

"Like a fucking baby. Not everyone had a happily ever after, which made the movie even more realistic. Have you seen these comments from last night?"

"Nope. After being without Wi-Fi for three months, I've learned that the Internet is nothing but a brain-draining cesspool."

"I agree, but it makes me wonder if some of these people should be locked up at Arkham Asylum."

Victoria snorted as she plated breakfast and said, "Okay. I'll bite. Read me some of the comments."

"Shit. Where do I begin?" I muttered, scrolling through the feed. "Here. This maniac wrote, 'I printed this picture and licked it. I have no regrets.'"

"That's not that bad," Victoria responded. My eyes nearly bulged out of my head.

"Not that bad? Okay. What about this? 'I want Zaddy Knox to knead my pussy like he kneaded that dough.'"

Victoria shrugged and hummed. "Also typical."

"Typical, she says. I'll show you. This future Arkham patient said, 'The toppings on the pizza spell out 'Help.' I cracked the cipher. Victoria is clearly being held against her will.' And if that wasn't enough, another user said, 'I zoomed in and enhanced the reflection on the wine glass. That is not Victoria. It's a clone.'"

Victoria sucked her teeth and set two plates on the table.

"That's what they always say when people lose weight. They did it to Gucci Mane and Fat Joe."

"Gucci who?"

Victoria rolled her eyes, tapped at her screen, and soon rap lyrics about a "very freaky girl" blared from the home's Bluetooth speakers. My head bobbed as my wife rapped and swayed.

"Dance with me, Gio," she suggested, offering a hand.

"I am talented and skilled in many things, but dancing is not my forte," I argued gently.

"Boo," she protested before turning off the song.

"It is for the best. I would've trampled all over these pretty pink toes of yours," I said, gathering her into my arms.

"Shut up."

"Make me," I murmured, caressing her jaw. Her lips graced mine, and my hand slid down to her ass. I cupped her harshly, lifting her onto her toes. She gasped, and I didn't hesitate to taste her tongue. It tasted like honey and reminded me of another sweet flavor I was missing.

215

I picked her up, maneuvering to the kitchen table.

"Gio, p-put me down. You're not supposed to—"

I silenced her with another kiss and sat her on the table. I kissed her fervently like a man starved for affection or like a man lost at sea. I pushed myself between her thighs and laughed when she mewled like her childhood feral cat, Nala.

"You feel that, Tori?"

"Fuck, Gio. Don't do this to me," she moaned pathetically.

"I'm gonna tell you how this is going to go, Mrs. Ramsey. I'll have you for breakfast," I said, sliding a hand underneath her dress shirt. I didn't stop until I reached her slick center. She hissed and jerked on the table when I slid a finger into her. She was so wet that I promptly added another. "And then you're gonna fuck me tonight for dessert," I demanded, slipping my fingers out of her.

"Knox, you can't—"

"*I* can't participate in any strenuous activity, but that doesn't mean that *you* can't."

That made her smile. "You're always looking for loopholes."

"No, that would be my accountant."

"Fine. How do you want it?"

"Oof. Tough call. No, it's not. I want to see that ass."

She giggled, saying, "Then ass you shall see. Now, are you gonna eat this pussy or what?"

"I'll take Eat the Pussy for $200.00."

"Make me squirt, and it's a Daily Double."

* * *

216

My cheeks hurt from all the fake smiling, and I felt I would be in a sling tomorrow from all the waving at my welcoming employees.

I don't know how much longer I'll be able to keep up the charade. I want to be home, annoying my wife, not shaking hands and accepting bone-crushing hugs. I wonder what she's up to.

I had my phone out, ready to text Victoria, when I passed her office. The door was slightly ajar, and the light was off. I pushed the door open and switched on the light. The room was untouched. Her chair was pushed in, and a coffee mug I bought her as a joke that said, "Best Worst Employee" still rested on a coaster in front of her desk phone.

It was quiet. Too quiet, and I wondered how I'd function without her if she never returned as my assistant. Victoria lit a fire under me like no one ever had, forcing me to strive to be better every day. But as I stood in that cold, desolate office, it became perfectly clear that she was the pulse of the office, and without her, I felt hollow.

I approached her desk and swiped the stapler off.

"Say one more word, and I'll staple your lips shut," I mimicked in a falsetto voice while clicking the stapler several times.

A throat cleared behind me.

I glanced over my shoulder to find a severe gentleman in an expensive charcoal suit. He stepped into the office like his name was on the fucking building, not mine. His suit was tailored, and his shoes were so polished I could see myself reflected in them.

His jaw locked, and his lips pressed into a thin line. He was furious. It was controlled, but barely. His eyes flicked from the stapler, then back to me.

"The tabloids claimed you lost your mind on the island. I thought I'd come see for myself before passing judgment, but it seems they might be right."

I set the stapler down and shifted my body to face the mysterious man head-on.

"Well, it's like they say, a broken clock is right twice a day."

The man's jaw tightened, and I quickly scanned to see if he had a weapon holstered to his hip. I was only slightly relieved when I didn't notice one.

"May I help you?" I asked, taking control of the confrontation.

"I wanted to talk to you about my boy."

"Your boy? Who is your boy? You'll have to be more specific than that."

The man's fists clenched at his sides as a flush of red climbed his neck, rising to his face like mercury in a thermometer.

"First Officer Joshua Lancaster."

* * *

"Tell me...everything," Mr. Lancaster demanded in a flat, unrelenting tone.

We'd moved our impromptu meeting to my office with security on standby in case Mr. Lancaster considered avenging his son's death.

I need to speak with my Head of Security because some incompetent son of a bitch allowed Mr. Lancaster free range of my building.

"Everything as in?"

"From the time you boarded the plane until my son's

218

demise." We locked gazes, and I could see it in his eyes—the hint of grief and vulnerability masked by pain and rage. "You're going to tell me everything," he said, voice tight, almost shaking. "From takeoff to the moment my son died."

I had a choice. I could tell the truth, or lie and tell the man his son died a hero swimming back out to sea to rescue the rest of the crew, and had gotten swept away. But I could tell from my brief interaction with Mr. Lancaster that he was a man who could see through bullshit like an X-ray machine.

"Are you sure you want the truth?"

"I didn't come here for comfort," he snapped. "I came for answers."

I nodded slowly before delivering the truth.

"The first leg of the flight went without incident. There were three pilots—Captain Lowell Charleston, your son, First Officer Joshua Lancaster, and a relief pilot, First Officer Brendan Holt. Captain Charleston and First Officer Holt completed the first leg of the journey. First Officer Holt did not return after our overnight layover, leaving Captain Charleston and First Officer Lancaster to complete the last leg of the journey. I felt turbulence. They weren't alarming at first, but I became concerned when the turbulence became more violent. I entered the cockpit to see what the hell was going on. Captain Charleston collapsed. Your boy said he suffered a seizure. Upon investigation, I found that Captain Charleston was deceased. Your son alerted me that there were catastrophic mechanical issues, and it was then that I knew we needed to prepare to land."

I paused to gather myself before continuing.

"I returned to the cabin and assisted Victoria into her life preserver before fastening mine. By that time, we were falling from the sky. The next thing I remember was swimming to shore with Victoria. Your son joined us shortly on land with a life raft and some staples and supplies. But the truth is… your son died because he was inexperienced, stubborn, and hardheaded. I'm not trying to slander his name, but that's the fact. The first several hours on the island were crucial. We were trying to scavenge for supplies, find water, and food. Victoria tried to guide him, but he panicked."

Mr. Lancaster's fists curled at his sides. "He was scared?"

"He was reckless," I said, voice low. "She warned him not to eat the berries that he had found. She told him they were toxic. He didn't listen. I guess he thought he knew better, and… welp."

A thick, suffocating silence stretched between us.

"Joshua was inexperienced, and he wasn't ready. And out there, not being ready gets you killed."

Mr. Lancaster's face twisted—grief, rage, disbelief all fighting for dominance. "You think he was a coward?"

"I think he made a fatal mistake," I said. "And I think you deserve to know that it wasn't anyone else's fault."

He stared at me like he wanted to swing, or scream, or collapse. But he didn't. He slouched in the leather armchair and looked as if he had aged ten years in front of me.

"Do you have anything to drink?"

"As a matter of fact, I do," I said, opening a desk drawer and retrieving a small unopened bottle of scotch Victoria had gifted me. I slid it towards him. He twisted off the cap and took a swig from the glass bottle, gaze dazed and nostalgic.

"The way you say he died-" Mr. Lancaster paused and shook his head. "-it's no surprise to me. Josh was always a coward and never took responsibility for anything a day in his life.

His mother overindulged his every whim. And when he said he wanted to be a pilot, she wanted to be Mom of the Year and throw all her support into him. I said it was a bad idea—a bad fucking idea. Don't get me wrong, Mr. Ramsey—I love my boy so much, but the boy had the attention span of a tumbleweed. He had no business flying a plane. But it was two against one, and I knew I was fighting a losing battle. So, what did I do? I wrote a check to the best aviation school in the country, and miraculously, he graduated with his pilot's license. He'd finally proven me wrong. Your flight was officially his first international flight. I wish I'd known it'd be his last."

I swallowed around the lump in my throat and wished I had one of those nifty pain pills to dull the edge of reality.

"How is your wife holding up?" I asked.

"Horribly. She hasn't been the same since the plane went missing. Sedatives have become her best friend," he replied, locking his watery blue eyes on me. "I lost them both on that day."

"I'm sorry," I croaked, incapable of reining in my emotions.

Mr. Lancaster lifted a brow.

"You're sorry for what?"

"For returning with less than favorable news."

"No need to apologize," he replied, climbing to his feet. "Take that $1 million you offered to settle and donate it to a charity for underprivileged aspiring pilots in Josh's name. Thank you for your time, Mr. Ramsey."

I stood and shook his outstretched hand.

"You're welcome. Please take care."

Security escorted him away just as Blakenship entered my office.

"Welcome back, Knox."

I smiled softly, leaning on my cane with both hands.

"That's five times already, which leads me to believe you're not thrilled about my return."

Blakenship sighed, and his shoulders slumped. His eyes guiltily landed on his loafers.

"I'm thrilled that you are safe—make no mistake about that." His eyes snapped up, along with his posture. "I love this job more than I thought I would, and it has been my pleasure to serve as the acting CEO during your absence."

I leaned harder onto my cane and smiled.

"The company has continued to flourish under your leadership. It was as if I never left," I said, tapping the handle with a finger. I glanced around the room I had spent years of my life in, and realized the accolades and awards, panoramic view, and designer furniture didn't mean shit. It was all bullshit that I could live without.

Is this my out? Can I walk away?

"Right. We have the meeting with the board," Blakenship reminded me.

"Yes, we do. Let's get this over with."

27

They Must Do Time

Victoria

"Those dirty bitches!" Alyssa shrilled as we stood in the aftermath of my apartment.

I stared at my destroyed diploma and tried to convince myself not to crash out.

How fucking jealous do you have to be to tear up someone's college diploma because you never accomplished anything in your life?

"I'm so sorry, Ms. Caldwell," the building manager apologized again. I glanced up from my shredded diploma and found Ms. Larkin nervously wringing her hands as she surveyed the damage. "Your family...they said they needed access to your apartment to get some items that could be used to locate you. They claimed there was a search party, and the dogs would need to pick up your scent. Initially, I was uncertain, but I wouldn't have been able to forgive myself if I impeded efforts to locate you."

I can't even be mad at her. At least she was trying to bring me

223

back home.

I waved her off and trudged towards the kitchen. My throat clogged up, and I was on the verge of tears again when I glimpsed the open cabinets and drawers. They took all my pots, pans, dishes, silverware, and whatever else they could get their greedy hands on. The bitches even took my fucking toaster.

The toaster, for crying out loud!

I cracked open the freezer, praying that the little fifth of vodka was still in there. I snorted and rolled my eyes at the empty icebox.

Now...I thought it was a sin and a shame to steal a toaster, but these hoes seriously took my damn ice molds.

"Ms. Caldwell, the management company is prepared to cover the expenses of replacing your belongings."

I stuck my head in the freezer when I felt a hot flash coming on. "I appreciate that, Ms. Larkin. My lawyer will be in contact with you."

"I'm aware that I am 100% at fault, but must we get legal involved?"

Her voice wavered as she attempted to plead her case, reminding me of a scolded child.

"Ms. Larkin, I don't hold any ill will towards you or the property management company and don't intend to sue you. Do I think you were gullible and naive? Absolutely, but your heart was in the right place. Trust me, you'd rather deal with Doug than Mr. Ramsey."

"Thank you. Thank you, Ms. Caldwell."

"Just cut me a check for $50,000, and we'll be squared."

Did I have $50k worth of shit in my apartment? Hell nah, but I had to add interest for my pain and suffering.

"Yes, ma'am. I have some calls to make."

She left, and Brittney returned from the bedroom where she'd been dutifully taking pictures on her phone.

"Is it bad?" I asked, still unable to bring myself to enter the bedroom. I already knew the devastation that awaited me.

"It is," she replied softly. I nodded.

"I need to step out and call Knox. I'll be back."

I stepped into the hallway, closing the door behind me and dialed. The first tear slipped when he answered.

"Just the woman I wanted to hear from. How are you doing, darling?"

"Th-th-they took everything!"

"Who took everything? What was taken?"

"M-my fucking sisters ransacked my apartment and stole everything valuable."

"Did you call the police?"

"Not yet. I called you first."

"I'm on my way. How did your sisters gain access to your apartment in the first place?"

I briefly explained, and if Knox was pissed before, he was DEFCON 1 now.

"The incompetence is absolutely mind-boggling. This isn't a mistake. I wouldn't be surprised if the property management were in on it."

"Let's not start pointing fingers. Ms. Larkin said the management company would cut me a check. I'm satisfied with that, and there is no reason to cause more drama."

"No promises. ETA 15 minutes."

"If you can't be kind, then be quiet."

"Again. No promises," he said before hanging up.

Welp... I tried.

* * *

The recipe book. They took the fucking recipe book.

I was staring at my empty wall safe when I heard Knox curse boisterously from the living room. I closed my eyes and took a deep breath when he began berating Ms. Larkin. She sobbed when he proclaimed he'd own the building by the evening.

"Damn. That man is really on one," Brittney commented.

"Can you blame him? Victoria, your sisters are thugs, and they need to do 10 to 15 in super max," Alyssa remarked with an aloof shrug.

"Let me go save this woman," I mumbled before poking my head out of the bedroom. "Giovanni, leave that woman alone."

Hearing his middle name called stopped him in his tracks, and Ms. Larkin had the good sense that God gave her to skedaddle out of the apartment when he was distracted. He sucked his teeth in annoyance and pointed me with a glare.

"You had no right to interfere while I was 'giving her the business,' as you would say."

"You didn't have to go in on her so hard. She's remorseful and realizes she made a mistake. What's done is done."

"Hmph," he huffed. "I was prepared for Tori Montana, not Diplomatic Victoria."

I smirked. "It takes less energy to be Diplomatic Victoria. Look at you, sweating and shaking and shit. You should sit down."

He threw his hands out in exasperation and yelled, "Sit down where, Victoria? The fucking couch cushion they generously left behind?" His cane thudded against the hardwood floors as he inspected the rest of my barren apartment. "Oh! Thank *fuck* they left the clothes hangers! Where would you be without clothes hangers?"

I stifled a laugh because my sisters were royally fucked.

"What did they take from the safe?" he shouted.

"My financial documents, Social Security card, some jewelry, and the recipe book."

"Have you checked your credit report?"

Alyssa began snapping her fingers. "He's asking all the right questions. Check your credit report ASAP."

"Do you need me to hold your hand?" Brittney offered genuinely.

"For what?" I asked, logging into my credit monitoring app.

"Your credit score is about to look like your IQ."

"I've never seen anyone with a single-digit credit score before," Alyssa ribbed, earning an eye roll from me.

"Haha. You got jokes."

"Victoria! Join me in the bedroom so we can lie down on the box spring and watch your invisible TV!" Knox shouted.

"All right. I think you've made your point," I commented as my credit report populated.

"Ooooo," Brittney said, staring down at my 289 credit score. Alyssa hummed the lyrics to "Locked Up" by Akon as I surveyed the damage. I found several delinquent credit cards that were opened in my name since my absence, and if I had to guess, they performed balance transfers for the cash.

Knox entered the living room looking like the devil himself.

"You're getting a security guard. Scratch that—a team of guards."

My brows crinkled in confusion.

"I don't need a security team."

"What if those crackheads were here lying in wait for you?"

"Crackheads?" I asked incredulously.

"I lived through the eighties—your sisters are crackheads."

My best friends cackled as I attempted to poorly hold myself back from laughing.

"Every day, you open your mouth and remind me of the significant age gap between us."

"Not only that, but crackheads are strong. My bike was stolen by a crackhead when I was twelve. Foolishly, I thought I'd fight her."

"She whooped your ass, didn't she?" Alyssa asked, amused by his confession. Knox huffed and ran a hand through his hair.

"I thought she was a damn Power Ranger by the time she was done with me."

A laugh ripped out of me, and I slid to the floor with tears streaming down my face as Knox tried to convince me his story "wasn't that funny."

"Oh, my God," I said, chuckling as I wiped away salty tears. "Thank you for the laugh. I needed it."

Knox's frown briefly tugged into a minuscule smile, and he seemed to relax before my eyes.

It would be awful of me to tell him about the identity theft now. The news will rile him up again. I'll tell him after I put it on him.

"You're welcome. I apologize for my earlier outburst. I'm sure that added to your stress, but this shit isn't right. Can you give me some insight on why they hate you so much?"

"They're jealous," Brittney piped up.

"That part," Alyssa added.

I blew a raspberry and pulled myself up from the floor.

"I'll tell you all about it after I finish filing a police report, but only if we pick up pizza from Vince's."

"Let's because I'm still considering rescinding my marriage proposal because you said his pizza was better than mine."

"It is. Did you want me to lie to you?"

"Yes," he replied without hesitation. "At least my feelings would've been spared."

"I'll remember that for next time."

Knox and I completed a final walk-through and took additional pictures per Doug's request after I promised to link up with my friends for brunch the following day. When we arrived at the police station, I was good and cried out—bloodshot eyes, snot dripping from my nose, salty tear streaks on my cheeks, and a hiccup that wouldn't quit no matter how many times I yelled, "I'm not a fish!"

Hope and Faith? I hope you enjoy your freedom while you still can.

28

Crackhead Chronicles

Crackhead Chronicles

Knox

"Okay. Tell me again—one more time."

"You said that the last time," I said with a huff, snatching another slice of pizza from the box.

My ego is bruised beyond repair. My wife won't stop laughing at the fact that I was roundhouse kicked by a crackhead at the tender age of twelve, and Vince's pizza is infinitely better than mine. Of course, I'll never admit that.

I told her it reminded me of frozen supermarket pizza, and she expressed that I was a liar and the truth wasn't in me. As she would say, I stood on business. I reiterated that the pizza was garbage while secretly signing up for the subscriber list to keep up-to-date with the restaurant and to score discount coupons.

What my wife doesn't know won't hurt her.

"This is the last time; I promise I won't ask again."

I sighed in annoyance and discarded the pizza on my plate.

"I came out of my favorite bodega after purchasing baseball cards and found a disheveled woman—"

"You know what? You deserved to get your ass kicked for trying to fight a woman."

"That's it. I'm done," I announced, leaving the couch with my pizza. Her laughter followed me into the kitchen, and the source of that laughter soon made its unwelcome arrival when she joined me at the kitchen sink. My mind swiftly changed when she wrapped her arms around my midsection and leaned into my back. Her body heat penetrated my shirt, reminding me of all those sleepless nights on the island. There was no doubt she'd keep me toasty through the winter. "Oh?" I said when one of her hands slid into my sweats. Her fingers circled my erection, and she stroked me languidly from the base to the tip.

"Aht, aht, aht; get back to those dishes," she ordered, squeezing her grip, nearly making my knees buckle.

I cleared my throat before asking, "Does my domestic labor turn you on?"

"It does, but this has nothing to do with that. This is me thanking you for dropping everything to see about me and an apology for laughing at your crackhead chronicles."

"As far—"

Shit, I can barely think.

"As far as your sisters go, you don't have to thank me for that, but if you think a hand job is enough to earn my forgiveness, then you have another thing coming."

She bit the shell of my ear. I shuddered.

"Wash those dishes faster, Gio. I'll be upstairs waiting for you," she whispered, giving me a final squeeze before sauntering away.

I finished the dishes in two minutes flat and took the elevator to the second floor. I entered our bedroom and found her gloriously naked and bent over the bed with her hands firmly planted on the mattress. Like a moth to a flame, I was drawn to her rounded ass perched in the air. My fingers skimmed the smooth flesh that felt like the finest satin before grabbing a handful of ass and pushing her forward. I spread her cheeks and lost myself in the view. She was already slick and juicy for me, dripping with need.

A soft moan escaped her lips when I penetrated her with my fingers.

"Tori, give me a preview, baby," I urged. She looked over her shoulder, made eye contact, and took my fingers. She rocked back and forth on my digits, slicking and coating them with her arousal. This went on for a few minutes until her arousal leaked from my fingers down my palm and wrist, and her moans became drawn out and more frequent.

With fervor, I abandoned my shirt, shucked off my sweats, and kicked them away before she warned me.

"Let me do the work. The last thing I need is you dying on top of me."

"The best way to go if you ask me," I said as I lined myself up.

"You've always been a selfish pig," she responded as she eased back on my engorged dick.

"You talk too much. Tilt your head back for me."

She did, and I didn't hesitate to slip my pussy-flavored coated fingers into her big ass mouth. She hummed apprecia- tively around my fingers as she fucked me.

"You like how you taste?" I asked through gritted teeth.

The urge to take over and fuck the daylights out of her was overwhelming.

"Mhmmm," she responded, her hum vibrating around my fingers.

"You sound so convincing. I think I need a taste, too." I wrenched my fingers from her mouth and slipped them into mine, sampling the last bit of her before probing her back door. She stuttered to a near stop. "Keep going; don't stop," I pushed, spitting on her hole.

I thumbed her asshole, and with each backstroke, the tip of my thumb sank further and further until I was past the first knuckle.

"Fuck," I muttered when her backstrokes started to sting my thighs, and my orgasm began to creep up.

Fuck it. She can be mad at me later.

I grabbed her shoulders for leverage and slammed into her. She yelped before burying her face in the comforter. I fucked her senselessly, not giving a damn about the consequences, and brought us both to completion a minute later. My chest heaved as my balls drained, and Victoria lost her footing and collapsed against the bed.

I pulled out, slapped her ass, and watched as my cum leaked out of her.

"Gi—"

"Shut up. It's your fault for having life-risking pussy. Let's hit the shower."

* * *

"Can we talk?" Victoria asked in the darkness.

"No."

"I'm being serious, Gio."

"Me too. I'm sleeping."

"I think we should open up the relationship."

I beg your finest pardon?!

I sat up as if ejected from the mattress and turned the side table lamp on.

"I'm sorry, Victoria. These old ears aren't what they used to be. What the hell did you just say?"

"I'm sleeping," she replied with a devious smirk. I picked up my pillow, held it inches from her face, shook it, and returned it behind my head. "What the hell was that?"

"Me briefly pretending to suffocate you. What do you wish to discuss?"

"Okay, psycho. I want to tell you about something else regarding my sisters."

Here we fucking go.

"You know how you told me to check my credit report when we realized my documents were missing?"

"Let me guess, they drove your credit into the ground."

"You'd be correct. I have a 289 credit score. Do you still love me?"

"Yeesh, that changes things. My feelings suddenly aren't as strong for you as they were two minutes ago." She pinched my side until I wriggled away from her.

"Be serious, Gio."

"What the hell do I care about your credit score, and fuck those bitches. I'm convinced your mother spread her legs for the devil, not once, but twice." Victoria snorted, but I was serious. "Tell me why they hate you so much."

"It's not that crazy of a story. Hope and Faith have the same father, and he cut out when they were young. My mother remarried, and I came along when Hope was seven and Faith was five years old. My father was good to them, but always doted on me."

"Favoritism?"

"Unfortunately. He didn't shun them, but…"

"His actions made it clear that there was a difference between his stepchildren and his biological daughter."

"And ever since I can remember, my sisters treated me like shit, and honestly, I couldn't blame them. Any child would feel jealousy and resentment if the father who stuck around started pulling away from them. He even bought me better toys, but my sisters would break them. It got to the point where I became anxious about receiving gifts. I remember this doll my dad bought me for my sixth birthday. I cried and clung to the doll all day because I knew I couldn't keep it. I threw it in the trash can when everyone was asleep. I made sure I tucked it under a pile of garbage so my parents wouldn't notice. I bawled my eyes out the next day when the garbage truck came, and no one could figure out why I was so upset. My child brain told me it was better to willingly give it up than to have it destroyed in my face. If I got rid of it, then my sisters couldn't hurt me. That was a different type of hurt."

"What did your mother say? Surely, she noticed the preferential treatment."

"I recall overhearing an argument late at night, and my dad gave her the 'I pay the bills and keep a roof over your head' speech and told her if she didn't like it, she could kick rocks. She was financially dependent on him and had to choose between raising two daughters on her own on a minimal income or staying."

"Two daughters?"

"He wasn't going to let her take me."

"Where is your father now?"

"Murdered when I was ten," she whispered. "It was so senseless. You know those office lottery pools?"

"I'm aware."

"My dad and a few guys from work participated in it religiously; however, the week they won, only my dad and one other guy pitched in. They didn't win a ton of money. It was only $50,000, and they were supposed to split it 50/50. The guy asked my dad if they could do a 70/30 split instead and started giving him some sob story about bills and whatever the fuck else. Of course, my dad refused. He followed my dad home and stabbed him to death before stealing the ticket."

"Oh, my God, Victoria. I'm so sorry," I said, pulling her into my arms. She cried softly as she continued to tell me about her sisters' mistreatment after the death of her father. The little witches taunted her mercilessly about her deceased father.

"And I just don't understand why I'm still paying for it all these years later. They're grown, and their father is still alive. I can't help that he abandoned them—that's not my fault."

"You're right. They need therapy. It's a good thing they can get that in prison. Those steel doors will shut on them, and their last taste of freedom would've been them watching you win."

She chuckled before wiping her face on my shirt.

"I'm so angry, Gio," she whispered.

"You have every right to be, but perhaps you might consider therapy to help you deal with those emotions."

"Will you go with me?"

"Of course," I said, reaching over to turn the light off. "I have a question, and please feel free to tell me to shut the hell up, but...what happened to the lottery ticket?"

"A neighbor witnessed what happened and called the cops. They found him quickly, and everything on his person was taken into evidence, including the lottery ticket. Would you believe me if I told you that ticket never surfaced again?"

"I guess there was some lucky cop out there with a brand-new boat or RV," I mumbled.

"I guess. We weren't wanting for anything, though. My dad had a hefty life insurance policy on himself and a will. He made my aunt the beneficiary and trustee of his estate. She gave my mother a portion of the money, and the rest was set aside for my college tuition and expenses."

"Ah, another source of contention between you and your sisters."

"Yep, but it'll all be over soon."

I kissed her lips softly in the dark and settled her against my chest.

"You're right, Tori. It will all be over soon. Also, is this a bad time to tell you that I submitted my resignation to the board, and we have dinner with my mother on Saturday?"

29

Crybaby

Victoria

I hesitated before stepping into the guest house like I always did, because each visit reminded me my mother's time was winding down. The box of chamomile tea shook in my hands as I gathered my courage.

I had psyched myself up to enter when I received a phone call from an unknown number from a Washington D.C. area code.

"Hello?"

"Am I speaking with Ms. Victoria Caldwell?"

"Yes. This is she."

"Ms. Caldwell, my name is Agent Carl Domer, and the Federal Bureau of Investigation has received your report regarding alleged wire fraud, identity theft, and conspiracy against Hope and Faith Brown. Do you have a moment to speak?"

"Wow. Sure," I said unsteadily.

"Is it a good time?"

"It is. I'm sorry. I hadn't expected a response this soon. I only filed the reports a few days ago."

"Correct. But due to the nature and severity of the crimes and the preliminary evidence submitted, we found it necessary to intervene as soon as possible."

"I just want to know if they'll do time."

"A wire fraud conviction can result in a prison sentence of up to twenty years and fines of $250,000.00 per count. Most federal cases end in a plea bargain—prepare for them to be given a lighter sentence."

"What preliminary evidence do you have besides my bank statements?"

"We have timestamps, IP addresses, device IDs, Geolocation, routing and account numbers, login history, personal account information changes, surveillance footage of withdrawals, and more."

I was impressed.

"That's a lot of evidence."

"It's enough indisputable evidence to have a warrant signed by a judge. I have a few follow-up questions if you don't mind."

"Sure."

I sat on a cement bench in the garden and provided the agent with as much information as possible. He informed me of his next steps, including officially interviewing the future jailbirds.

"Do you have any questions for me, Ms. Caldwell?"

"I would like to retrieve my personal items—particularly my Social Security card, birth certificate, and a recipe book. How can I go about getting that?"

"Any stolen personal items will be logged, taken into

evidence, and released to you at a later date."

"Perfect. One more question: would I have to testify?"

"The probability of testifying is low because more than likely they will accept a plea deal. However, you can provide a victim impact statement for sentencing."

My shoulders sagged with relief. Doug and Amelia had worked tirelessly to keep my legal battle with my sisters out of the headlines, and I clung to the hope that everything would be resolved quietly so I could finally move on. It was bad enough that the press had branded me a gold-digging thot, and the so-called "carefully crafted" statement Amelia issued only poured gasoline on the fire instead of putting it out.

"We have enough for probable cause. After I interview your sisters on Monday, we'll present the case to the U.S. Attorney. If they sign off, we'll get a warrant and pick them up."

"Thank you for your diligence, Agent Domer."

I signed off and deliberately ignored a text from Knox summoning me to the bedroom. Ever since announcing his retirement and ditching his cane, the man had turned into a full-blown menace. He'd warned me he'd drive me crazy once he stepped back, and he wasn't wrong. Luckily, he still had a few transitional months left before officially handing the reins to Blankenship and sliding onto the advisory board. And because I was a glutton for punishment, I'd agreed to shepherd Knox through the hand-off and train Blankenship's new assistant myself.

Amelia: *I hate to interrupt your time with your mother, but caterers have arrived. Mrs. Ramsey should be here soon.*

Me: *Thanks. Be there soon.*

I entered the warm, dimly lit guest house and was greeted by the soft hum of the air purifier and the occasional creak of the floorboards. Nurse Linda was at the kitchen island, documenting medical notes on her laptop. She paused when she noticed me.

"Good afternoon, Mrs. Ramsey."

"Good afternoon, Nurse Linda. How's she doing today?"

"According to Nurse Brenda, your mother was a little agitated last night, and it took her a minute to get her settled. I think your mother wore herself out last night because she's as cool as a cucumber now."

I smiled softly.

"Good to hear. Has she been eating?"

"Not as much as I'd like. She only drank a quarter of her meal replacement shake this morning and had a few bites of soup."

"That's it?" I asked incredulously, moving to the stove to put on the kettle.

"I'm afraid so," Nurse Linda answered earnestly with the gentleness of a grandmother.

"Has she been speaking?"

"A little, but everything is unintelligible."

"Her blood pressure?"

"Lower than normal today. I messaged Dr. Fitzgerald about lowering her dosage."

I prepared our tea while Nurse Linda gave me her full report; however, I knew she was skirting around the truth. My mother was declining.

I offered her a cup of chamomile tea before entering my mother's bedroom. My breath caught at the sight of her frail body, wrapped in an afghan while a soap opera droned in the background. Her eyes flickered towards me, and briefly, I had the sense that she vaguely recognized me before her eyes dulled again.

I smiled anyway.

"Hey, Mama," I said, sitting in a love seat beside her bed. I carefully balanced the cup and tucked my legs beneath me. "Nurse Linda said you haven't been eating that much today. You need to eat your dinner," I mentioned as I blew into the steaming cup of tea. She didn't respond—just turned her head to gaze out the window. I allowed the silence to stretch. We didn't need conversation. I just needed her safe.

Amelia: *Mrs. Ramsey's ETA - 15 minutes.*

I rolled my eyes and shoved my phone into my pocket.

"I'm sorry to cut this short, Mama, but I have to meet my future mother-in-law," I explained, rising from the chair. I raised a brow when she started humming. I moved closer.

"What are you trying to say?" I asked, grazing her shoulder with as much gentleness as I possessed.

"Knnnnnnn-knnneeeees."

"Knees?" I mumbled, shocked by her choice of words until it clicked.

Knees!

"No, Mama. He's gone!" I exclaimed, laughing while wiping away tears. "Nah. I ain't gotta deal with him or his crazy ass mama no more."

She smiled faintly before returning to a blank canvas. Just like that… she was gone again. But that little spark was enough to give me solace.

"I love you, mama," I said, leaning down to kiss the top of her head. I grabbed her hand and allowed my thumb to trace the veins. "I'll see you soon."

* * *

"I need more pictures of you and Mr. Ramsey," Amelia's high-pitched voice rang through the kitchen as I added the final touches to the dining room table.

"You have enough," I grunted, adjusting the stemware.

"As your publicist, I strongly disagree."

"You know what?"

"What?"

"Why are you here? Today is meant to be a private family gathering."

"Again. I need more pictures."

"So that you can sell them to the highest bidder? How much are you getting on the back end from those tabloids?"

"I need photos showing a stable, happy home, and your mother-in-law's blessing," she replied, ignoring my accusation.

"The headlines must be brutal today."

"You don't know the half of it," Amelia commented. She sighed and sipped from her bedazzled pink tumbler, which I was certain was filled to the brim with Cutwater.

Don't ask me how I know, I just know.

Out of nowhere, a wave of emotion dragged me into the undertow.

"Um... Victoria," Amelia said with an uneasy chuckle.

"Fuck," I mumbled, realizing that I was crying. I snatched up a folded linen dinner napkin and dried my face.

"You know what you need?"

"A blunt?" I blubbered.

"I would not suggest getting high less than five minutes

243

before your mother-in-law's arrival. You need a Crying Room." The next thing I knew, Amelia was shoving me into the pantry and consoling me while I cried. "What's going on, Victoria?"

"I don't know. I'm so overwhelmed. There's too much to do and not enough hours in the day. I feel like I'm barely keeping my head above water. Mom is fading, my sisters are likely going to prison, Knox is retiring, and social media is a drag. I wasn't big on it before the island, and I'm certainly not fucking with it now. Everyone is in our fucking business and wants to know every move we make. I have to smile for the camera and tap dance for these strangers when I only want to feel my toes in the sand again."

"You can always move to Florida."

That made me bawl.

Of all places to suggest! Not Mexico, not Bora Bora—fucking Florida.

"Have you told Mr. Ramsey how you feel?" I shook my head. "Why not?" she pressed.

"He has a lot to deal with already with the transition."

"I think a husband should know if his wife is depressed."

"You think I'm depressed?" I questioned, wiping my nose with the napkin.

"Depressed, anxious, stressed—you name it. We should get you a therapist as soon as possible."

I sighed, and my shoulders nearly sagged to the ground. "Knox and I had discussed going to therapy. Add it to the list."

"I know what can fix most of your problems."

"What?"

"Quit your job."

My body went rigid.

Quit my job? I can't do that.

"No."

"Literally quitting your job will resolve most of your issues. You'll have more time in the day to focus on what matters: self-care, your friends, and your mother."

"I can't leave my job. What about Knox?" Amelia frowned and chewed her bottom lip as if she were looking for a way to put something delicately and still have her job. "You may speak freely."

She heaved a sigh of relief. "He doesn't matter." My eyes widened from the unexpected response. "Don't look at me like that, Victoria. *You* matter. You already saved the man's life, and now you need to save yourself. The two of you have an obvious codependency, which isn't abnormal given your situation. I don't know much about your life before the crash, but if I had to guess, the two of you were codependent on each other back then. Mr. Ramsey doesn't need you to babysit him; he can function without you. You two need to learn how to function independently."

"You may no longer speak freely," I joked through a sniffle. She grinned widely, showing off a dazzling smile that made me feel better. Despite her preppy and fluffy appearance, she kept it real.

"Don't think about tomorrow, Victoria. Let's just get through today."

I nodded.

"Now, take a minute to gather yourself, and join me in the foyer," she demanded before leaving my crybaby ass in the pantry.

My stomach curled into a tight ball of nerves. I'd already had my share of bitchy mother-in-laws and prayed I'd catch a lucky break with Lorena Ramsey.

30

Knoxovanni

Knox

My phone vibrated on my desk right as I tapped the golf ball into the tipped coffee mug.

Polly Pocket: *Your mother is 5 minutes out.*

I sighed and rotated the golf club in my hand, stalling for time.

I was anxious because Lorena Ramsey was a little high-strung. She'd either welcome Victoria with open arms or dismiss her without a second glance. The truth was, my mother would be wary of any woman after Naomi's failed murder-for-hire plot, and she wasn't thrilled when I told her about our engagement. But what my mother had to realize was that Victoria was genuine and would take the direct approach and murder me with her stapler to my face.

"Here goes nothing," I muttered, returning my putter to my golf bag and eventually joining Victoria, who was pacing in the foyer. "Amelia, can you explain to me why you made my wife cry?" I said when I noticed Victoria's red, swollen eyes.

A gasp ripped out of her, and her phone dropped to the floor. "I-I-not me! You!" she stammered.

"Me?" I asked, pointing at myself. "I don't see how. I've been on my best behavior."

"Not *you*," Amelia responded, seeming to recover. "But *you*," she said, flailing her arms about as she tried to get her point across. "Victoria is crying because she's overwhelmed, overworked, and underpaid."

"Severely underpaid," Victoria chimed in.

"Underpaid?" I muttered in disbelief. "That woman's benefits package is through the roof. She's overpaid if you ask me."

"You would overlook overwhelmed and overworked," she mumbled. "Mr. Ramsey, Victoria is in a delicate position right now. Maybe you should speak to her."

"Maybe you should go work on your little TikTok dances, and give me and my wife a moment of privacy."

Amelia smirked at me evilly, and I knew I'd regret poking the PR Beast later.

"I'll be outside, waiting to receive your mother."

Amelia left in a swirl of cotton candy perfume and glitter, closing the front door behind her.

"Just for that, she's going to have you doing TikTok dances," Victoria warned.

"Fuck that. I'll pull the leg card so fast. But let's focus on what matters. My mother isn't that scary of a woman, you know. Back in the day, she could pinch like a motherfucker, but I'm sure her decrepit, gnarled fingers can barely grip nowadays."

"Ramsey."

"It's That Man Over There. That's what you call me when

248

you're cross," I reminded her.

"You do not have to disrespect your mother to make me laugh."

I anxiously scratched the back of my neck, feeling like a scolded child. She was right, of course.

"I apologize, Victoria. I'm a little nervous myself. I haven't seen her in a while, and I want the two of you to get along. Seriously, I'm a mess on the inside."

She nodded.

"I'll be on my best behavior," she promised.

"I know you will. Polly Pocket mentioned that you're overwhelmed, and I'd be lying if I said I hadn't noticed, but I didn't want to suggest that you step down from your duties because not having you by my side is—quite frankly—a terrifying thought. I like having you near because you're the only person in this world whom I can trust. Hell, sometimes, I can't even trust myself. The day goes by faster when you're there."

"Why is that?" she asked curiously.

"Because I can fantasize about fucking you in those pencil skirts. As they say, time flies when you're having fun."

"Where's Detective Benson and Stabler when you need them?" she commented, already tired of my mischief.

"Busy with other predators, I suppose. Look, let's cut to the chase. I know we have this dynamic between us. It's unshakeable, but it's about time we've learned to cut the cord before our bond does more harm than good. It's scary and uncomfortable thinking you'll no longer be a shout or instant message away during the day, but it's only six months until I'm officially out. It sucks, but it's for the best. We're not on the island anymore, Victoria. We don't have to live each day

249

in fear—"

"We don't?" she interrupted. "Because sometimes I feel like I live in Gotham City."

"Can you not interrupt my monologue? I was on a roll."

"My apologies. Continue."

"As I was saying—fuck. What was I saying?" Victoria shrugged.

She's a menace!

"I was trying to be nice to you, but I see you don't appreciate pleasantries," I said, groaning as I pulled myself to my feet.

"My grandmother always said people don't take you seriously unless you're cussing them out."

"Well, I think I will take a page from your grandmother's book. Fuck you, Ms. Caldwell. You're fired effective immediately, and I'll be seeing you in couples therapy. I love you."

The gasp that escaped her was glorious; too bad my gloating was interrupted by the front door opening.

Victoria quickly recovered.

"I swear to God, Gio. Your mom better act right because my days of dealing with difficult-to-please mother-in-laws are over."

I grabbed her shoulders and massaged them. "Everything will be all right, Tori. She'll love you. I promise."

"If you say so."

I heard Amelia animatedly talking, and the sound of my mother's kitten heels against the floor made my stomach tie in knots.

My eyes stung from unexpected tears as I laid eyes on my mother. She looked exactly how I remembered, save for more gray streaks in her dark hair and deeper crow's feet. She was a slight woman who stood 5'3" in stature but still appeared as strong as an ox.

"Oh, Gio. You look as handsome as ever—just like your father," she said with outstretched hands. I grasped them gently in mine and kissed both of her cheeks before enveloping her in a hug.

"You flatter me. It's good to see you again, Ma."

"You, too, Gio. I'm so happy you're home!"

She pulled away and stared up at me with brown eyes, shiny from tears. "My handsome boy."

"Ma, I want you to meet my wife, Victoria."

"Wife? When did you get married?" she asked, sounding appalled.

"On the island."

She waved her hand around like she was swatting at flies—something she always did when I used to tell her something foolish when I was a child.

"If you weren't married by a priest, then it doesn't count," she argued. "You shouldn't make a mockery of marriage."

"There were no priests on the remote island we were stranded on. This is my wife, Victoria," I introduced, smoothing a hand down Victoria's back.

"It's lovely to meet you, Mrs. Ramsey. We're so glad to have you in our home," Victoria greeted graciously. Victoria's broad and dazzling smile made my heart skip a beat, as it always did. My mother? Her lips were screwed tighter than a butthole.

This won't be good.

"Hmph. *Our* home? This is my son's home. Don't get beside yourself."

"On that note, I'll be dining upstairs."

* * *

I trotted behind my wife, who made a beeline for the stairs.

"Okay. Let's hit the redo button," I pleaded, hoping I could convince Victoria to give my mother another chance.

"I warned you, Knoxovanni," Victoria said as she ascended the stairs.

Knoxovanni? She's efficient. I've always admired that about her.

She was gone before I could try to persuade her again. I should've known better and taken her at her word. When she said something, she meant it.

I shook my head and left, finding my mother surveying the spread of food.

"Let's talk, Ma," I said, pulling out a chair and motioning for her to sit.

"Gi—"

"Sit or get out of *our* house," I demanded, leaving no room for argument. My mother took my strongly worded suggestion and promptly sat with her hands in her lap and her legs crossed at the ankle.

"A very wise, loving, and caring person once told me that you should treat everyone with dignity and respect, and that person was my mother. So, you can imagine how your rude behavior toward my wife within three seconds of meeting her might make me a little unsettled."

"I'm—"

"Let me finish, Mother."

She snapped her lips together, and I was prepared to continue my lecture when Amelia came through with her fingers plugged into her ears.

"Don't mind me. Don't mind me. I'm not even here," she proclaimed. "Carry on."

I refrained from chewing my mother out and offered to help, but Amelia refused my assistance and quietly made a plate of food I imagined was for Victoria. She snagged a bottle of wine from the wine fridge before dashing out of the kitchen with a tray laden with food.

"I didn't quite get who she was when she introduced herself. She spoke so fast that I couldn't keep up. Who is she, Gio?" my mother asked, pointing in Amelia's direction.

"The help. Let's continue. You may not acknowledge Victoria as my wife because, as you said, we didn't get married before a priest, but we will be married soon enough once we get our lives back on track. I plan on making Victoria the mother of my children, and somehow, I think I can convince her to allow us to have ferrets."

"Ferrets are disgusting, and they smell. You should give up this obsession you have with those creatures."

"Maybe if I had parents who loved me and bought me the ferret I asked for like clockwork for my birthday and Christmas, then I would be over my obsession."

"You're still overdramatic and long-winded. Please finish making your point."

"Sure. I'll cut to the chase. My point is that I love Victoria, and as her husband, it's my duty to provide, protect, and all that other wholesome shit. You have to decide right now if you want to be a part of my family. If not, then it was nice knowing you."

She gasped and clutched the base of her throat.

Look who's being overdramatic now. On another note, I feel like a parent scolding a child. It's euphoric, and now I realize why my parents constantly fussed at me. I can't wait until I have my own children and can drop the D-word. Let me test it out.

"I'm disappointed in you, Ma."

She nearly crumpled.

Yep. That hit the spot.

"May I speak?" she asked, nearly in tears.

I didn't want to make my mother cry, but I had to let my boundaries be known.

"You may."

"Giovanni, I apologize for behaving in an untoward manner. I have some concerns."

"Let's hear them," I said, finally taking a seat when my leg began to ache.

"What do you know of this woman?"

"Everything I could possibly ever know. Trust me—a lot is revealed when you're stuck on an island with no cell or Wi-Fi reception."

"What if she has ill intentions towards you, like—"

"Like Naomi? I can assure you, she doesn't, or she would've left me for dead on the island. What is your next concern?"

"How do you know you love her and you're not suffering from White Knight Syndrome or something similar?"

"White what?"

"White Knight Syndrome; it's when someone falls in love with their rescuer," she explained.

"I loved her before I was injured. Next, and please make it interesting."

"She's only with you for your money."

I rolled my eyes and reclined in my seat, elevating my leg with another chair.

"You know, I do have other shining qualities besides my wealth."

She snorted. "If you say so."

"Where did you get this idea that Victoria's only with me for my money?"

She opened her purse and pulled out a glossy magazine, showing me the cover. It was a gossip rag with our faces on the front and a headline that read, *Barely legal secretary snags millionaire! Inside sources claim she's bleeding him dry!*

Well, that's a defamation suit if I've ever seen one.

"Gio, is what this magazine is saying true?"

"I don't know, Ma. It looks like they also wrote an article expressing that Tupac and Anna Nicole Smith are alive and well, living their retirement together on a private island. You tell me," I said, drawing my words. I was over the ridiculous conversation and miffed about the article.

Victoria's my executive assistant, not my secretary. And I'm a billionaire, not a millionaire. Doesn't anyone fact-check anything anymore?

She huffed and folded the magazine before returning it to her purse.

"May I offer a suggestion?"

"Go ahead," she said.

"How about you put the magazines down, turn off your television, trust your son, and get to know Victoria for yourself? You might actually enjoy her. I see a lot of you in her."

She perked up with interest. "How so?"

"You should apologize and find out for yourself."

My mother looked ashamed of herself, and I was confident she wouldn't cause any issues moving forward.

"Very well. I'll apologize."

I smiled warmly.

"Good. I'll see if she's up for company."

31

Hussies

Victoria

I ate a few bites of my meal and set it aside when I lost my appetite. I knew there was a 50/50 chance Mrs. Ramsey and I would get off on the wrong foot, but it still sucked. Could I have slapped a smile on my face and ignored the slight hostility? Sure, but I allowed myself to be a punching bag for too long for the sake of peace.

I stared at my phone and tried to convince myself not to call my sisters and give them a piece of my mind. It was tempting, but what would that achieve? What would be the outcome? They'd probably try to gaslight me and claim they did what they did because they thought I was dead, thinking there was no harm.

"Mrs. Ramsey is under the impression you're a gold digger," Amelia relayed, her ear pressed against the crack of the door.

I rolled my eyes. I had expected the cliche gold digger label. I was young and hot, and Knox was a crusty older gentleman with the personality of a mop head.

"Get away from the door, Messy Boots," I chastised.

"Very well," Amelia agreed with a disgruntled sigh. She closed the door before dramatically dropping onto the bed. She retrieved her special drink tumbler from the nightstand and took a long pull from the pink straw. "We need to talk strategy. We have to spin this around."

"No, we don't."

"I beg to differ."

"Listen, Knox's mom will either come around or she won't. Either way, that's her business. I won't be the first woman in the world to be disliked by her mother-in-law. And that's okay. I understand that your job is to make our lives seem glamorous and hunky dory, but it's irrelevant at this point. As of twenty minutes ago, I received my pink slip, and That Man Over There is retiring. Who are we trying to impress? We'll both be bums in six months."

Amelia blew out a frustrated breath through her nose and sipped from her tumbler again.

"I understand where you're coming from, but can I be frank?"

"Please."

"I see everything you don't see—the viciousness, the hate, the scrutiny, the microaggressions, the racism—you name it. I'm consumed by it. And while I haven't been your publicist for long, I feel protective of you and Knox. I don't want to witness anyone mocking or vilifying you if I can help it. You and Knox have been through enough and deserve to be happy and stress-free, not under fire every time you turn around."

I softened in understanding.

"You're not superwoman, Polly Pocket, and you won't be able to shield us from everything. Let them speculate, let them talk, and let them hate because meanwhile, I'm making Knox's pockets hurt and living my best life."

We laughed until knocking interrupted us.

"What's good?"

"My love. Do you have a moment?" Knox asked through the door.

"I might. What's up?"

"My mother would like to apologize. Would you spare her a moment of your time?"

"Sure."

The bedroom swung open, and I almost laughed when Knox gently shoved his mother into the room. Lorena seemed less confident than when she first arrived and tried to put me in my place.

"I guess that's my cue to leave. Good luck, Victoria," she wished before slipping out of the room.

We were alone, avoiding the obvious elephant in the room.

Lorena clutched her leather handbag so tightly, I swore her knuckles cracked.

"I don't hear apologizing," Knox said through the door.

Lorena rolled her eyes and muttered Italian under her breath.

"I was pregnant with twins, you know," she said suddenly.

My eyes widened in disbelief.

"No, I didn't know that."

"Mhm. Knox was originally a twin; however, he absorbed his twin in the womb, and now this is what I'm left with."

I snickered, and soon she joined me.

"Of course Knox is the evil twin."

I'm sorry for her loss, but thank goodness there aren't two of them. I can't imagine. I would've had double the dick, but double

259

the headache.

Lorena sat in an armchair by the window, set her purse on a side table, smoothed her hands down her skirt, and crossed her ankles.

"I apologize for my behavior, Victoria. I was cold, dismissive, and didn't give you a chance. I've lived with a knot in my stomach for years after what Naomi attempted to do to my boy. She had us both fooled—me more than him—and it almost cost him his life."

"I understand, Mrs. Ramsey."

"No," she whispered. "You don't understand. Even when the evidence was presented, I thought the cops had gotten it wrong. Naomi wouldn't do something heinous like that. She loved Knox. It wasn't possible, but there it was in black and white. The future I thought they would have dwindled away into nothing."

Tears crested the woman's eyes, and my heart lurched for her.

"And poor Knox. He was devastated. I thought he would remain a bachelor forever, and I had made peace with that. Sad to say, but I was a little gleeful that he'd given up on love. But then, you came along and changed his mind. I panicked. Especially after reading all the headlines, and I formed an opinion of you before meeting you, and that was wrong." She took a shaky breath. "I'm sorry for disrespecting you, Victoria. Truly. You didn't deserve my suspicion. Knox deserves happiness, and so do you. I hope you'll forgive me."

The tightness in my chest eased. "Lorena," I said softly. "Thank you. That means more than you know. And for what it's worth, I don't want anything from him except to love him and be loved back."

"Thank you, Victoria. I want to spend some time getting to know you if you don't mind."

"I don't mind at all," I replied, returning her smile.

* * *

"My Heavens! Who needs enemies when you have sisters?" Lorena exclaimed after I gave her the cliff notes of my long-standing feud with Hope and Faith.

"You can say that again."

"My sister and I no longer speak," Loreno mentioned..

I raised a brow.

"Word?"

"Word."

"Well, spill the tea," I urged. I held back my sigh when she gave me that blank, owlish look Knox gave me when I said something and was reminded we grew up decades apart. "Tell me what happened," I rephrased.

"Oh! The hussy stole my boyfriend right from under me. His name was Rocco Romano." I folded my lips in to hide my smile and prevent myself from asking if Rocco had beef with Elmo.

Focus, girl. You're supposed to be bonding with your mother-in-law over your ain't shit siblings.

"Tell me more."

"He was the most handsome man in Little Italy. He had the most lustrous dark, wavy hair, these beautiful amber eyes, and a smile that could make your heart skip several beats."

"Not one beat?"

"Several," she reiterated.

"And how did you and Rocco cross paths?"

On Sesame Street? Ha! Let me stop.

"He worked at the local butcher, and his body showed it, too."

"I bet."

"When I visited, he'd always wink and smile at me. He'd tell me he put a little extra for me in my order and suggested I visit closer to closing so we could get to know each other better."

"Please tell me you didn't fall for that."

Lorena tutted under her breath. "Of course not. I was young, not dumb. He wanted to slip me his salami."

"Not slip you his salami," I drawled.

"Pun intended!"

Lorena continued telling her story about her sordid love affair that ended in heartbreak, betrayal, and humiliation when her younger sister set her hooks—pun intended—into her man.

"They married, and a few years later, they were swimming with the fishes."

Wait... did this woman put a hit on her sister?

"Hold on. You said you don't talk to her any longer."

Lorena shrugged casually. "She's deceased; therefore, we don't speak."

"I mean... hell yeah. Continue."

"Rocco thought making an honest living was beneath him and became mob-affiliated."

"Say less. You live by the streets; you die by the streets."

"That's a lovely way of putting it, Victoria," she said, patting the back of my hand. At one point, I had pulled up a chair and we had cracked open a bottle of wine while trading stories.

"So, tell me about you and Mr. Ramsey."

"I met my late husband at a pizzeria. He could make one hell of a pie."

This explains so much....

"I remember walking into the shop after the funerals, and he was doing the tricks with the dough, twirling and tossing it above his head. He took one look at me and forgot to catch the dough. It fell on his head, and I couldn't stop laughing. He was as red as a tomato when he finally got himself out of that mess. He apologized and said that it'd never happened to him before. I said, 'What? Dropping dough on your head?' He said, 'No. A woman's never taken my breath away like that before.'"

I wiped away a stray tear.

Why the fuck am I crying?

Lorena sighed and reclined in her chair.

"Dante was a beautiful man inside and out, and we shared many wonderful years together. He always made me laugh, and he had a penchant for mischief. There wasn't a serious bone in the man's body."

That's peculiar because the way Knox tells it, his dad had his foot on his neck. But, then again, at Knox's big age, he still needs a foot on his neck.

"Dante was a little strict with Knox because that boy always found himself in the most absurd predicaments."

"Like battling it out with a crackhead outside a bodega?"

My mother-in-law threw her head back and laughed. "I didn't want to believe the story when he told me. I thought he was telling a little white lie. A few days later, I walk to

263

the bodega and see the woman on my son's bike. Gio's bike was very distinguishable with the embellishments he put on it. Plus, I'd seen that bike in the middle of the damn driveway so many times that it was imprinted in my mind.

"Did you get the bike back?" I asked excitedly.

"Of course, I got it back. We weren't wealthy, and we couldn't afford to replace his bike at the drop of a dime. Plus, we needed Gio to have a bike because he needed to burn off all that energy. I fought that woman for my child's bike. I was losing badly until I found a steel pipe in that alley. I gave her all I had," she boasted pridefully. "I returned home before Knox came home from school and pulled myself together. I had to put makeup on because that bike thief gave me two black eyes."

I snickered.

"Damn. Not y'all both getting your asses kicked."

She smiled genuinely. "I didn't mind. I'd do whatever I could to protect my son. That's why I took—" She paused and swallowed around a lump in her throat. "I didn't handle the Naomi situation well. I was so excited that this woman who seemed perfect for my son appeared in our lives, but I was so blinded that I failed to protect him and led him to the lion's den."

"You have to let that go, Lorena. The important thing is that you're here now, and you're willing to make me pasta a minimum of twice a week."

She smiled widely before saying, "I think I can manage that, but may I ask you a question?"

"Sure."

"You're not with my son for the money; I can accept that, but why are you with him?"

I chewed my bottom lip and thought of the most poetic way to tell her I loved her son.

"No, I'm not with Knox for the money. I'd still be with him if he only had two seashells to rub together because even on the worst day of my life, when we were stranded thousands of miles from home, Knox made me feel like a millionaire. He made a hut feel like a mansion and a turtle feel like a feast fit for a king. I'll be honest, Lorena, I despised your son before the island, but I fell in love with him because he's the most selfless, caring, and capable man I know. I suspect he was all that before the crash, and the island drew it out of him. I love him more with each day, and let's face it, Giovanni is the only one who can handle Tori Montana."

32

Jailbirds

Victoria

I was putting a dent in Knox's credit card when I received an incoming call.

"Hello?" I answered, not paying attention to the caller ID. I was more concerned with figuring out which store I'd hit up next.

"Ms. Caldwell, this is Special Agent Domer."

I froze. Even through the line, he sounded like someone who was about to deliver bad news. I tightened my grip around the phone and the shopping bags.

"Special Agent Domer. Did you... did you get a chance to speak with my sisters?"

There was a pause before he replied.

"We attempted to; however, things didn't go as planned." My heart sank, fearing the worst. They were cruel to me, and I wanted justice, but that didn't mean I wanted them harmed.

"What happened?" I asked breathlessly.

"When we arrived to conduct the interview, your sister Faith became combative with an officer, and Hope was attempting to destroy evidence. Both were immediately taken into custody."

The words slammed into me like a bus.

"Taken into custody? They're arrested?"

"Yes, ma'am. Given the seriousness of the fraud and identity-theft allegations, and the new charges, including tampering with evidence and assault of an agent, they will be held, likely without bail. We've recovered several items matching the personal belongings you described in your statement, including your identification, electronics, and a recipe book. We're cataloging them now."

I leaned against the storefront window in a daze. I was shocked. You always heard how sluggish the legal system was, and here it was, three weeks post-island, and my sisters were already incarcerated.

"You're welcome to come down to our field office this afternoon to identify and collect the recovered property. It will help us close the evidence chain."

I swallowed hard. I was getting the closure and the justice I wanted, but it was still painful—painful but necessary.

"Text me the address. I'll be there."

"Of course. I'll meet you in the lobby."

"Will I be able to speak with them?"

"That can be arranged."

"Thank you, Agent Domer. I'll see you soon."

I hung up, and my first thought was to call Knox, but I quickly abandoned that thought. I needed to handle this myself.

* * *

By the time I pulled into the concrete parking lot of the federal field office, my palms were slipping and sliding against the steering wheel from the dampness. The building had looked exactly how I expected—nondescript with a flag pole outside with a flag lowered half-mast, snapping in the wind.

I threw up a prayer and asked God to calm my nerves before venturing into the office. My teeth chattered as soon as I entered the office, and the air smelled faintly of citrus disinfectant, coffee, and toner.

"May I help you, ma'am?" the officer at the reception desk asked.

"Yes, I'm Victoria Caldwell," I said, voice coming out steadier than I felt. "Special Agent Domer is expecting me."

"I need to see some identification. Please sign in, here," he said, extending a clipboard with a pen attached by a silver chain.

I fished my ID out of my wallet, slid it over to him, and signed in while he contacted Agent Domer.

"Thank you, Ms. Caldwell," he said, nodding towards the metal detector. "Place your bag on the belt, remove any metal, keys, watch, belt, et cetera, and step through."

I did as I was instructed and walked through the detector. I'm handed back my belongings along with a visitor badge that was clipped to a lanyard.

"Please have a seat," he said, pointing to a set of plastic blue chairs. "Someone will be down to collect you."

My feet tapped on the gleaming tile floor as I waited. I didn't have to wait long until a man in a suit appeared, calling my name.

"Ms. Caldwell?"

I stood and took his outstretched hand.

"Yes, sir."

"I'm Special Agent Fuentes, Special Agent Domer's partner. I have been assisting him with your case. Will you please follow me?"

We rode an elevator to the third floor, and when the doors opened, we were met by another suit with tired eyes.

"Ms. Caldwell. I'm Special Agent Domer. It's nice to meet you. Thank you for coming."

We shook hands.

"Thank you for your diligence."

He gestured for me to follow him down a corridor lined with closed doors and security cameras. "We've logged the items, and they're ready for you to view and sign off on. But before that, we can take you to see your sisters. They're being held for processing."

"Do they know that I'm here?"

"They are aware you're coming," he answered.

We stopped at a door with a small window. Special Agent Domer swiped a badge against the card reader, and the lock clicked open.

The room was exactly how I pictured it—cold, sterile, white walls, a bolted-down table, plastic chairs, and a glass viewing wall. Through the glass, I see Hope and Faith sitting side-by-side, looking annoyed and disheveled.

I sucked my teeth.

They couldn't even bother to pretend to be remorseful.

"Can I go in?"

"You may," Agent Domer confirmed. "You can speak with

269

them for a few minutes. There will be an officer present in the room with you at all times. Once you're finished, I'll bring you to evidence to identify your property."

"Okay."

"Are you ready?"

I nodded.

He opened the door and motioned me inside. I stepped forth, Hope and Faith's eyes lifted. For a second, the years fell away, and I felt as if my childhood was staring back at me. It wasn't all bad. Not every day was a nightmare, but it was enough to leave a permanent stain. But then I saw the handcuffs and was snapped back to reality.

I pulled out the chair opposite them and sat, setting my handbag on the table. We sized each other up—taking in the differences. Before the island, I hadn't seen them for three months. The difference was jarring, especially Faith's chest, which was no longer a modest B-cup. Her new breasts looked to be a voluptuous DD. She always complained about her "small boobs" and had picked on me growing up because I was more developed than she was. Hope's waist was snatched to the gods—she'd finally gotten that lipo she'd always wanted.

These bitches really stole my money and had their bodies done.

"I wish that things could've been different. I wish that you two had made better choices and weren't facing twenty years in federal prison. I wish that Mom could've been surrounded by her daughters one last time before she passed, but that's not going to happen. I didn't come here to scream at you," I said, looking from one to the other. "I came here because I need to understand why. I need to know why you hacked my accounts, stole my identity, and raided my apartment. Do you know what happened to Mom after you stole from me?"

Faith cracked immediately.

"I'm sorry! You weren't supposed to come back!" she cried out, tears spilling out of the corner of her eyes. They zig-zagged down until they dripped onto the metal table.

My throat tightened, but I pushed the words out anyway.

"Are you even aware of the shit you caused when you stole from me?"

They didn't respond. Instead, Faith kept sniffling, and Hope stared at me like she smelled sour milk.

"Mom was evicted from her memory care facility, but you know this. You both were out trying to look like IG models on my dime while Mom was shuffled from the facility to the hospital to some raggedy nursing home I wouldn't put my worst enemy in."

"How's Mom doing?" Faith asked.

My throat tightened, but I pushed forward.

"She's safe, and she is receiving the best care money can buy. She's with me. But…I don't think she'll be around much longer."

"I'm sorry," Faith whispered softly, lowering her head.

I nodded because I genuinely believed her.

"Victoria, what we did was fucked up. I'll admit that, but why are you doing all of this when you're with a fucking billionaire!" Hope seethed, lurching forward in her chair.

"Back up!" the guard barked.

Hope instantly complied, and from her hardened expression, I knew I'd never get through to her.

"When will you get it through your head that it's not about the money? It's about the principle. You stole from me—down to my fucking ice molds, and when you stole from me, you put our mother's well-being in jeopardy. She wasn't Mom of the Year by any means, but she was the only parent we had, and she loved us and did the best she could to raise us on her own. For too long, I let the shit you did to me slide because I held out hope. I thought that one day, we'd get older, become wiser, and a real conversation could be had. But one thing the island taught me was survival. And survival isn't clinging to the people who keep hurting you. It's knowing when to let go. I'm done being your safety net. You made your choices, and now you have to live with them. I won't be posting bail or depositing money into your commissary account. I won't be making any further statements, and I won't write the judge a letter begging for leniency. Take care of yourselves."

* * *

Tears swam in my eyes as I flipped through the pages of my mother's recipe book while sitting in my driveway. A page slipped out, and I nearly burst into tears as I read the lemon bar recipe.

"Sh-she burnt the shit out of these damn lemon bars," I said to myself, choking on a sob that eventually turned into laughter.

I jumped when Knox knocked on the window with his cane handle. I rolled down the window with a tearful scowl on my face.

"Can't a woman cry in peace?"

"Not my woman," he said, affectionately tracing a tear away with his thumb.

God, I love this man.

"How did it go?"

"It… it felt good. It was cathartic in ways that I never imagined."

"Good. I see you have the recipe book back."

"I did. I'm thinking about letting my mom hold onto it for now."

"That's a good idea, love. It might bring back a fond memory—even for a second."

"Will you go with me?" I asked, hoping he'd say yes.

"I go where you go, Tori Montana. Lead the way."

33

Therapy

Knox

Victoria shifted in her spot and tugged down the hem of her dress for the twelfth time—no exaggeration—I counted.

I grabbed her hand and squeezed it gently.

"Someone has ants in her pants," I whispered.

"I'm anxious," she admitted.

"Me too. Therapists aren't my favorite," I shared.

She snorted.

"What you meant to say was that *accountability* isn't your favorite."

"You took the words right out of my mouth."

The door opened, and Dr. Matthews strolled in with a warm smile on her lips, displaying deep laugh lines from decades of smiling and laughing. Her silver-streaked hair was piled high on top of her head, secured in place by a pencil. She gracefully dropped into the leather chair opposite us after retrieving a notepad and pen from her desk.

"Good afternoon, Mr. and Mrs. Ramsey. How are you?"

"Fine," we both muttered.

She nodded and scribbled on the pad. I couldn't imagine what she possibly garnered from "fine" that required writing, but she was the expert, with her many glowing recommendations, degrees, and accolades on the walls.

"I hadn't expected to see you again, Mr. Ramsey," Dr. Matthews stated.

"Neither did I. I had left your office a little excitable."

Victoria snorted.

"I already know what happened. You told him about himself and he acted a donkey. I'd apologize on his behalf, but you should see who raised him."

I rolled my eyes.

"Oh? Do you not get along with your mother-in-law?" Dr. Matthews questioned.

"She's a liar and can't be trusted."

I laughed and folded my arms over my chest before turning my attention to our therapist.

"My lovely wife is upset with my mother for missing dinner this weekend; however, they have a spa day arranged next Wednesday."

"What upsets you about your mother-in-law missing dinner, Victoria?"

Victoria sighed and mimicked my posture, crossing her arms over her chest.

"Knox moved my mother from a memory-care facility to our guest house that he converted into a medical suite. She has full-time around-the-clock care, but I'm still involved with her day-to-day care." She shrugged. "Since her arrival... well... we started making arrangements."

"I'm sorry to hear of your mother's decline," Dr. Matthews

sympathized.

"Rapid decline," Victoria added. "I don't know. A part of me feels like she held on long enough for me to return home."

I reached for the tissues on the table beside me when I heard her voice crack. She accepted it from me and wiped away her tears.

"How does that make you feel?"

"I feel...like I'm not in control. I don't know how to explain it, but I feel that my life has been predetermined and—I don't know what the hell I'm saying."

"Take your time," I voiced reassuringly.

"I think I'm trying to say that everything happens for a reason, but I don't feel I'm making the decisions. Do you think I wanted to be an executive assistant to this nut?" she asked, shoving her thumb in my direction.

"From the disdain in your tone, I'd guess not," Dr. Matthews replied.

"I did not. I'd been applying for marketing jobs left and right, but the employment ad for Ramsey Acquisitions Group kept popping up everywhere I turned—the newspaper, numerous online job boards, LinkedIn—you name it. Eventually, I stopped fighting it and applied. From there, I was stranded on an island. I fell in love. Knox was bitten, and we were rescued in the nick of time. We returned home, and now my mother is about to check out. My entire reason for working for Knox was to care for my mother. I feel like a chess piece on a board, and someone is moving the pieces."

"Hm. I see. I admire the analogy you used. Are you spiritual, Victoria?"

She smirked.

"I am, but in that cliche, you've hit rock bottom kind of way, and you need hope."

"So, you found spirituality on the island?"

"Yes."

"Did it serve its purpose? Did you have hope you'd be rescued?"

"At first, but I stopped hoping to be rescued at some point and started searching for peace and acceptance instead."

"Tell me more about that."

"There's not much to tell. I felt content. I had shelter, water, food, good loving, and entertainment. The way I see it, if I wasn't supposed to make it, then I should've died in the crash."

I nodded, agreeing with her statement.

"I feel that I'm clinging to my mother-in-law because my mother will pass away soon. I wish I had more time with her, and I feel she was taken away from me too soon."

"I see. You mentioned making arrangements?"

Victoria dabbed at her eyes again.

"Everything is taken care of—plot, casket, flowers, repast, and eulogy."

"And how have you been coping with this?"

"As well as I can. I have a great support system."

"That's good to hear. How are you feeling mentally and emotionally? Any signs of depression or thoughts of harming yourself or others?"

"No."

"Victoria, be honest," I whispered.

"I am a little depressed, but I'm working on it," she admitted.

"How are you working on it?" Dr. Matthews pushed.

"I have my morning devotion, work out, share my experience on social media, and volunteer. I think my depression would resolve if I had an emotional support animal."

I sighed heavily.

"Victoria, for the last time, you don't need an emotional support animal."

"Emotional support animals have proven to ease anxiety, depression, and some phobias," Dr. Matthews chimed in.

"I'm not denying any of that. She just wants a fucking dog. Go get the damn dog. You don't have to put a label on it. Just say you want a dog."

"Is this upsetting to you, Mr. Ramsey?" Dr. Matthews asked.

"He's just a crotchety old man," Victoria teased, tugging on my earlobe.

"I'll show you just how crotchety I can be when I get home," I said, squeezing her thigh.

Dr. Matthew's gaze slid down to my hand and back up again.

"I guess that answers my next question, but I have to ask: Do you have any issues with intimacy?"

"None whatsoever—minimum twice a day, Monday through Thursday, and three times a day Friday, Saturday, and Sunday."

"That's very healthy," Dr. Matthews commented. "Victoria? Are you all right?"

"What?" she asked as if she were breaking out of a daze.

"Where did you go?"

"I-I have to go," Victoria said before gathering her purse and running out of the office, leaving me and Dr. Matthews dumbfounded.

What the hell is going on?

Victoria

I tore into the bodega like a mad woman, scaring the cashier, who was probably wondering if I was about to stick him up.

"Do you have any pregnancy tests?" I asked breathlessly. His shoulders seemed to slump in relief.

"Yes, ma'am. Do you need just one?" he asked, reaching behind him to the wall I hadn't noticed of contraceptives, lube, stimulants, and pregnancy tests.

"Give me three—just to be sure."

I paid for the tests and cringed when he congratulated me as I raced out of the store. I'd forgotten to get my Depo shot when we returned and had been letting Knox shoot the club up left and right.

I'd barely whipped the illegally parked SUV away from the curb when I received a call from Alyssa.

"Hello?"

"Um…is everything okay, Victoria? Knox sent me a text message saying to check on you because you bolted from therapy and took off with the vehicle."

"Everything is so fine."

"You don't sound fine," she replied.

"It's all starting to make sense!"

"What's making sense because it's not you?"

"Hold on, this asshole is driving like I don't have somewhere to be," I said before laying on the horn. He rolled his window down and stuck out his middle finger.

I planned on ignoring him when he switched lanes and rolled down the passenger window.

"Lord have mercy, Jesus," I mumbled when we approached a stoplight.

"What's going on?" Alyssa asked.

"Nothing. Nothing at all," I lied, reaching into my purse for my gun. I hadn't planned on using it, but the guy was doing the most over a little toot-toot, beep-beep. I laid the weapon across my lap and faced forward as the man berated me.

"Who is yelling like that?" Alyssa questioned, sounding more concerned than when I first answered.

"Some idiot driver."

"Are you safe?"

"I'm safe, but if he steps out of his vehicle, then I can't say he will be."

"Suck my dick, bitch!" he yelled. I closed my eyes and prayed for the light change because I was tempted to brandish my weapon, but I couldn't unless I was in imminent fear for my life.

I can't be so reckless. I possibly have precious cargo onboard.

Finally, the light turned green, and the car made it through the intersection, losing the guy who didn't know how to find the gas pedal.

"Victoria, what's going on?"

"I…I may be jumping the gun here, but these mood swings have been killing me, you know? And I have been more tired than usual, but I chalked it up to stress, but—"

"Do you think you're pregnant?"

I shrugged my shoulders as if she could see me.

"Maybe?"

"Will I be a godmother?"

"Maybe," I repeated.

"Are you on your way home?"

"I am."

"Do you need someone there with you?" she asked.

"No. I'm fine, but you can stay on the line and talk to me until I get home."

The forty-minute drive home was grueling. Traffic was a nightmare, of course, and the anxiety made my bladder fill, and I was damn near pissing down my leg when I threw the SUV in the garage.

"I think if you have a boy, you should name him Chastain," Alyssa suggested.

"Chastain Ramsey? That sounds like a fucking horse. I gotta go," I rushed out before hanging up on her.

I tore open the pregnancy test as I sprinted to the downstairs powder room.

"Ohhhhh, God, I didn't think I was going to make it," I moaned as I peed. The relief made me so delirious that I had nearly forgotten the pregnancy test. I stuck it under the stream and capped it before laying it flat on the counter.

I finished my business and left the bathroom for the living room couch. I lay on the sofa and laced my fingers on my stomach while staring up at the ceiling. I closed my eyes and imagined how our lives would change with the potential new addition. One minute, I was playing scenarios in my head, and the next, Knox was shaking me awake.

"Victoria? Are you okay? I've been worried sick about you," he said with deep concern etching his face.

"I-I'm fine. I'm sorry I worried you."

"Do you want to talk about what sent you running out of therapy?"

I pulled myself up and patted the cushion next to me.

"Oh, boy. We're having one of those moments." I nodded. "Well, I guess after therapy would be the best time to do this while the coping techniques I learned are still fresh on my—"

"I never went in to get my Depo shot."

Knox stared at me blankly until it finally sank in.

"Oh…*oh*."

"Yes…*oh*."

"I see….Do you think you're pregnant?"

I shrugged.

"Anything's possible."

"When do you want to take a test?"

"I took one already."

The shock and anticipation made his breath catch slightly.

"And? What was the result?"

"I haven't checked. The test is on the vanity in the powder room. Will you go get it?"

"Sure. I'll return shortly."

True to his word, Knox returned in less than a minute.

"What does it say?" I whispered. My heart thudded in my chest as I waited for him to put me out of my misery.

"Mrs. Ramsey, I think we should gas up the jet and go to Las Vegas this weekend. My mother would have a conniption if we had a child out of wedlock."

"It's positive?" I asked in disbelief, even though I knew it was a high probability.

"We're pregnant," he confirmed, turning the test for me to see the two solid pink lines.

I jumped from the couch.

"I'm pregnant."

"We're pregnant," he repeated.

"*I'm* pregnant. I'm the one carrying this child, fuck face."

"Ooh. That's a new one; I like that. Are we replacing That Man Over There with fuck face?"

I slowly paced the living room, my hands on top of my head, as if I had just lost the rent money on a parlay.

"This is my fault."

"What's your fault?" Knox asked incredulously.

"I should've remembered to schedule my appointment, but we had so much going on that it completely slipped my mind."

"You didn't remember because you didn't want to remember, Victoria."

I rolled my eyes and allowed him to envelop me in his arms.

"Why aren't you freaking out? Not that you would be upset, but I kinda expected you to be jumping on the couch Tom Cruise-style or something."

"It's basic biology, darling. I've been coming in you gratuitously. I'm surprised it took this long."

"Hm," I hummed. "Do you mean it about going to Las Vegas and getting married this weekend?"

"I do. Take your friends and Polly Pocket and go shopping for our trip. Get whatever your heart desires, and I'll take care of the rest."

"Stop it, Knox. I love you so much, but I will run up your credit card."

"I love you, too, and that's what it's there for. I'm so happy, Victoria," he said, sighing as he swayed with me in the living room.

"Me too."

"We finally have an excuse to get ferrets. I know our child will want one, and you'll be powerless against their pleading eyes."

I pushed him away gently and returned to the foyer. "Where are you going?"

"We are going on a field trip. Let's go, Knox. I'm driving."

* * *

I stood with a satisfied grin on my face as Knox pinched his nose and stole small sips of breath when he could.

"What's the matter, Gio?" I asked coyly.

"I don't—Jesus, do they always smell like this?"

"Yep!" I boasted proudly.

"I don't believe it. I think the pet shop owners have severely neglected these ferrets. Shame on them."

"Nope. Ferrets are stinky sock puppets, like I told you."

"I thought you were exaggerating like you usually do when you're trying to rain on my parade."

"Go ahead and pick it up."

"I'd rather not," he snapped.

"Why not?" I asked, smiling wider.

"I fear the stench will never leave my fingers."

"So, we agree that stinky sock puppets won't enter our home?"

"I agree."

The true definition of 'I can show you better than I can tell you.'

"Let's get out of here before I lose consciousness. Are you hungry?" Knox inquired, returning his handkerchief to his pocket.

"I can eat."

"Good. What do you think about Vince's?" he asked, slinging his arm over my shoulder and leading me out of the pet shop.

"That sounds like a wonderful plan, but I want wings, too."

"All flats?"

"You got it, baby."

34

Bali

Knox

My wife ripped her lips away from mine and squeaked when my dick caressed her spot. I smirked, knowing it wouldn't be long before she climaxed and sent me spiraling after her. I found her lips again and laced my fingers through hers as I sluggishly plunged in and out of her.

It was day three of our honeymoon, and nothing short of a small miracle would drag me out of bed.

She can withdraw her consent, but the chance of that happening isn't likely. The sex is just that phenomenal.

"This is the last round. I'm tapping out," she mumbled before nipping my ear.

You know what? It's my fault for saying something. Fuck. I didn't even say anything—I thought it. But that shows how in-tune we are. Thus proving that we are perfect for each other.

"C'mon, Tori Montana. I know you're not giving up that easily," I taunted as I sped up my strokes.

"Fuck you, Gio," she moaned as she began to meet my

strokes.

"And you do it so well," I replied. I laughed when she snatched her fingers from mine and placed her palm over my mouth.

"Just be quiet, ho. You're gonna mess up my nut," she hissed. *We can't have that.*

I pulled out of her toxic embrace and placed her legs on my shoulders. We began to compete at who could moan louder than the other, but of course, my wife always had to best me. She drowned me out easily as I delivered stroke after stroke as my climax built at the base of my dick. I tried distracting myself from coming early by reminding myself we only had four more days of paradise before returning home, but that self-control went out the window when we made brief eye contact.

My wife's eyes were deep and soulful, and I'd always been weak to those long lashes that she'd bat at me to get her way. But my ultimate undoing was when she mouthed that she loved me, sending me tumbling over the edge.

I emptied into her and dropped down to kiss her, wrapping her legs around my hip, and I prayed I didn't soften before she came.

"Come on your husband's dick, Mrs. Ramsey," I said through gritted teeth, hoping her pussy would comply.

"I'm fucking coming," she squealed, letting me have it. I closed my eyes and marveled at how her pussy gripped me for the hundredth time.

I lazily rocked in and out of her as she rode out her orgasm, eventually stopping when her muscles relaxed and she went boneless. A long, drawn-out sigh escaped her when I pulled out and buried my face in her perspiring neck.

"Tell me you didn't mean it," I mumbled.

Even though I wasn't looking at her, I could picture her brows scrunching together in bewilderment.

"Tell you I didn't mean what?"

"That you're tapping out."

She patted my shoulder three times.

"I'm tapping out, Gio," she said firmly. "We've been in Bali for three days, and I don't even know what it looks like outside."

"You're a fucking liar, and the truth isn't in you. I fucked you on the balcony yesterday in front of a magnificent view. You didn't catch the ocean as I had you bent over the railing?"

"You know what?" I smirked, knowing she was about to let me have it. "I should've guessed triflin' as your middle name because you're never beating the allegations."

"I might be triflin', but at least I have knees."

"The bar is in Hell where that snake nearly sent you," she whispered as she attempted to wiggle from beneath me. I swiftly rolled off of her when I was reminded of Mini Montana.

I remained silent as I watched Victoria leave the bed and groaned when my dick started to perk up again. The shower cut on, and instead of joining my lovely wife and attempting to "talk her out of her panties" as she would say, I returned some neglected text messages.

Ma: I haven't heard from either of you in three days. I'm getting a little worried. Did Victoria finish what that foul woman didn't?

I snorted and rolled my eyes.

Me: I'm replying from the bottom of a ravine.

Ma: No one likes a smartass.

Me: I'd beg to differ. I wouldn't be married otherwise.

Ma: A woman doesn't have to like you to marry you.

Me: I'll keep that in mind.

Ma: Send pictures when you can.

Me: I will.

Ms. Linda (Nurse): I don't mean to interrupt your honeymoon, Mr. Ramsey, but you told me to notify you if Mrs. Caldwell's status changed. As of yesterday, she's no longer eating.

I sighed once I realized my mother-in-law wouldn't make it to see her grandchild. We'd be lucky if she lasted until our return for Victoria to say her goodbyes.

Me: Very well. Please ensure she is comfortable.

The Defamers: We haven't heard from our friend in three days. She better FaceTime us today by noon.

I put those two well-intentioned knuckleheads in a group chat because I was convinced they were functioning on one shared brain between them, and I didn't want to have to repeat myself and answer multiple text messages.

Despite my slight disapproval of their smear campaign against me when Victoria and I went missing, even I had to acknowledge they were the best friends a woman could have. I'd forgive them... eventually.

Me: I will have her FaceTime you both once she's out of the shower.

The Defamers: Okay, purr!

"What the fuck does that mean?" I spat, narrowing my eyes at the screen.

Polly Pocket: Where are the honeymoon pics that you promised? I'll send the paps to your location if I don't receive a Safe for Work picture for social media of you and Victoria frolicking on the beach by 5:00 PM.

Me: I can't promise it'll be suitable for work.

Time had gotten away from me as I responded to some crucial work emails regarding my grand departure. I glanced up from my phone when I heard an "ahem" in the background.

"Yes, dear?"

"You're not supposed to be working during our honeymoon. That's what Blakenship is for," she reminded me.

"I'm not working. I'm transitioning," I replied with a taunting smile.

"Hand over your phone," she demanded, holding her hand out.

"No. I'm looking at porn."

She quirked a brow.

"Really?" she questioned, folding her arms over her damp breasts. My eyes traveled down her physique, taking in her dark, moist skin and the short towel that barely stopped beneath her ass.

"Really."

"What kind of porn?"

"My favorite kind—ebony BBW. I especially like the pornos that are in an office setting."

She bit her bottom lip to prevent herself from bursting out in laughter. Eventually, she turned away when she couldn't hide it any longer. She could call me every name in the book and tell me how trifling I was, but unbeknownst to her, I could see her very clearly in the mirror, and she wore a grin from ear to ear.

"You're so childish, and I regret ever setting foot on that plane with you."

If she wants childish, then wait until she gets a hold of this....

"Okay, purr!"

I yelped when Victoria jumped on me and started hitting me with a pillow. We wrestled for a few seconds before we called a truce because we were cramping with laughter. We lay side by side, staring into each other's tear-filled eyes. I slipped my fingers between hers and brought her hand to my lips.

"I wanted you, and I got you," I mumbled against her skin.

"And it only took a plane crash to get me."

"Shhhh. The story we tell our child is that we had a passionate office romance—get with the picture."

"I apologize. I forgot it was love at first sight, and I definitely never threatened to staple your lips together."

I smiled.

"I like that version," I agreed, kissing her luscious lips.

"You'll never live to tell the story if you don't feed me and take me to the beach."

"Noted. Please dress inappropriately in one of those revealing bikinis you packed, return your friends' calls, and join me on the balcony for breakfast."

The mention of breakfast had her scurrying out of bed. I raised my hand up, stared at my wedding ring, and released a sigh of contentment.

I hadn't lied when I said I wanted her and got her. My methods might have been a little unconventional, but the outcome was amazing. We were *officially* married, had a child on the way, and we finally made it to Bali. I couldn't ask for anything else.

35

Epilogue

Ten Years Later

Monty

"Sock? Puppet? Where are you guys?" I hissed, dropping to my knees to check under the bed for the millionth time. They were nowhere in sight, and the last thing I wanted was for Mom to have a meltdown.

My ears are still ringing from the last time they went missing, when she found them swan diving into the rice bin.

"What are you doing down there, Monty?"

"Nothing!" I exclaimed, suspiciously yanking the comforter back down and climbing to my feet.

"Uh-huh," my mother said as her critical eyes scanned my bedroom.

"Don't you have to leave for your spa day soon?"

She glanced down at her watch and cursed.

"I'm canceling."

"You can't cancel. It's your tenth wedding anniversary," I

291

said, easing her out of my bedroom and closing the door behind me. "Dad would be disappointed."

"I can never relax when we go to the spa together because he talks too damn much."

I rolled my eyes.

She's one to talk. She talks just as much as him!

"It'll be perfect, Mom. You guys will spend the day at the spa, have a little lunch, and go shopping on me," I said, slipping her my prepaid debit card that my weekly allowance was kept on.

"Monty... how much you got on this little card?" Mom asked with a hand on her hip.

"Around $150."

"One fif—here take this back. That'll barely cover lunch," she said, handing the card back to me. I scoffed and slipped it into the back pocket of my jeans.

"This wouldn't be an issue if you found somewhere more affordable to eat."

"I swear you act like you grew up on stamps," she said under her breath.

"What are stamps?" I asked curiously.

"My point exactly," she commented.

"Montana Gianna Ramsey!" my dad yelled from somewhere in the house.

He only calls me Gianna when I'm in trouble. My goose is not only cooked, but it's deep-fried.

"Ooooo, you're in trouble," my mother taunted childishly. "What did you do?"

"I didn't do anything," I lied.

"That Man Over There doesn't call you by your government name unless you did something."

292

"Hold on. Is Dad in trouble?" I asked, raising a brow. She only called him "That Man Over There" when he had to sleep in the guest room.

"He didn't do anything wrong. But he's so damn old that he wouldn't remember if he did. I can milk him for all he's worth today."

I shook my head.

"He's not old," I argued.

She stared at me blankly and asked, "Then what would you call it?"

"He's... he's... um... he's mature."

"He qualifies for senior citizen discounts at chain restaurants. He's old as dust."

"That's rude."

She winked at me.

"Good thing your father likes me rude. You better go see what your dad wants. You're sitting here judging me and you might not have a tablet in a few minutes."

Oh, God. Please don't let Dad take my tablet. He might forget to return it like last time. I had to go an entire month without it!

A voice crackled over the intercom.

"Montana Gianna—my office—now."

"Tell That Man Over There that I'll be *impatiently* waiting for him downstairs," she said before bailing on me, which sucked because she typically ran interference when I was in trouble. You'd think she'd be the strict parent, but she was a pushover. It was Dad you had to watch out for.

I journeyed through the mansion until I finally arrived at his office.

"It's fine. He's just an old, crochety man like Mom says."

I knocked on the door and waited for him to respond.

"Bring your ass," he commanded. I rolled my eyes and regretted my mother's influence on him.

"Here goes nothing," I whispered, opening the door and poking my head in. "Hi, Daddy."

He snorted and waved me in.

"That 'Hi, Daddy' shit isn't going to work on me. Sit down," he said, pointing at The Chair of Doom in front of his desk. It's where Mom and I had to sit when we were about to get chewed out. Usually, she'd get an earful about going on elaborate trips with her friends and ditching him for long stretches of time. As for me? It could be anything.

He glared at me, and instead of meeting his judging gaze, I stared at the picture of him and Mom grinning on the island they'd crash-landed on years ago. I dreamily sighed as I thought about their passionate office romance and how their love saw them through the worst of times on the island.

I wish I could have a love like that someday.

The best part was that Dad purchased the uninhabited island a few years ago and named it after my mother. It was called Tori Island, and they took a yearly pilgrimage to the island with minimal supplies and the clothes on their back. I thought it was ridiculous, but they always returned crispy, slimmer, and in love two weeks later.

"Are you missing something, Gia?"

"Mmmmm. I don't think so," I replied with a shrug.

He shook his head solemnly, and I knew I had to come clean. "I can't find Sock and Puppet."

"Well, they happened to find my golf bag," he said, spinning in his office chair and grabbing the bag. He set it in front of me. I peered at the mesh side pocket and sure enough, my albino ferret, Sock, and my black ferret, Puppet, were nestled in there, resting peacefully.

"Uh-huh," I replied, sitting back against the chair.

"Uh-huh? Is that all you have to say?" he growled.

"Not really."

"Let's hear it then."

"No, thank you."

"Don't be shy, Gia."

"Well… technically they wouldn't be in your golf bag if you left your clubs in the garage like Mom asks you."

"Get out," he said, waving me off. "And take these rank ass bendy straws with you. I can't believe your mother allowed you to get those vermin. My office smells like an outhouse."

"That's probably because you farted," I teased, picking up my beloved pets.

"I swear to God I will ship you off to boarding school," he threatened.

"Mom wouldn't allow that, and you know it."

He smacked his lips and ran a hand through his salt-and-gently peppered hair.

"I know. I'm full of shit. You know I wouldn't send you away, baby. Just make sure you latch their cages properly. I don't want them getting into the rice bin again. Your mother nearly screamed the roof off the house."

"You're telling me. Oh, what did you do to Mom?"

He peered at me curiously.

"What do you mean?"

"She told me to tell you that she was waiting for you downstairs, and she called you That Man Over There."

"What the hell?" he mumbled, gazing off into space. "I don't remember. But I had to have done something for her to call me That Man Over There. Don't worry about it, Monty. I'll buy her something extra nice with a lot of zeros in it today. Be good for your nonna."

"I will. Have fun."

A few minutes later, Sock and Puppet returned to their habitat, and I waved my parents off with my nonna beside me.

"Okay, Chef Gia. What are you whipping up today?"

"Don't worry about it, nonna. Just sit back, relax, and watch me work my magic."

I ran to the kitchen, washed my hands twice since I'd handled Sock and Puppet, and donned my favorite apron. I disinfected the countertop before retrieving the recipe book from the pantry. I flipped through the book and beamed when I found my next challenge.

"Tell me a story, Nonna," I insisted, separating egg whites into a copper bowl.

She smiled softly.

"You want a story, huh? Have I told you about my sister who stole my man?"

I gasped dramatically.

"Your sister did what?"

She sat on the stool beside me and proceeded to tell me how her sister was a hussy who stole her man and was now sleeping with the fishes.

I smiled and started beating the meringue for my Baked Alaska. My family was a little crazy, and sometimes a little extra, but I wouldn't change them for the world.

About the Author

I started writing back in 2018 as a way to escape the daily grind of my high-stress social services job. I'd always loved reading, but writing was new territory—one that quickly became a passion. What started as a hobby turned into a career four years later, and I've never looked back.

People often describe my writing style as comedic and sexy, with witty dialogue, unexpected twists, and characters you can't help but root for. I love bringing interracial romance and thrillers to life—stories that mix passion with plot twists, and, of course, plenty of laughs along the way!

Sign up for my newsletter and receive a FREE copy of *Teasing the Crime Lord*!

You can connect with me on:
- https://www.anboydenbooks.com
- https://www.inkitt.com/anboyden
- https://www.instagram.com/anboyden

Subscribe to my newsletter:

✉ https://dl.bookfunnel.com/h5q29x1nhz

Also by A. N. Boyden and Em Jay

Thank you for reading "Anyone But You"! Sign up for my newsletter at www.anboydenbooks.com or Inkitt to receive one shots of Knox, Victoria, and Montana, and updates on future releases!

Exclusive Content on Inkitt!
Gain early access to weekly updates on fan-favorite stories, including *The Teacher, Secret Lovers, Hunt Me, Anyone But You, Squeak I & II*, and new releases like *Squeak III* and *Ice Me Out*. Inkitt subscribers will enjoy sneak peeks, one-shots, in-line comments, and exclusive giveaways!

www.inkitt.com/anboyden

Spouse Swap

Charlotte (Charlie) Davis is a successful divorce attorney who agrees to participate in a social experiment where she swaps lives with another wife and mother, leaving behind her emotionally unavailable husband and four-year-old daughter. Her "new" spouse, Taylor Scott, is an electrician by trade who agrees to participate in the spouse swap program for the $10,000.00 to be paid out after the program. Charlie and Taylor have an instant connection when they first lay eyes on each other. Throughout the program, they realize their marriages have been missing the love and affection they've been craving. Taylor finds out a devastating secret about his wife that forces him to face reality and make moves for the safety and well-being of his family.

There was one itsy bitsy detail in the spouse swap contract that both Charlie and Taylor missed...the couple has to sleep in the same bed....

Mail Order Groom

Nina thought she was marrying her dream man—a mail-order groom to fulfill her fantasies. What she didn't expect was a man with a past and secrets that run deep. Will Nina take the risk, or is it time to cut her losses?

The Widowed Nanny

Recently widowed, Kierra Houston is ready to give up all hope of getting justice for her husband's death when she walks into Jonathan Baker's office with her three-year-old daughter, Kiyah. Before Jonathan, she was turned away by sixteen lawyers who refused to represent her wrongful death suit against Vance Oil, who claims her husband's death was due to a critical error on his part.

Jonathan eagerly agrees to represent Kierra, confident that he could win her case with some strategic thinking outside the box. Meanwhile, Jonathan is looking for a live-in nanny after being awarded sole custody of his children, and Kierra fits the bill. Kierra moves into Jonathan's home with her daughter and helps wrangle his three rambunctious children.

It doesn't take long for Jonathan and Kierra to seek refuge in each other when they discover how caring and nurturing they are, despite Jonathan's failed marriage and Kierra's grief.

The sexual chemistry between the two is explosive, leading to many instances of bedroom swapping and quiet lovemaking in the middle of the night to avoid waking the children.